The sylphlike figure of Helena Vaughn took another step down the stairwell toward him

Kane squeezed the trigger on his Sin Eater, unleashing a stutter of 9 mm lead bullets. The shots sounded loud in the enclosed space of the stairwell, and bullets rattled off the concrete walls and steps beside and behind the naked girl. She seemed unaware of them.

Kane gritted his teeth as his discharge passed through her pale, ethereal flesh.

"You aren't real," he spat out. "You can't be."

Helena Vaughn just stood there amid the barrage of bullets that pummeled her body, the dark shadows of the stairwell obscuring her sad expression, turning it into something much more haunting.

Kane eased his index finger from the blaster's trigger. The girl looked up at him through her bangs, the blond hair tangled and in disarray. Kane watched as her mouth opened and she let loose a soft sigh before drawing a tiny stutter of breath…as if in pain.

Other titles in this series:

Parallax Red
Doomstar Relic
Iceblood
Hellbound Fury
Night Eternal
Outer Darkness
Armageddon Axis
Wreath of Fire
Shadow Scourge
Hell Rising
Doom Dynasty
Tigers of Heaven
Purgatory Road
Sargasso Plunder
Tomb of Time
Prodigal Chalice
Devil in the Moon
Dragoneye
Far Empire
Equinox Zero
Talon and Fang
Sea of Plague
Awakening
Mad God's Wrath
Sun Lord
Mask of the Sphinx
Uluru Destiny
Evil Abyss
Children of the Serpent
Successors

Cerberus Storm
Refuge
Rim of the World
Lords of the Deep
Hydra's Ring
Closing the Cosmic Eye
Skull Throne
Satan's Seed
Dark Goddess
Grailstone Gambit
Ghostwalk
Pantheon of Vengeance
Death Cry
Serpent's Tooth
Shadow Box
Janus Trap
Warlord of the Pit
Reality Echo
Infinity Breach
Oblivion Stone
Distortion Offensive
Cradle of Destiny
Scarlet Dream
Truth Engine
Infestation Cubed
Planet Hate
Dragon City
God War
Genesis Sinister
Savage Dawn

James Axler
Outlanders®

SORROW
SPACE

A GOLD EAGLE BOOK FROM
WORLDWIDE®

TORONTO • NEW YORK • LONDON
AMSTERDAM • PARIS • SYDNEY • HAMBURG
STOCKHOLM • ATHENS • TOKYO • MILAN
MADRID • WARSAW • BUDAPEST • AUCKLAND

Recycling programs
for this product may
not exist in your area.

First edition May 2013

ISBN-13: 978-0-373-63878-9

SORROW SPACE

Printed in U.S.A.

Let us beware of saying that death is the opposite of life. The living being is only a species of the dead, and a very rare species.

—Friedrich Nietzsche,
1844–1900

The Road to Outlands—
From Secret Government Files to the Future

Almost two hundred years after the global holocaust, Kane, a former Magistrate of Cobaltville, often thought the world had been lucky to survive at all after a nuclear device detonated in the Russian embassy in Washington, D.C. The aftermath—forever known as skydark—reshaped continents and turned civilization into ashes.

Nearly depopulated, America became the Deathlands—poisoned by radiation, home to chaos and mutated life forms. Feudal rule reappeared in the form of baronies, while remote outposts clung to a brutish existence.

What eventually helped shape this wasteland were the redoubts, the secret preholocaust military installations with stores of weapons, and the home of gateways, the locational matter-transfer facilities. Some of the redoubts hid clues that had once fed wild theories of government cover-ups and alien visitations.

Rearmed from redoubt stockpiles, the barons consolidated their power and reclaimed technology for the villes. Their power, supported by some invisible authority, extended beyond their fortified walls to what was now called the Outlands. It was here that the rootstock of humanity survived, living with hellzones and chemical storms, hounded by Magistrates.

In the villes, rigid laws were enforced—to atone for the sins of the past and prepare the way for a better future. That was the barons' public credo and their right-to-rule.

Kane, along with friend and fellow Magistrate Grant, had upheld that claim until a fateful Outlands expedition. A displaced piece of technology…a question to a keeper of the archives…a vague clue about alien masters—and their world shifted radically. Suddenly, Brigid Baptiste, the archivist, faced summary execution, and Grant a quick termination. For Kane there was forgiveness if he pledged his unquestioning allegiance to Baron Cobalt and his unknown masters and abandoned his friends.

But that allegiance would make him support a mysterious and alien power and deny loyalty and friends. Then what else was there?

Kane had been brought up solely to serve the ville. Brigid's only link with her family was her mother's red-gold hair, green eyes and supple form. Grant's clues to his lineage were his ebony skin and powerful physique. But Domi, she of the white hair, was an Outlander pressed into sexual servitude in Cobaltville. She at least knew her roots and was a reminder to the exiles that the outcasts belonged in the human family.

Parents, friends, community—the very rootedness of humanity was denied. With no continuity, there was no forward momentum to the future. And that was the crux—when Kane began to wonder if there was a future.

For Kane, it wouldn't do. So the only way was out—way, way out.

After their escape, they found shelter at the forgotten Cerberus redoubt headed by Lakesh, a scientist, Cobaltville's head archivist, and secret opponent of the barons.

With their past turned into a lie, their future threatened, only one thing was left to give meaning to the outcasts. The hunger for freedom, the will to resist the hostile influ-ences. And perhaps, by opposing, end them.

Chapter 1

It wasn't here yet, but already Domi could feel it. Its approach played at the edge of the albino woman's heightened senses like the half-remembered words to an old, old song. The woman's pale nose twitched and her ruby eyes darted left and right as she searched for the source of the irritation.

"Something's coming," she murmured, giving voice to her thoughts.

Domi had always been sensitive to changes so subtle that others failed to detect them: changes in temperature and air pressure, changes in the electromagnetic fields. These were the signals that sent animals scurrying to their nests and burrows prior to an eclipse, that made cows lie down before a storm broke, and Domi felt them all.

Domi had grown up a child of the Outlands, and some mistook her highly tuned senses for evidence that she had more in common with animals than with civilised humans. Certainly she didn't appear entirely human. An albino, Domi stood a little over five feet tall. Her skin was the pale alabaster of chalk, and her short-cropped hair was the creamy color of bone. Her hair was arranged in a ragged, pixie-style cut, framing the sharp planes of her face and drawing attention to her eyes, twin pools of a vibrant scarlet the color of blood.

Domi's clothing, too, was unusual in comparison

with the other people in the cavernous operations center of the redoubt. There were almost twenty personnel working diligently at the twin aisles of computer terminals that ran the length of the room. Each technician wore a standard uniform, a one-piece white jumpsuit with a vertical blue zipper running down its center. Domi, however, was dressed in cut-down denim shorts and a crop top that left her legs, arms and midriff bare. Her feet were also bare, and like the clothes she wore, showed smudges of dried earth, tree sap and berry juice, traces of some personal jaunt beyond the corridors of the Cerberus redoubt. A combat knife was strapped to Domi's left calf just above the ankle, its wickedly serrated blade a solid nine inches of razor-sharp steel. The knife was a memento from Domi's previous life, where she had been held as a sex slave in the Tartarus Pits of Cobaltville.

The busy operations room was the central hub of the Cerberus complex, a fully-staffed facility hidden from prying eyes in a former military redoubt high in the Bitterroot Range, where it had remained forgotten or ignored in the two centuries since the nukecaust. In the years since that nuclear devastation, a strange mythology had grown up around the mountains with their dark, foreboding forests and seemingly bottomless ravines. The wilderness area surrounding the redoubt was virtually unpopulated. The nearest settlement could be found in the flatlands some miles away and consisted of a small band of Indians, Sioux and Cheyenne, led by a shaman named Sky Dog.

The redoubt was manned by a full complement of staff, some of whom were cryogenic "freezies" from the twentieth century who had been discovered in sus-

pended animation in the Manitius Moon Base and many
of whom were experts in their chosen field of study.

Tucked beneath camouflage netting, hidden away
within the rocky clefts of the mountain range, concealed
uplinks chattered continuously with two orbiting satellites that provided much of the empirical data for the
Cerberus team. Gaining access to the satellites had
taken many man-hours of intense trial-and-error work
by many of the top scientists on hand at the mountain
base. Now the Cerberus staff could, at any time of the
day or night, draw on live feeds from the orbiting Vela-
class reconnaissance satellite and the Keyhole Comsat.
This arrangement gave the staff in residence a near
limitless stream of feed data surveying the surface of
Earth, as well as providing almost instantaneous communication with field teams around the globe.

Domi's eyes flickered once again, ignoring the hus-
tle and bustle of the operations room as she felt a subtle
change in the atmosphere. The room was a vast space
carved out of the mountain itself, and it was dominated
by the two rows of computers that were used to monitor and process the satellite feed data.

Across the back wall, a huge Mercator relief map
stretched high above the operators' heads, showing
the topography of the planet prior to the nukecaust of
2001. On that fateful day, the borders had been redrawn
and fault lines had been shocked into action, plunging
vast chunks of the West Coast of the United States of
America—and elsewhere—into the ocean.

The Mercator map was dotted with glowing points
that were connected by a web of colored lights like
decorations on a Christmas tree. These lights showed
the available pathways of the mat-trans network, an
advanced transportation system that involved shunt-

ing matter through quantum space to a chosen destination. The Cerberus redoubt had been involved, from its earliest stages, with research into the transfer of matter from one location to another. Later, the mat-trans units were involved in exploration of other planets and even alternate dimensions.

While the other Cerberus personnel continued to monitor their feeds and analyze the data they were receiving, Domi's piercing red eyes fixed on the mat-trans unit itself, her gaze playing across the brown-tinted armaglass that surrounded it. The mat-trans was located in a separate chamber that stood as an adjunct to the ops room. Hexagonal in shape and eight feet in height, the chamber featured a locked door set within the protective armaglass structure. The device was operated by a control terminal located outside of the mat-trans chamber itself, where a specific destination could be selected by inputting destination coordinates.

Most recently the unit had dispatched a field team to meet with an arms supply ring that was threatening to destabilize the already volatile area of the western United States.

There was something about the mat-trans, however, that served to unsettle Domi right now. She padded toward it on her bare feet, sniffing at the air as she felt that eerie wrongness wash over her. The mat-trans tampered with quantum energy, but it also involved standard mechanical processes, including the automated air-filtration system that functioned when the unit was in use, clearing the gases that were expelled during teleportation.

As Domi brushed past him, a Cerberus operative called Farrell peered up from his post. Farrell had a shaved head, a thin, goatee-style beard and a gold hoop earring in one earlobe, and he had been poring over a printout. "Domi?" Farrell asked, peering over the papers. "Everything okay?"

"Who's coming through the mat-trans?" Domi asked, addressing Farrell without looking at him.

"No one," Farrell assured her. Then, as if in afterthought, he checked the monitor before him, confirming his statement. "No one."

Domi's eyes remained fixed on the chamber. "Wait," she said in a low voice.

"Domi," Farrell began, "there's nothing coming. The unit's powered d—"

He stopped, the words drying in his mouth as he heard the familiar hissing and whirring that accompanied the activation of the mat-trans chamber.

"Incoming!" Farrell shouted, glancing across the operations center for the security detail that waited close to the room's main door. "The mat-trans is live."

From his post at the back of the ops room, Mohandas Lakesh Singh rose to his feet. The founder and director of the Cerberus operation, Lakesh had been a part of the original team of scientists who had operated here in the twentieth century, when it was a military research facility dedicated to matter-transfer research. Visibly in his fifties, Lakesh was of medium height with dusky skin and clear blue eyes that were the product, as was his longevity, of organ replacement. Lakesh had sleek black hair with just a trace of white at the temples and sides, slicked back from his forehead, and an aquiline nose over a small, refined mouth. In his time as Cerberus director, Lakesh had seen many strange things, so it took more than an alert regarding the mat-trans to shock him.

"Mr. Farrell, status report," Lakesh demanded as

Edwards and Sinclair came charging along the double aisles of computer terminals, their weapons drawn. "I heard no request from Kane's team. Why did you activate the mat-trans?"

"I didn't activate it," Farrell confirmed. "It just… activated."

"Troubling," Lakesh murmured.

Edwards, a former Magistrate, was a muscular man with a bullet-bitten ear and hair cropped so close to his skull that he appeared almost bald. Sela Sinclair was a slender, dark-skinned woman with a fierce expression and short black hair in ringlets. Both Sinclair and Edwards had served with Cerberus for a long time, and they well understood the mat-trans procedures. The incongruous figure of Domi stood before them in a semicrouch, her nose twitching as the chamber powered up. Behind this group, the remainder of the Cerberus staff watched from their designated positions behind their terminals, with several of them standing up to better see what was occurring.

And then the mat-trans chamber seemed almost to shake. Lightning streaked through the air within the hexagonal chamber, joining the ceiling and floor tiles in bent lines of dazzling whiteness as something solid was dragged from the quantum ether to materialize within. The whole operations room suffered a dramatic temperature drop at that instant, as if struck by an icy blast of air. Hidden motors hummed and chuntered as the chamber powered down again, the familiar whine of whirring fans drumming from their hidden alcoves.

Still in her semicrouch, Domi stretched forward, peering into the chamber as the mists cleared, feeling the coldness like a weight on the atmosphere. As the fog parted, Domi and the others saw a figure standing within. No, it wasn't standing—it was moving, propelled toward the door.

Unconsciously, everyone in the operations room reared back as the thing in the chamber slammed into the locked door, making not the slightest sound through the barrier of the armaglass.

"Open it," Domi instructed, not looking away.

When Farrell questioned the order, Lakesh consented with a single nod of his head. "It's the only way we're going to find out what's come through," he reasoned. As he spoke, he reached for a small rebreather that was located in one of his desk drawers, and he watched as other personnel in the room did the same. From its operating specs, the mat-trans chamber should not open until the filtration system had cleared any toxins from the air, a fail-safe to prevent the units from accidentally carrying a biological weapon to the heart of the military redoubts where they were located.

At the control desk, Farrell ran his eyes over the system's stats, confirming that the air within had been cleansed. "Opening now," he advised. "We are live in five…in four…in three…"

Impatiently Domi leaned a little closer, watching the dark figure within the mat-trans chamber, still obscured by the transport mists.

"Domi," Lakesh reminded her. "Be careful." The two of them were romantically involved, but Lakesh knew better than to try to persuade Domi to back off when there was danger near; she was too brave and too much of a free spirit for that.

A highly skilled hand-to-hand combatant, Domi pulled her knife from its ankle sheath as she stepped closer to the door of the chamber. The seal hissed, vent-ing air as Farrell tapped the fail-safe code into the control terminal. Then the door opened.

The first thing that hit Domi was the smell of rotting meat that poured from the mat-trans chamber like a storm front. The stench made Domi gag, and before she could do anything else, the lone figure emerged from within, shuffling forward in a stumbling, staggering abruptness of limbs. She was tall, female, five foot ten and wearing a sheer body stocking of inky black. Her dark hair had fallen over her face. Beneath the body stocking, her frame was so slender it left every muscle on display. There was not so much as an ounce of fat on the whole of the woman's figure, and the shining body stocking only accentuated that fact.

The woman took four staggering steps, her movements angular like a stop-motion animation in a film, her long limbs jutting and awkward. Her face was still hidden by her drooping hair, and Domi saw now that her hair was black and wet, matching the body stocking exactly. Her arms poked out behind her, elbows bent, wrists turned backward, gloved fingers taut. And then, before Domi could say a word, the woman fell at her feet, sagging to the floor amid a forming pool of oil.

Domi stepped closer as the woman slumped to the floor, two guns trained on her by the Cerberus security staff. The woman's hair was in disarray over her face and Domi saw more clearly that it was streaked with black gunk, the same oily stuff that seemed to sheath her body. It was not clothing, Domi recognized now. Rather it was a tarlike substance, thick and viscous, covering the woman's body entirely and creating a second skin that blocked every pore.

Domi leaned down to address the woman, but before she spoke, the dark-sheathed woman started to shud-

der violently. Her body trembled as black gunk poured
from it, oozing across the floor like an oil slick on water.
Domi skittered backward, careful to not let any of the
gunk touch her bare feet. Then the woman lifted her
head, revealing for the first time that her face, too, was
covered in the dark sludge. It shone beneath the fluo-
rescents, obscuring the woman's features, turning her
eyes into smooth bulges like eggs, covering her open
mouth with a taut skin like the top of a drum.

Domi watched with a growing sense of unease as
the woman opened her constrained mouth wider and
began to scream. It sounded strained and penetrating,
like a distant seagull's caw. The awful scream seemed
to reverberate through Domi's bones, punching through
to her core.

"Who is she?" Edwards asked as the mysterious
woman shook more violently still.

But before anyone could answer—if, indeed, they
had an answer—the woman's scream turned into a wet
gurgle, that sounded as though she was being drowned
in a basin of water. Then—quite impossibly—the dark
sheathed woman's body lost its solidity and she deteriorated into a spreading pool of blackness in a matter of
moments, merging with the gloop that had been pouring from her body in its shadowy waterfall.

As one, the Cerberus personnel in the room held
their collective breath, all eyes fixed on the mat-trans
chamber door and the dark stain where the woman had
collapsed.

Chapter 2

The Chinook helicopter cut through the air over the Panamint Range, the pilot skimming close to the tops of mountain ridges where powdery snow dappled in white buds. It looked as if the whole range had been dusted with powdered sugar, just enough to give the top of each ridge a white coating of indifference.

The loud thrumming of the helicopter's rotor blades made conversation difficult but not impossible. As it was, Kane had to shout to be heard over their drumming sound, which made something of a mockery of the idea that this was a clandestine meeting.

"So, where was it you say you found this stash?" Kane asked in a raised voice. He was a tall man with eyes like blue-gray steel whose intensity demanded a man's attention when he spoke. His dark hair was cropped close to his head, and his square jaw was clean-shaven. He wore a dark-colored suit, its neat lines clinging to his broad chest with precision. A pair of shiny black boots with well-cushioned soles finished the ensemble. There was something of the wolf about Kane, both in his physicality and his manner—he had broad shoulders with rangy limbs. He displayed a natural instinct to lead and often to act alone.

Kane was a member of the Montana-based Cerberus organization, a group dedicated to the security and welfare of the human race. Ever since their emergence as a resistance group years ago, Cerberus had been spear-heading an ongoing war against the Annunaki, a group of alien invaders. The Annunaki had been involved in mankind's affairs since the days of prehistory, in an era when man was still cowering in trees from saber-toothed tigers. When they had first come to Earth those millennia ago, the Annunaki had been mistaken for gods, and their superior technology had become tran-scribed into mankind's myths and legends.

Following the nuclear holocaust at the start of the twenty-first century, the Annunaki reappeared dis-guised as the nine barons, hybrid human creatures who ruled over nine spectacular walled cities amid the rav-aged remains of the United States of America. It took many years for the hybrids to reveal their true nature and assume their proper forms as the entrancing, rep-tilian Annunaki, like butterflies shedding their chrys-alis state.

But internal rivalries among the Annunaki had proved their undoing, and over the past year they had been in retreat, appearing only irregularly in scuffles with the brave Cerberus warriors. Kane and his team had been caught dead center, however, in the Annun-aki's most recent skirmish, the so-called God War be-tween the cruelest of their number.

To a lesser man, one who placed undue emphasis on his own ego, it might have seemed a demotion to be aboard this scratch-built helicopter now, endeavor-ing to track the missing technology of one of the nine villes that those same Annunaki had abandoned. But the Cerberus organization had been on this trail for months now, and Kane and his two-man field crew knew how important it was to shut down the operation before a new batch of guns flooded the black market, bringing with them the old savageries that had once defined the landscape.

Kane sat in a bucket seat facing the negotiator aboard the patchwork Chinook helicopter. The negotiator, Bucks, was an amputee in his late twenties whose legs had been cut off at the knees and replaced with scythe-like blades of fiberglass on which he walked with surprising, insectile grace.

Buchs had black hair slicked back from his forehead revealing a widow's peak, and a neatly trimmed mustache brushed his top lip. He wore a silky black shirt, wide open at the collar to show three buttons' worth of chest hair down his sternum, and abbreviated combat pants that ended in ties just beneath his knees, leaving his bladelike leg attachments free from obstruction. The chopper belonged to the negotiator's people, one of a number of treasures they had acquired during their scavenging of the fallen baronies.

"Oh, it's more than a 'stash,' my friend," the negotiator hollered back in his singsong voice. "We're talking database material here, whole plans for how to fashion the old tech. Blasters, ammo, even a rig like this one." He pointed vaguely in the direction of the whirring rotors above them.

Kane raised his eyebrow. "Deathbirds?" he queried.

Buchs nodded. "D-birds, screamwings, Tomahawks, Apaches. Did you know the prenukecaust people named all their helicopters after old Indian tribes?"

Kane gestured a nonanswer, taking the man's point with only passing interest. "How long 'til we reach the drop point?" he shouted.

The negotiator narrowed his eyes in confusion, cupping a hand to his ear.

"How long?" Kane repeated.

"Minute, maybe two," the paraplegic assured him. "Not long. Look out this side—once we cross over the ridge you'll be able to see it."

Kane peered as indicated through a square window that sat in the middle of the side door, straining forward a little to get a better perspective on the ground. The chopper was crossing the Panamint Mountains that bordered Death Valley, an area that Kane and his partners knew well. Kane had once been a Magistrate in the nearby city of Cobaltville, an enforcer of the law within its strictly regimented city walls. That was before he had learned the truth about the hybrid barons, and with his partners, Brigid Baptiste and Grant, defected to join the Cerberus agency.

Those same two partners were with him now, assuming the roles of science and finance advisors for the scam they were trying to pull on the negotiator and his boss. They hoped the scam would put them in position to close down this poisonous network of gunrunners and weapons-makers.

Grant was a hulk of a man, with ebony skin and shoulders so wide he had to hunch over just to fit into the bucket seats of the retrofitted chopper. Several years older than Kane, Grant was dressed in casual wear, a dark sweater over a wine-colored shirt and heavy canvas pants that featured low pockets that bulged out along the length of his hips.

Grant's head was shaved and he sported a goatee-style beard above which he currently wore a pair of round-framed spectacles. The glass in the spectacles was clear, a concession to his role as advisor rather than to correct defective vision. The simple but effective trick made this brute of a man appear marginally less menacing. Grant, like Kane, was an ex-Magistrate from

Cobaltville—in fact, the two had worked together for several years before being exiled from the ville's walls following a terrible showdown with its ruler, Baron Cobalt.

Grant sat silently in his seat, eyeing the armed guards who were poised beside and behind the paraplegic negotiator. There were five in all, and each one had a mini-Uzi or MP-9 cradled in his or her hands. Grant had no doubt that all of them had other blasters about their persons, too, as befitted arms dealers, and he did little to disguise his interest as he made a mental note of the bulges in their clothing where weapons likely lurked.

Grant and his two Cerberus teammates were traveling unarmed, of course—that was part of the arrangement of meeting Mr. Buchs and his paymasters, and there was no room for negotiation with regard to that. All three Cerberus operatives had been marched through a portable metal detector and frisked with professional precision before they had been allowed to board the private Chinook. None of them had come armed—this was a reconnaissance mission; they weren't looking to start a war. Not yet.

Sitting beside Grant was the final figure of the field team, the beautiful Brigid Baptiste. Tall and slender, Brigid wore a figure-hugging black one-piece that left little to the imagination, accentuating the swell of her breasts and the curve of her hips. Peeking above the high-buttoned collar of the suit, Brigid's pale face wore an expression of disinterest behind her small square-framed glasses. Brigid was both an academic of prodigious intellect and a passionate romantic, and her features seemed to reflect those characteristics. Her eyes were a brilliant emerald-green beneath a high forehead, while her rose-petal lips were full and sensuous.

However, Brigid's most striking feature was her red-gold hair, which curled about her head like a sunburst.

Unlike Kane and Grant, Brigid had never trained as a Magistrate. Her discipline had been as an archivist in the vast history project of Cobaltville. Unfortunately for her, she had happened upon evidence of a grand conspiracy that had led to her expulsion from the ville. But while Brigid was an archivist by training, she had become highly skilled in the arts of combat, having learned from Kane, Grant and others to defend herself during the fraught missions that the Cerberus trio found themselves engaged in with alarming frequency.

Though Brigid appeared bored, she was in fact taking in everything—and in more detail than one might expect. Brigid had an eidetic—or photographic—memory, and was able to retain and reproduce the slightest detail of anything she had seen or read, recalling it perfectly after a single glance.

As the chopper pitched around, Kane watched through the small window and he drew in a breath as their destination suddenly came into view.

There, between the mountainous lines of the Panamint Range, crouched a long black building of sturdy construction. It looked like an upturned table with four towering chimneys, one on each corner, all four belching white-gray smoke into the atmosphere. The temperatures were always in flux in this region, Kane knew, roasting in the daytime but dipping into the minuses with nightfall. With such extremes and the lack of roadways, the factory sat in what was without doubt an inaccessible spot, free from casual discovery. Quite how its owners had managed to construct it tucked among the peaks like this, he could not imagine, but the evidence before his eyes could not be disputed.

"There she blows," Buchs told him, leaning across for a closer look.

Kane glanced at the man for a moment, smelling mint julep on his breath as he spoke. "Mighty impressive," he commented. "You find this place or build it?"

"Built it," Buchs shouted with a proud, toothy smile. "The air around here is real clean, good for manufacturing the kind of stuff we wanted, free from dust and junk like that."

"And prying eyes," Grant added from over Kane's shoulder. Even raised as it was, Grant's voice was a low rumble like approaching thunder, emanating from somewhere deep in his chest.

The mustached negotiator nodded. "Life's easier that way, isn't it?"

The Chinook dipped lower, circling the vast factory. Oblong in shape, Kane estimated that the factory stretched the length of a thousand feet. Veering around, the Chinook's pilot located the landing pad—just a square of smoothed rock among the otherwise uneven ground—and brought the craft down into a swift drop. There were roads here, Kane saw as they descended, rough paths cut through the uneven terrain. Perhaps not so inaccessible after all, then.

Recognizing the landing pattern, the paraplegic shimmied back in his seat and clung to a handhold that jutted from one wall. He gritted his teeth as the chopper came down, landing with the violence and abruptness of a prizefighter's punch.

Kane had taken the cue and braced, too, as the craft came to land. Behind him Brigid lurched forward in her seat, tumbling toward Kane's seat back until Grant grabbed her with one of his big paws, his well-muscled arm stopping her like a safety bar on a fairground ride.

An experienced chopper pilot and passenger, Grant dismissed Brigid's thanks with a smile. "Gotta know when to hold 'em," he told her.

"And when to fold 'em," Brigid finished, smiling back.

An instant later, two of the armed guards hurried forward to unlatch and draw back the doors before their leader, Buchs, made his way out of the craft on his gracefully curving fiberglass limbs. His artificial walk reminded Kane of a grasshopper, with a bouncing gait that made it appear he was walking on a springy surface like an old bouncy castle.

Kane stepped from the helicopter and joined the negotiator while Grant, Brigid and the other security officers followed. They were thirty feet from the outside wall of the factory, where a set of rollback doors had been opened wide. The sunlight turned the brown paint of the doors a pleasing shade of umber. People and machinery could be seen working inside the building, sparks flying like film scratches on the air where metal was tooled and cut, whining and screeching like a choir of cats. Beside the rollback doors, a line of jeep-type road vehicles had been parked, six in all, roofless and each one painted black. They looked new and Kane suspected they had come from the factory's production line.

"So, what is it you make here, Mr. Buchs?" Kane asked as he kept pace beside the negotiator.

"Little of everything," Buchs told him, trudging along with his strangely bounding steps. "Your people said you'd be able to fund us through to the year after next, but I have to warn you it's a pretty big production line we have going now."

Kane smiled. "All to the good," he said, "if it means a better return on our investment, right?"

The negotiator laughed. "Sure."

Stepping past the jeeps—and noticing their wet-paint smell even as he did so—Kane made his way through the wide doors and into the factory. Three stories high from the outside, the factory was four deep within, another story carved into the rock itself. It appeared to be just one gigantic room split in two down the middle. Vast conveyor belts snaked through the room, rising to a height of fifteen feet or more, many of them wider than the vehicles at the doors. There were more vehicles inside, including several jeeps in use, a flatbed truck and two helicopters. The helicopters were still in the process of being built, their exposed shells looking like something ravaged by locusts.

There were other things being constructed in the factory, too. Kane recognized several types of weapons, including his favored Sin Eater, trundling along a production line and spewing from a buzzing mechanical unit overseen by a half-dozen women in overalls. The whole factory was a cacophony of noises, buzzing and hissing and clanking and whirring, as various units pressed and popped and moulded and shaped a plethora of items. Despite the harshness of that wall of noise, it sounded somehow tranquil after the heavy thrumming of the Chinook's rotors.

Striding with the grace of a swan in flight, Kane's paraplegic liaison led the three Cerberus teammates across the vast room, past the groups of packers and checkers who huddled at various points around the conveyor belts like trained rats in a maze awaiting their food reward.

"Looks like a broad variety of items being constructed here," Brigid observed, raising her voice over the discordance of the factory floor.

Buchs nodded. "Guns, ammo, rigs—you name it," he trilled with pride. "We're looking to start up a line of Sandcats."

"How can you produce such variety?" Grant asked. "Stuff like this involves a lot of technical know-how."

"We acquired one of the databases out in Cobalt," Buchs explained. "Computer full of designs, just needed to get things up and running here so we could start making them wholesale. Took eighteen months to get this far—and we're only just getting started."

"But all of this takes money," the paraplegic continued as they passed a production line of minicannons, portable antitank devices that required two men to move them. "And that's where you boys come in, Mr. Kane."

Kane nodded. "Well, let me assure you, I like what I see here. Reckon we can make a solid return on our investment."

The mustached negotiator slapped Kane on the back. "We ain't in the Deathlands now—people expect to get paid for working. But you'll get back double, mebbe even triple what you put in in the first year alone. I can guarantee you that.

"Let's go meet the chief."

With that, Buchs led Kane and his companions up a flight of wrought-iron stairs that ran alongside the wall of the factory. The staircase led up two flights to a high L-shaped platform that abutted two adjoining walls of the factory, running the full length of both, high above the workstations. Buchs's fiberglass legs clanged against the iron stairs.

As they ascended, Brigid called out to Buchs from

behind Kane. "I'm wondering how you manage the distribution once your product is complete, Mr. Buchs."

Buchs peered back over his shoulder as he reached the midlevel flight of the staircase. "There are tracks through the ravines," he explained. "Hard to spot from the air, but they're there. The smaller stuff we can cart out of here on people or mules. The larger items—well, they make their own way mostly."

"Sounds like a tidy arrangement," Grant muttered as he trudged up the clanging stairs behind his companions, the five sec men following.

While Kane, like his companions, took pains to conform to the illusion that he was a businessman looking for an investment opportunity, he also used the walk up the stairs to surreptitiously secure a better idea of the factory layout. A conveyor belt of newly completed guns ran beneath the edge of the staircase, their smooth bodies each made of a single vacuum-molded piece. Given the rate of the conveyor belt, Kane estimated that this factory was pumping out upward of two thousand of the handblasters a day. He knew then that he and his team were right to shut this place down; whatever came out of the factory, its ultimate result was more human misery.

Buchs reached the top of the staircase and turned, directing Kane and his entourage toward a single office that was located here among the rafters overlooking the works.

The metal catwalk ran along the walls of the factory, lit only by the sunlight that streamed through a series of horizontal slit windows that traced a line around the whole plant. Lights dangled from buzzing fixtures, running off some hidden generator. Up here among the shadows, the owner's office ran fifteen feet of frosted glass and boards, the latter painted black. The posse walked beside it to reach its lone door. The door, like the walls, had a pane of glass in it, though this one was clear.

Buchs grasped the office door handle, and Kane glanced through the panel of glass before the door swung back. A wide table ran the length of the room and a man sat dead center in a leather chair. He was shuffling papers but looked up at the sound of the opening door. The man had thinning brown hair drawn back in a ponytail. His face was so gaunt it looked like a skeleton's, with thick ridges of acne scarring running down both cheeks. His eyes were a blue so pale they appeared almost white. Kane recognized him as soon as he looked up, and his heart began to race. Jerod Pellerito was one of the earliest lawbreakers that Kane had arrested in his career as a Cobaltville Magistrate. If Pellerito should recognize him, Kane knew, then they were probably in a lot of trouble. A whole lot of trouble.

Without realizing it, Kane held his breath as Buchs pushed the door open for him and encouraged him inside. Kane entered the room at the man's urging, with Brigid and Grant following close behind.

The pockmarked man at the desk took a moment to scrutinize his guests, then Kane's heart sank as the professional smile on Pellerito's gaunt face drained away.

"You're shittin' me!" Jerod Pellerito exclaimed in disbelief. "Magistrate Kane, you motherless bastard."

Chapter 3

Kane had been younger back then, and much more impulsive. The crimes hadn't mattered so much, just the hunt and its conclusion. Following in his father's footsteps, Kane became a full-fledged Magistrate, and he already had that drive to be better, to *do* better.

Smart drugs had been appearing in the upper levels of Cobaltville, distilled herbs and plant extracts that appealed to the intelligentsia. Kane and Grant, already partners, had been following the trail for a while, conscious that the problem was increasing. Someone was importing this stuff from beyond the ville walls, but they were moving it quickly, deftly able to sidestep the ville patrols.

The case had taken on a more serious tone when one of the abusers died from taking a dose. Until then it had been a few privileged kids getting high, but a death made it all much more urgent, raising the stakes and drawing the baron's attention. Kane had been the responding officer when the call came in. It had been raining when he arrived at the school, dark clouds leering heavily overhead. The school catered to the children of well-heeled parents, doctors and dentists and division supervisors, the professionals and administrators who kept Cobaltville running.

Kane arrived alone at the principal's office, the heels of his uniform boots sounding loud in the silent corridors. The whole school had an atmosphere, a weight to it that Kane could feel as he strode the corridors, a kind of misery that was every bit as real as the lime paint on the walls.

The principal, an open-faced woman with graying hair cut in a long bob, had jumped with surprise when Kane entered her office. He hadn't knocked; he was a Magistrate, so it was his prerogative to go where he pleased.

The principal had been sitting at her desk, and Kane could see she had been crying. She dropped the paperwork from her hands as she looked at Kane, eyeing him with fear. Kane wore the standard Magistrate uniform beneath a long black raincoat; black leather polycarbonate armor with a red shield on the left breast to signify his office, a solid black helmet with a visor that came low over the bridge of his nose, hiding his eyes. The uniform had been designed to menace, to create a presence, to instil dread in those who saw it. Clearly the Magistrates were not in the business of making friends.

"Magistrate—?" the principal began, flustered.

"Kane," Kane said helpfully. When she said nothing, he continued. "You're Principal Neighley. You called the division about a death on the premises. A student."

After a moment, Principal Neighley nodded. The movement was confused, as if she had just been woken up. "Yes, Helena Vaughn. Dear Helena." Then she sighed, shaking her head.

Sensing that the woman was about to cry again, Kane turned and made his way to the door. "Where is the body?" he asked.

Principal Neighley followed, sniffling quietly to herself. "Room 2-B, Helena's homeroom."

Neighley walked with Kane, directing him even

though it was unnecessary; he could read the signs on the wall that had been written for kids to understand. The woman came up to Kane's triceps, but he made no allowance for her shorter stride, just hurried on, yearning to see the crime scene and to get started.

The corridors were quiet, the classroom doors closed. But Kane could sense the eyes watching him, the students talking in heavy whispers, peering through frosted glass at the leather-clad Magistrate among them. Death in a school changed things, changed the school. Five years from now these kids would have left and the student body would have regenerated, and no one here would remember what the girl Helena Vaughn was like. They would just tell the story, and tell ghost stories about her, how she haunted the classrooms, turning the air ice cold, killing students who got stuck here at night.

"She's in here, where we found her," Neighley explained as they reached the door to room 2-B. She looked at Kane for a moment, as if waiting for him to dismiss her, to remove her from this nightmare come to life.

Kane said nothing, and his helmet made his emotions impenetrable, as if he wasn't really human.

Reluctant but resigned, Principal Neighley opened the door into the classroom and she and Kane stepped inside.

Kane saw her right away, sprawled in her seat, head lolling back so that her long blond hair draped behind her, brushing the floor with its tips.

"She was an excellent student," Neighley explained. "We never expected…"

Kane ignored the woman, stepping closer to the body. A pencil case was open on the girl's desk, its contents strewn across a personal jotter. A computer dominated the rest of the desk, a modern DDC, equipped for vocal and retinal commands. Kane peered at the screen for a moment but it was blank. Little surprise, it had shut off in the time it had taken for the Magistrate Division to be called in, for Kane to arrive. He looked then at the corpse, taking her in for the first time.

She was fifteen and beautiful, thin but with the shape of a woman, a subtle touch of makeup on her pale face. Her ash-blue eyes were open, staring vacantly, while her lips were drawn into a moue that made her seem almost to be listening, awaiting her turn to speak in some dangling conversation.

Removing one black glove, Kane reached down with his bare hand and felt the girl's neck, confirming there was no pulse. She still felt warm, but Kane could tell she was cooling down, rigor mortis setting in. Without turning back to Neighley, he asked what had happened.

"We don't know," the principal answered. "One minute she was fine, and then she started rocking back and forth and—this. We don't know."

Kane turned, eyeing the room and the principal, his eyes masked by the visor he wore. "Who found her? Was it you?"

"Instructor Levy," the principal explained. "It was her form. I think one of the other girls first noticed that dear Helena was behaving strangely and then…" Neighley didn't go on, instead she broke down in tears, the emotional floodgates finally giving out.

"I'll need to speak to them both," Magistrate Kane said in his professional voice, emotionless.

Principal Neighley was sobbing, a handkerchief clutched in her tiny, cold hand, the sounds coming around it like the squeak of a rodent. Between sobs, she promised Kane she would find them, and Kane waited while she left the room to locate them.

Alone now, Kane stared at the girl's corpse. Sprawled in the chair, Helena didn't look serene or peaceful to Kane; she simply looked dead. He strode around the body and the desk as the rain lashed the windows, examining the scene through the medium of his visor. Swirling handwriting curled across the open page of the jotter, and tiny pictures had been drawn down the margin, hearts and flowers. Three pens lined up beside Helena's open pencil case, her name inscribed along their shafts close to the apex.

And then Kane saw it, peeking out from just under the open mouth of the pencil case itself—a little package of pills. He reached inside, drew the package out with the tip of his index finger, clawing it across the desk's surface until it could be seen properly. It looked like an ordinary bag, transparent and waterproof with a resealable plastic zipper across the top. Kane peered through the plastic at the contents, three white pills like chalk bullets. They could have been painkillers, but she was dead, right here. Whatever these drugs were, they were sitting right here, too, right inside the lip of her pencil case.

Kane was still studying the bag's contents when Instructor Levy and the student who had first alerted her to Helena's distress walked into the classroom.

"Magistrate—?" Levy began. She was a young woman with an olive complexion and a jaw that made her face seem too long.

Glancing up, Kane told them both to sit. Then he took the package of pills and, ignoring Levy, showed it to the kid, a brunette with tousled hair as if she had just gotten out of bed. The girl looked intimidated even before he began.

"You recognize these?" Kane asked.

The brunette visibly swallowed, her eyes flicking left and right before she broke down in tears. Ten minutes later, Kane knew everything, from what they were to where they came from and who was supplying them. Smart drugs, chemicals designed to make their users more intelligent. They were supposed to enhance a user's concentration, ensure a greater level of recall, make the brain run quicker.

Whether they did or not, Kane could certainly see the appeal. Cobaltville was a strictly regimented society where prestige was bound up with status. As a rule, its people were born into their class with very little room for movement—those who were close to the baron lived in the highest levels of the Residential Enclaves; those designated the dregs of society would have a tough time escaping the Tartarus Pits at the base of the structure. In between, the other tiers all had their checks and balances, ensuring a society that remained static and docile. As a Magistrate, Kane saw more of it than most ever would.

To maintain social status, the pressure was on to succeed, to stay smart and beautiful so you would fit in, retain your family's position. These schoolkids knew that better than most; they felt it every day, in every lesson, at every family meal.

Kane had grown up the son of a Magistrate, and it was expected that he would follow in his father's footsteps. His father had drummed that into him over and over when he was just a child. These kids would be getting that same speech every night from their parents, assuring that they, too, must become doctors and dentists and supervisors in the Historical Division. It didn't take much for a kid under that kind of pressure to get sucked into drugs, especially the kind that promised a shortcut to their goals.

"Ain't no shortcuts," Kane muttered as he exited the school premises, back out into the driving rain.

THE KID RAN IN THE SAME social circle, but he was smart already. Smart enough to know what his classmates wanted and how to package it for them in bite-size chunks that he could sell for a tidy profit. Where he was getting the ingredients from was still a mystery to Kane, but he would find that out in time.

Magistrate Kane didn't bother to knock when he reached the Pelleritos' apartment; he just walked right in. The Program of Unification had decreed that no citizen of the villes could have a lock on his or her door; trust was expected of every person if society was to function.

Jerod Pellerito wasn't home, and his parents, well, they weren't anywhere at all. Later, Kane would discover that Jerod had slipped through the net after his parents had been hurt in an engineering accident at the plant where they both worked. Now, the mother was dead and the father was in a coma in the medical facility, just as he had been the past seven months and would probably be for the next seven, at the very least. Their son, the fourteen-year-old Jerod, had been left with a lot of time to explore Cobaltville without supervision, and he had made some new friends in the undercity where things were a little closer to lawlessness than the Magistrates would care to admit.

Kane stood at the open door, listening. A short corridor stretched back from the front door, tunneling into the meager apartment in the residential complex, the same rabbit warren as everyone else. The apartment was all straight lines, dominated by a large living area with a single, flat window that looked out over west Cobaltville. The light from the far window was filtered through the heavy rainclouds, casting the interior in a miasma of shadows and gloom.

Stepping over the threshold, Kane powered his Sin Eater handgun into his hand from its hiding place in the wrist holster beneath his right sleeve. The weapon seemed to take shape in Kane's hand, extending to its full fourteen inches in length, a stubby muzzle jutting from its cruel, black body. The official side arm of the Magistrate Division, the Sin Eater was equipped with 9 mm rounds. The trigger had no guard, as the necessity had never been foreseen that any kind of safety features for the weapon would ever be required. A Magistrate's judgment was, after all, above suspicion. Kane held his finger straight as the weapon slapped into the palm of his hand; if his index finger had been crooked the pistol would have begun firing automatically.

Warily, Kane took a step into the apartment. He didn't expect trouble, but that didn't mean it wouldn't come. Kane nosed into the dark apartment, the Sin Eater stretched out before him in a two-handed grip. Kane listened with preternatural intensity, his fabled point-man sense reaching out to try to detect possible dangers. The apartment buzzed and clicked as the hot water churned in the tank and the refrigerator hummed to itself, but there was nothing out of the ordinary.

"Magistrate business," Kane called out, breaking the silence. "Anyone home?" His words echoed back to him from hard walls and empty rooms, but no one else made a sound.

Pushing the front door closed silently behind him, Kane entered the apartment, the Sin Eater still poised in his hands. As he reached the end of the short corridor, Kane brushed one hand close to the wall, triggering the motion sensor that fed the overhead lights. The lights snapped on, dimming for a moment as they found a comfortable lighting level to complement the rain filtered gloom.

The apartment was empty; Kane was sure of that now. It smelled of dust and unwashed clothes and of something else—grease and oil, like a mechanic's bench.

Kane looked around. Though it was empty, the apartment was not without interest to a Magistrate. Few were. The main living space had been converted into what appeared to be a workshop, reminding Kane a little of the Magistrate garage where the mechanics worked on the Sandcat vehicles they used outside the ville's walls. There were hunks of greased metal lining the floor, what looked like an industrial turbine resting on the deflated couch, and pots and jars of screws, each carefully sorted by diameter and length.

Kane checked the other rooms of the apartment: two bedrooms, a basic bathroom, an open-plan kitchen. It was untidy, with worn clothes and dirty towels strewed on both bedroom floors, but otherwise there was nothing especially notable about the residence. He'd unearthed evidence of the smart drugs that would be found in Helena Vaughn's body when the coroner completed her analysis later that week. The components were scattered across a desk in the smaller bedroom—standard viral radiation blockers and some plant extracts. In fairness to the Pellerito kid, Vaughn's reaction had been extreme; it was a one-in-a-thousand freak happenstance.

Kane returned to the living room, sending his Sin Eater back to its hidden holster with a well-practiced flick of his wrist tendons. He looked around at the pots and jars, the greasy metal slabs that lay on the couch and floor.

Intrigued, the Magistrate reached down, turning over several of the metal parts—machined cogs and gears, something that looked like it could be armor plate. There was paperwork here, too, smeared with oil-stained fingerprints, a line of penciled workings neatly written down one side, adding personal notes to the printed-out design. Removing his helmet, Kane read the words that were typed in bold there: *Signal block.*

The term was followed by a series of numbers and reference codes and accompanied a cutaway diagram of what appeared to be an octagonal drum or box. It meant nothing to Kane. The only part of it he recognized was what appeared to be a radio transmission unit attached across the upper section of the octagon.

Kane glared at the strange design for a moment. The paper was new but the plan that had been printed on it could be ancient. There was no way to really tell.

Kane looked up as he heard a sound coming from the front door at the far end of the apartment. As he watched, the door pushed open and a scruffy-looking teenager strolled in, hair an unruly dark tangle, a carpet of acne bubbling red and white across his chin, forehead and both cheeks. The lad had a sneering smile, the smile of one raised in privilege who thus valued nothing.

The Sin Eater was back in Kane's hand before the kid even realized he was there.

"Freeze," Kane instructed.

The kid froze, not even knowing what he was doing.

Fear of the Magistrates had become ingrained in the populace, their dark uniforms designed to instil terror.

Kane gestured with the Sin Eater. "Get on your knees, Pellerito," he ordered. "Down on your knees."

Wild-eyed, the kid did exactly as Kane told him, his hands raised up at shoulder height. "Who are—?" he sputtered, struggling on the words.

"Magistrate Kane," Kane told him. "And you're Jerod Pellerito, right?"

The kid nodded, watching as Kane retrieved his Magistrate helmet and placed it over his head with single-handed precision.

"Girl by the name of Helena Vaughn is dead. Know her?"

Pellerito nodded again.

"Then you're in a lot of trouble," Kane told him.

Jerod Pellerito laced his hands behind his head and Kane cuffed him amid the mechanical debris that littered the apartment.

Chapter 4

It was a given that Jerod Pellerito had always been interested in technology. It should perhaps not have come as a surprise to Kane to find him the spider at the center of this factory web.

Standing two paces inside the room above the factory floor, Kane held his hands loosely at his sides and offered his most sincere shit-eating grin. "I'm sorry, I don't think we've met."

"Don't remember me? Jerod Pellerito?" Pellerito scoffed. "Don't you Magistrates remember everyone you screw?"

"Ex-Magistrate," Kane corrected smoothly. "Lot of water under the bridge since then, Mr. Pellerito."

As he spoke, Kane surreptitiously surveyed the rest of the room. Although the large table that dominated the room held fourteen seats, there was only one other individual there besides Pellerito himself: a bald man in a neatly tailored suit wearing dark glasses that completely obscured his eyes. The bald man had a pale complexion and a facial expression that gave so little away that he seemed almost drained of any personality. His suit was tight, clinging to his narrow-shouldered frame in an unflattering way that made him seem almost rodentlike in proportion, its high collar tightly cinched about his throat. The bald man had a large book before him, open at a handwritten page.

Pellerito eyed Kane warily for a moment, his acne-scarred face distorting as he tried to second-guess the man standing before him. Then his eyes flicked across to Kane's companions and his calm facade seemed to return, in control once more. "Well, you're not hanging around with Magistrates, anyway," he decided. "These two know what you used to do for a living?"

Brigid voiced her assent, while Grant just nodded, putting a hand up self-consciously as if to adjust his glasses.

"You left Cobaltville when it started to crumble, I take it?" Pellerito suggested.

"Little before that," Kane corrected. "Difference of opinion with some of my other Mags. Seemed they didn't like the laws I was enforcing."

Pellerito nodded. "Probably for the best," he lamented. "Cobaltville's like the rest of them now. Pesthole with benefits." He shrugged. "So, Robert here tells me you're in the investment game these days. That right?"

Kane nodded, and Pellerito offered him a place to sit opposite him across the vast boardroom table. He introduced the bald man at its far end as his accountant. "A necessary evil, I'm afraid."

Kane took his seat while Brigid and Grant took up positions to either side of him. As they did so, Pellerito swiveled back to a small octagonal unit that rested on a window ledge behind him. Made of unmarked plastic, the unit was no bigger than a hardcover book. Despite its blank appearance, Kane saw three diode strips running across the side, and he watched these come to life as Pellerito flipped a button at the top of the box. For a moment, Kane felt a strange vibration inside his ear, and he realized that the hidden Commtact there had been triggered.

Surgically embedded beneath the skin of the Cerberus field personnel, the Commtact was a radio communications unit that defied conventional detection. Each subdermal device was a top-of-the-line communication unit, the designs for which had been discovered among the artifacts in Redoubt Yankee several years before by the Cerberus exiles. Commtacts featured sensor circuitry incorporating an analog-to-digital voice encoder that was subcutaneously embedded in a subject's mastoid bone. Once the pintels made contact, transmissions were funneled directly to the wearer's auditory canals through the skull casing, vibrating the ear canal to create sound. In theory, even a deaf user would still be able to hear normally, in a fashion, courtesy of the Commtact device.

Kane twitched momentarily as he felt the Commtact snap. Something was playing up and down its frequencies, dispersing any signal it might broadcast or receive. Grant and Brigid felt the same effect as Kane, and were careful to give no outward indication as the radio spectrum buzzed through their ear canals. After a moment, the disorienting effect passed.

"Little something for our protection," Pellerito explained as he took his seat. "Ensure no one's listening in."

Before him, Jerod Pellerito had spread a sheaf of paperwork, which included spreadsheets, tables of figures and a series of three-dimensional construction drawings. Brigid's emerald eyes glanced across the paperwork for less than a second as she adjusted her position to sit, and with a slow blink she digested the information that she had taken in. As she did so, Pellerito continued to speak, running his hand across the papers to tidy them into a neat pile. It was a nervous gesture, contradicting his facade of confidence.

Then Pellerito picked up a metal nail file that lay beside his notes, working its roughened length over his fingernails as he spoke. "We're producing some stuff here that your old Magistrate buddies wouldn't appreciate very much," he explained.

"So we saw," Kane acknowledged.

"But it's a big operation, and there's a huge market for this stuff out there now," the pockmarked trader went on, his eyes still fixed on the fingernail he was filing down. "Seems everyone's arming themselves up the wazoo just now. Between the fall of the baronies and all that religious crusade stuff that floated around, who can blame folks for being scared?"

"It can be brutal out there," Kane agreed, and Pellerito laughed.

"Yeah, it's scary once you're outside of ville walls, ain't it?"

"Touché," Kane replied.

As the two men sparred verbally, Brigid Baptiste stared blankly at Pellerito, apparently offering him the politest minimum of attention. In her mind's eye, however, she was mentally reviewing what she had seen on his desk. The tables of figures gave an idea of the scale of the operation. More interesting, however, were the line drawings she had seen. These showed the inner workings for two different types of antiaircraft missile launchers, with blowback projections and comparisons.

There had been a third sheet, Brigid saw in her mind, obscured by the others. It looked like a construction diagram for some sort of road vehicle, but all she had made out were the tire treads and suspension informa-

tion for the back wheels before Pellerito had covered it.
That information suggested the vehicle was designed to
take a lot of weight—something big, then.

"So, what are we looking at?" Kane probed, glancing across to the bald accountant. "You need investment
for what exactly?"

Pellerito fixed him with his pale eyes. "Come on,
I'll show you."

With that, Pellerito pocketed the nail file and got to
his feet. Buchs and the two sec men waiting by the door
stiffened. Taking his cue, Kane pushed himself away
from the table and stood as Pellerito ambled toward the
door, and Grant and Brigid joined him a moment later.
Remaining seated, the accountant in the corner didn't
even bother to look up from his busy paperwork.

THERE WAS NOTHING INSIDE the Cerberus mat-trans chamber now, just the same six walls, tiled ceiling and floor
that Domi had seen a hundred times before. Behind the
riblike struts of the ventilation ducts, fans whirred, filtering the rank-smelling air from the room. It still re-
tained the faint odor of rotting meat.

"Smells bad, but there's nothing else here," Sela
Sinclair confirmed as she followed Domi, the 9 mm
Smith & Wesson in her hand. The metallic lines of the
handblaster glinted beneath the harsh lights as Sinclair
trained it across the room, turning in a smooth arc to
check the familiar staging area that she had used dozens of times before.

Outside, Edwards was kneeling down at the oily pool
of gunk that had moments ago been a woman. The pool
was spreading across the floor at his feet, shimmering
lines of red, gold, green and blue webbing across its
oily surface, reflected from the Mercator map. "Let's

get this…leak…contained," Edwards growled, shuffling back as the puddle oozed gradually closer.

Behind Edwards, the ops room remained in a shocked silence, almost two-dozen personnel still trying to process what they had just seen. A woman had died here, disintegrating before their eyes.

Standing by his desk, Lakesh cleared his throat, drawing everyone's attention. "Okay, people," he said. "We'll get a cleanup crew in here and have Reba do an analysis of whatever is left of that woman. Mr. Farrell, I also want a full analysis of the mat-trans algorithms before and during the rogue delivery."

Farrell assented and turned back to his terminal, pulling up the relevant data for analysis.

"Mr. Philboyd," Lakesh continued, "run through the current functionality. Full system check."

Hunched at another of the terminals, Brewster Philboyd, a lanky figure with dark-framed glasses, receding blond hair and pockmarked cheeks, nodded his acknowledgment of the request, his fingers already playing across his computer keyboard.

"Donald?" Lakesh continued.

From close by, Donald Bry—Lakesh's right-hand man—came marching over with a half-full cup of coffee in his hand. He wore a fretful expression beneath unruly copper curls of hair, and his brow was creased with concern. Coffee stained the front of his tunic, evidence that the sudden appearance of the mat-trans traveler had surprised him. "Yes, Lakesh."

"Organize a team to do a complete check of the mat-trans network. Find out if this has been happening elsewhere," Lakesh instructed. "We may just be one of numerous mat-trans facilities that have witnessed this phenomenon."

A computer expert by training, Bry inclined his head in agreement before scurrying off to select his research team.

"As for the rest of you," Lakesh said, raising his voice to be heard. "Get back to work. We have a field team out there right now, and they need our support."

Beth Delaney, the blonde comms op, called to Lakesh from the communications hub. She wore a commset hooked over one ear, its pickup microphone jutting out on a thin wire just beyond the extent of her jaw. The flesh around her jaw was puffy where a wound was still healing. Her jaw had been broken a couple of months ago during a brutal invasion of the Cerberus redoubt. "Shouldn't we warn CAT Alpha?" she asked. "They intend to return via mat-trans at some point today."

Lakesh considered this for a moment. Kane's team— CAT Alpha—had accessed the mat-trans to reach their current destination, where they were investigating a conspiracy to supply arms. "For now we must maintain radio silence," Lakesh decided. "To tip their hand too soon, to alert their foes to our presence, could prove even more dangerous for them than whatever has happened here."

Beth nodded, returning to her monitoring of the communications network.

KANE KEPT PACE AS Jerod Pellerito led the way, walking beside him as they made their way along the metal walkway that arched over the factory floor. Brigid and Grant followed, surreptitiously observing everything that was proceeding in the factory while Robert Buchs kept a rear guard with two of the security officers, bounding along on his scythelike leg extensions, the guards exuding bored efficiency.

"Makes sense you getting into the weapons game," Pellerito opined as they strolled along the catwalk. "Ex-Magistrate like you knows his firepower."

Kane gave a cruel smile. "Formally trained," he said. "Had to put it to some use when I got out of the system."

"So how did that come about, again?" Pellerito asked. "You were a pretty fearsome bastard when I met you."

"Just a disagreement," Kane said dismissively. "Personal stuff."

In less than a minute, Pellerito had led the group the full length of the catwalk to the far side of the factory. From up here they could see the conveyor belts churning, transporting glinting shafts of metal along their trundling lengths, the familiar burn of acetylene torches illuminating the factory floor in lightning splashes, grinding wheels spinning and howling as workers smoothed the rough edges off their wares. Beyond the buzz of workers, one area had been effectively fenced off by curtain-draped scaffolding. Beyond it, a single large operation was in progress with several whitecoats moving back and forth to examine specific parts of the construction.

"See that?" Pellerito said, gesturing to the enclosed area.

Kane placed his hands on the catwalk's safety rail and peered over the edge. Below him, over the lip of the curtained-off area, he saw a massive tubelike structure in the process of construction. A metallic cylinder with a two foot diameter was being put together piece by piece, sections of it waiting to be attached, workmen running metal files over its surface to smooth the edges where they would join. Because it was still in pieces, it was impossible to judge how long the cylinder would ultimately be, but it looked huge.

Kane's gaze worked over the parts for a half minute, recognizing the flaring tail fins and the nose cone with its bed of circuitry. The ex-Mag's stomach clenched as he realized what Pellerito's men were constructing.

"What is that?" Kane asked, to confirm his worst fears. "A missile?"

Smiling wickedly, Pellerito nodded. "Guided missile," he explained. "Nuclear payload, the works. I have several buyers lined up who'll pay a lot for one of these."

"What are they hoping to do?" Grant asked, peering over the edge of the walkway. "Start a war?"

Turning to him, Pellerito shrugged. "I'm just supplying the goods, not playing Magistrate. The baronies are in disarray, villes are starting to make their own laws now. Guess you never know when you'll need more firepower than your friendly—or not-so-friendly— neighbor."

Turning back from the platform edge, Brigid addressed Pellerito. "You said this thing was nuclear?"

"Nuclear capability, yes," Pellerito clarified.

"And you have the load material?" Brigid asked insistently.

Pellerito offered a broad smile. "What is this, the third degree?" He was becoming suspicious, Kane could see, uncomfortable with the direction Brigid's questions were leading.

Kane reached one strong arm around the man's shoulders before he could step away. "We're planning to give you a long line of credit, Jerod," he said. "We want to know what we're getting into. Stands to reason, doesn't it?"

Pellerito nodded, as if convincing himself. "Yes, that does make sense," he said after a moment.

"So?" Kane probed. "Are you ready to go nuclear or not?"

Pellerito smiled, and it was the ugly smile of the school bully. It was the same smile Kane had seen all those years before, back when he had arrested Jerod Pellerito as a rebellious teen. "We're all set, Kane. Nuclear strikes on command."

Chapter 5

Kane stared at Jerod Pellerito with his steel-gray eyes like bullets. If Pellerito could supply nuclear missiles, this situation just went from disquieting to catastrophic. Kane and his team had come here to assess an arms factory, not to halt a nuclear conflict.

"Have you supplied many of these—what did you call them—guided missiles?" Kane blustered.

"We only tapped into the designs last week," Pellerito explained. "What you see here is fresh off the production line."

Removing his arm from Pellerito's shoulder, Kane leaned over the edge of the railing, letting out a long sigh as he scanned the missile construction area. Suspecting that he was losing his backer, Pellerito sidled next to him and said conspiratorially, "There's interest out there. A lot of interest. This'll sell, Kane. With the right backer, we could take this to the next level."

"No," Kane said, turning back to the arms dealer. "I'm sorry, Jerod, but I can't back this. We're out."

Pellerito looked astounded, but he composed himself swiftly. "That's too bad," he lamented. "You could have been a kingmaker."

"Not my style," Kane told him, signaling to Grant and Brigid that they were leaving. Kane was uncomfortable here now, standing this close to the very type of weapon that had set humanity on the road to self-destruction two hundred years before. That time, the population had been cut down to a fraction of its former size, and left the survivors living in a virtual hellscape. Seeing the building blocks laid out, seeing it all start again like this, did not sit well with him. He wanted to get out of there, ponder his next move, bring in Cerberus and shut this operation down, root and branch. How the hell did this kid come out of Magistrate incarceration to end up like this?

"There's just one problem, Kane," Pellerito said as the Cerberus team gathered themselves up. "You've seen the operation now—and perhaps my people weren't clear to your people about this—but we can't let you leave."

Kane turned back to face Pellerito, and as he did so he heard the distinctive click of safety catches being switched on the sec men's weapons.

"We need money," Pellerito said, "not friends. You've come too far to back out now."

CERBERUS MEDIC REBA DEFORE had never wanted to play coroner, and she had done too much of that over the past six months. Now she knelt before the inky stain pooled across the operations room floor outside Cerberus's mat-trans chamber—the one that had been a woman—with a portable lab beside her.

DeFore was a stocky woman with long, ash-blond hair that she had tied behind her in an elaborate French braid. Besides the standard-issue white jumpsuit, DeFore wore a pair of thin rubber gloves with which she could sift through the oily detritus without contaminating it.

The area of the inky stain had been cordoned off using a couple of well-placed chairs, allowing Reba to work undisturbed as standard procedures continued all around her in the operations center. The black liquid had spread to a rough circle pattern that ran about nine feet in diameter, and it glistened under the fluorescent lights of the room, an oily rainbow shimmering across its surface as DeFore collected her samples.

The circle still had four struts poking from it, a vestigial hint of how the limbs had been spread when the mysterious woman had dropped to the floor here. The farthest edges of the stain were dry now, and the remainder was evaporating as DeFore worked, scraping the coal-black residue from the floor. The dark material had a powdery quality, clotting from the liquid into tiny islands of solid matter that adopted an almost crystalline appearance, like flecks of onyx littering the floor. She leaned closer, running the metal tip of her scraper across the lumps, pulling a few more away to analyze under the microscope.

As DeFore continued to work, running a battery of tests on the samples, Lakesh strode across the room to join her, standing on the far side of the carefully placed chairs that formed the barricade around the stain. "Have you found anything, Reba?" he inquired gently.

The Cerberus medic looked up from her work, a serious expression on her striking features. "It's genetic matter," she summarized, "which appears to be going through the standard stages of decomposition far faster than one would expect. I wish I'd been here when the—woman, you said?—when she came through the mat-trans."

Lakesh stroked his chin pensively. "You said the material was experiencing decomposition at a faster rate than normal."

"'Normal' is too specific a term," DeFore corrected,

"but certainly, the body has deteriorated far faster than a human should in this environment. Normally, the human body passes through five stages of decomposition once it has died.

"In stage one, once the blood stops pumping the flesh will take on a bluish hue and rigor mortis will set in, stiffening the tissues and making it difficult to move the limbs.

"That is followed by the bloat stage, where anaerobic metabolism begins to break down the body, resulting in the accumulation and dispersal of gases.

"Stage three is active decay, which involves the purging of decomposition fluids. This is typically the period of greatest mass loss, when what had been a corpse moves to resemble something more like a skeleton." DeFore fixed Lakesh with her steady brown eyes. "The body here has passed through that stage with incredible rapidity. From what you've told me, it appears to have reached that stage less than a minute from the woman's arrival in the mat-trans."

Lakesh peered down at the inky stain. "What are the other stages?" he inquired.

"Stage four is characterized as advanced decay, where the carcass breaks down more slowly as less cadaveric material is available." DeFore informed him. "That's followed by the dry stage, basically where the corpse is just dried-out skin and bones with no flesh remaining.

"In this case, the woman seems to have liquefied, such was the speed with which stage three took hold. What we're looking at here are decomposition fluids, albeit turned a rather nasty color on expulsion."

"She was covered in an oily sheen of unknown nature," Lakesh clarified.

"It appears to have mixed with the body during breakdown."

"Do you have any idea what it's made of?" Lakesh asked.

"Hard to tell without a proper analysis," the medic admitted. "There's nylon in there, along with Mylar and something that resembles Nomex."

"Nomex?" Lakesh blurted in surprise. "The fire-resistant material?"

DeFore nodded. "Whatever it was your visitor was covered in, it was most likely intended for her protection."

Lakesh looked thoughtfully down at the inky stain that had expanded across the ops room floor. "If that is the case, then I think we can say it failed. This time."

"You believe it will happen again?" DeFore asked.

Lakesh nodded solemnly. "Somebody went to a lot of trouble to send this woman here. I would wager they won't give up at the first failure."

ON THE CATWALK IN THE Panamint arms factory, Kane had turned to face Jerod Pellerito as twin guards covered his Cerberus teammates.

"Now, back up a minute here…" he began.

"Sorry, Kane," Pellerito mocked, "but we can't risk you leaving here now. The deal was that you came to view the investment. There was no provision for you to reject the deal. You were just here to talk terms, and if there aren't any terms to discuss then I'm afraid we've reached the end of our relationship. But I'm sure your employers will pay handsomely for your safe return. You'd better hope so, eh?"

Kane was only half listening. Already his senses

were reaching out, analyzing possible options, searching for his best escape route.

"If it makes you feel a shitload happier," Pellerito concluded, "I had a terrible time inside, thanks to you. So I suppose this is kind of karmic payback."

"You know what?" Kane growled, slapping his hands against the safety bar that surrounded the catwalk. "That ain't gonna do it for me."

Before Pellerito realized what was happening, Kane vaulted over the side of the catwalk and disappeared from view.

"What th—?" Pellerito blurted as Kane dropped down to ground level.

Still on the catwalk, Grant and Brigid took their cue even before the guards could react. Grant's muscular right arm swung back, grabbing the barrel of the nearest guard's blaster and yanking it forward, dragging blaster and man toward him.

The guard reacted by pulling the trigger, but the weapon—a modified MP-9 submachine gun—was out of his grip before the first bullet had left the chamber. Grant cursed as a blur of bullets blasted from the weapon, feeling the barrel shudder in his grip as he yanked it away from its previous owner. His other arm was already snapping back, driving the pointed ram of his elbow into the surprised guard's face. The guard crashed backward with the impact, blurting out an abbreviated yelp of pain.

To Grant's side, the red-haired Brigid dropped low and brought her right leg around in a rapid sweep that knocked the second guard off his feet. Continuing her sweeping arc, Brigid spun back to a standing position in a feat of athletic prowess.

Below his teammates, Kane had dropped two stories

to land beside the guided missile with a hard thump, the cushioned soles of his boots absorbing the shock. A surprised whitecoat stumbled as Kane landed beside him in a crouch, but before the man could raise the alarm Kane was rearing up, driving a ram's head punch into the man's jaw. The blow was so hard it knocked the whitecoat from his feet, and the bespectacled man went colliding into a round segment of the missile housing with a metallic clang. The missile tolled like a bell with the strike.

"Stop him!" Pellerito called at the top of his voice, his face turning an angry shade of red as he glared over the edge.

Kane ignored him, shoving another of the whitecoated workers aside as he ducked through the curtains. In a second he was on the factory floor proper, sprinting past whirring blades and trundling conveyor belts as he hurried toward his objective.

"Grant, Brigid," Kane said, engaging his Commtact. All that came back was the whine of a feedback loop, and Kane cursed as he toggled the unit back to standby mode. Whatever Pellerito had done in his office, it was still blocking the signal.

Kane kept running, shunting another of the factory workers aside.

On the catwalk above the factory floor, Robert Buchs was hurrying toward Brigid with loping strides as she recovered from felling the guard. Behind him, more guards were running toward them along the catwalk, newly minted Ruger knock-offs in their hands.

As Buchs drew close, some sixth sense kicked in, and Brigid turned as one of his scythelike legs swept through the air toward her. Buchs had brought his center of gravity low, Brigid observed as she turned, extending his artificial leg like a sword to its maximum reach. The bladelike limb brushed past Brigid's face, slicing through a few rogue strands of her red-gold hair even as she twisted out of its path.

In a moment, Brigid found herself pushed back against the safety bars that ran the length of the catwalk. "Dammit, Kane," she muttered. "What have you walked us into this time?"

Though he may not have voiced his concerns aloud, Grant was thinking much the same as his impulsive partner. Kane seemed to have a knack of getting them into dangerous situations that sprang out of nowhere. It had been the same for as long as Grant had known him, dating all the way back to their days as Magistrates in Cobaltville.

Grant turned the stolen MP-9 over in his hands, adjusting his grip and resting his index finger on the trigger as more guards appeared. Grant didn't like the MP-9, but it would have to do—the cast-iron rule that had been insisted upon before this visit was that the Cerberus team arrive unarmed.

Having checked the breech in a split-second glance, Grant looked up at the cluster of armed guards who were sprinting down the catwalk toward him.

"Put down the weapon and get your hands up where we can see them," the leader called as he halted beside some packing crates, at last spying what Grant was holding.

"Must think I was born dumb," Grant muttered as he swept his glasses aside and raised the weapon. Without hesitation, Grant squeezed its trigger, admiring its smooth action as he sent a lethal volley of 9 mm slugs down the catwalk toward the approaching guards. He smiled grimly as two of them fell, while the remain-

ing three scrambled back, ducking for cover behind
the crates.

Down on the factory floor, Kane was ducking and
weaving through an obstacle course of potential foes,
expending as little energy as possible to reach his objective. He clambered over a moving conveyor belt, kicking aside a half-dozen ammo cases as the workers there
struggled to grab his ankles. One worker went flying off
his stool as a booted ammo case smacked the dead center of his forehead, while another grabbed at her bloody
mouth as an ammo clip knocked her front teeth out.

Kane bent down for just a moment, snatching up
two of the familiar ammo clips from a stuffed box. It
was 9 mm, just what he wanted. Then he was leaping
back to the floor, ducking under a moving cauldron that
was poised to fill a mold with molten metal. Kane felt
its heat blasting against his face as he ran past, driving
himself on toward something he had noticed earlier. He
knew it was around here somewhere—if he could just
figure out where.

ABOVE KANE, BRIGID'S BACK was pressed against the
metal bar of the safety balcony as Buchs rushed at
her, his arms pumping at his sides, his artificial legs
stamping out an angry tattoo against the metal walkway. Brigid leaned back, lifting her body and kicking
out in the blink of an eye.

Buchs saw the move too late, and he found himself
reacting after the event, turning aside even as the sharp
toe of Brigid's booted foot clipped the side of his head.

Brigid brought herself back to a standing position as
Buchs sank dizzily to the floor. But the liaison-cum-
bodyguard was still moving, thrusting one of those

brutal-looking leg attachments out at her like some lethal version of jump-the-rope.

Miss Suzy had a steamboat, the steamboat had a
bell. Miss Suzy took some dynamite and blew the bell
to hell-o, operator, give me number nine...

Brigid leaped, bounding above the first kick of those
legs, only to meet with the second kick-sweep as Buchs
redoubled his efforts.

Brigid tumbled to the floor with a shuddering crash
of bone against metal, her red hair flying loosely about
her head like a flaming halo. Buchs scrambled across
the catwalk, snagging the front of her tunic and shunting her back. There was another awful clang as Brigid's
head struck one of the support bars that held up the catwalk, and she felt the blow ring through her skull like
the steamboat's bell.

Buchs dragged Brigid's bloodied head close and
snarled at her. "You think I'm going to say something
clever?" he growled. "Not my style."

Brigid took that moment to kick him in the crotch
with all her might, and Buchs doubled over with a
strained yelp. Then Brigid pushed herself up from the
catwalk, sweeping a trickle of blood from her mouth
as she loomed over the hunkered and sobbing form
of Buchs. He was in agony. "Think I wouldn't kick a
cripple in the balls?" she challenged. "Not my style."

Down on the factory floor, Kane rolled beneath a
twisting two-ton turner mechanism before bringing
himself up at its far side. The turner kept rolling on its
spindle as Kane ran past.

In another second, Kane was at the production line
he had spotted on entering the building. Six women
were working at the trundling conveyor belt, deftly putting parts together to form the familiar Sin Eater hand-

gun. Kane assessed the line in an instant, reaching for one of the units as the woman working at it completed the construction. "'Scuse me, ma'am," Kane blurted as he reached over her shoulder and snatched up the assembled weapon.

The woman swore in surprise, cursing Kane in Spanish.

Kane ignored her, securing the fourteen-inch hand pistol in his grip and snapping one of the stolen ammunition clips into place. Then he raised the blaster high in the air, pointed it in the direction of the ceiling and snapped off three quick shots. The Sin Eater sounded like a sudden thunderclap in the busy factory, and once Kane had finished everyone on the factory floor had stopped to stare fearfully at him, their assembly lines forgotten.

"We're shutting the hole down," Kane shouted over the harsh whines of the machinery. "Everybody out— *now!*"

Some of the workers stood and stared, but most just grabbed their personal effects and scampered toward the open doors of the factory. Those who did remain took one look at the grim expression on Kane's face and decided not to argue. They knew the factory was illegal, and it was not worth getting involved with this fracas for the paltry sums they were being paid.

On the catwalk overlooking the factory floor, Jerod Pellerito was red-faced with anger as his staff left en masse. "Somebody stop them," he screeched. "We're not—"

But before he finished, Buchs came crashing into him where Brigid had dropped the paraplegic over her shoulder. Pellerito staggered against the wall, shrieking as his delirious aide knocked him off his feet. When he looked up again, Brigid was looming over him, her red-gold hair framing her face like a lion's mane.

MEANWHILE, ON THE FACTORY floor, Kane rushed back to the metal staircase that ran up the side wall of the busy factory. A moment later, he was at the top of the stairs, coming up behind the remaining guards who had been forced to seek cover when Grant began firing. The rearmost guard turned as he heard Kane's heavy footsteps thumping up the metal stairs. The Sin Eater in Kane's hand spit fire, drilling a 9 mm slug into the guard's leg, shattering his kneecap before he knew what was happening. Clutching his ruined leg, the guard let out a scream as he dropped to the metal walkway, his head slamming into it with the clang of a clock-tower bell being struck.

As the other guards realized that they were now under attack from two directions, Kane flitted into Pellerito's office, ducking out of sight. A smattering of impacts came from beyond the room where the remaining guards had turned their blasters on this new enemy, but Kane had a new problem. Without warning, the bald-headed accountant tossed his glass of water at Kane, liquid and glass spinning through the air until they struck the wall just inches from Kane's head.

Kane spun on his heel, bringing his Sin Eater up to target this new attacker.

"What is it? Double cross?" the accountant asked. "Rival outfit wanting more? Think you're going to cut a deal?"

As the accountant spoke, he threw a hard-backed notebook at Kane's face. Kane swept it aside without thought, knocking it to the floor with his free hand.

Then the accountant was on his feet and running across the long table, and Kane saw the flash of something in his outthrust hand. Before Kane knew what was happening, a jointed length of metal cut the air toward his face, striking his cheek with a stinging blow.

Kane spun, dropping away from the strike as the accountant drew the strange missile back to his hand. It was some kind of whip, Kane noted, made up of flexible links of metal that could extend to almost three feet. The odd weapon must have been hidden in the man's sleeve, tucked away in much the same manner as Magistrates would habitually carry their Sin Eaters. It should have come as little surprise to learn the man was armed—this was, after all, an arms factory. Kane cursed himself for naively expecting otherwise.

Before Kane could counterattack, the bald man's other arm snapped up, and the distinctive scent of cordite whispered in the air along with a crack like a book being slammed shut.

Gun, Kane realized even as the bullet zipped past him and shattered the glass in the office door.

OUTSIDE ON THE CATWALK, Brigid grabbed hold of Jerod Pellerito as he pulled himself up from the tangle of limbs, realizing too late which way the tide of battle was turning.

"Pit bitch!" Pellerito screamed, baring his teeth.

Before Brigid knew it, Pellerito was driving one crooked elbow at her face. Brigid reared back, bringing her head just barely out of reach of that outstretched elbow. Fingers clenched in an arrow shape, Brigid jabbed her attacker in the side, striking the nerve cluster. Pellerito screamed in agony, stumbling back against Brigid.

KANE SPUN RAPIDLY ASIDE as the bald accountant snapped
off a second and third shot from his tiny blaster. The
pistol was a tiny 18 mm, its barrel no longer than a
man's index finger.

Kane grunted as one of the bullets clipped his
flank, breathing through his teeth as the impact was
dulled by the armorlike weave of the shadow suit he
wore beneath his clothes. Clinging to its wearer's body
like a second skin, the shadow suit was made of incredibly flexible material with the capacity to deflect
a blade or small-arms fire. The durable suits had other
properties, too, including acting as an artificially con-
trolled environment, regulating the wearer's body temperature and ensuring comfort in the most extreme of
locales. Just now, Kane was thankful it could stop a
small bullet.

Kane brought the Sin Eater up, squeezing the trigger
and sending a burst of fire at the accountant as he leaped
from the table. The shots followed the man, boring into
the back wall as Kane ducked aside. The accountant's
weapon was also firing, blasting bullets at Kane as he
continued moving in the confined space.

The metal whip jabbed through the air at Kane's
throat, lashing against him as he endeavored to weave
out of its path. Then the accountant's blaster was firing again, its stream of bullets tracing across the wall
behind the long table as Kane ducked. One of those
bullets struck the blank, octagonal box that resided
on the sill behind the table, and Kane grimaced as his
Commtact went haywire, sending a high-pitched burst
of static through his skull. Kane tumbled down, slamming against the boardroom table as the echo jabbed at
his brain, cutting through him like a hot knife.

ON THE CATWALK outside the office, Brigid and Grant both howled as their own Commtacts stuttered that same electronic shriek.

The sound was so penetrating that Grant's vision blurred, and he dropped the MP-9 he had snagged from the guardsman. "What the—?"

Brigid, meanwhile stumbled backward, letting go of her grip of Jerod Pellerito. As she struggled to recover, Pellerito moved toward her, the five-inch metal nail file appearing in his hand, wielded like a dagger.

"You fight like a wildcat," Pellerito snarled as Brigid writhed in place, the Commtact howling through her skull. "Now, let's see if you scream like one."

Chapter 6

Things had settled down in the Cerberus ops room. The puddle of goop that had started as a visitor had been cleared away at Reba DeFore's insistence, leaving only a dark mark where it had been. Beth Delaney was back monitoring the communications feeds, and Farrell and Philboyd had joined Lakesh at his desk to report their initial findings.

"I'm afraid I haven't located the source of the rogue incursion," Farrell said. "I've tracked back as far as the mat-trans log can go, but there's no indication of where she entered the system."

"Same here," Philboyd agreed. "And without that information we're going to have a hard time blocking anyone else who utilizes the same pathway."

Lakesh tapped at his front teeth absently as he worked this over in his mind. "No 'in' point," he summarized. The mat-trans system required a sender and a receiver point. In this instance, the latter was the mat-trans chamber at Cerberus. So where was the sender? "Could there be another source behind our visitor?" Lakesh pondered.

Philboyd shrugged. "You know the workings of the mat-trans better than any of us," he stated. "If anyone can answer that question, I'd say it's you."

Deep in thought, Lakesh fixed his eyes on the mat-trans chamber. "Every traveler requires a starting point," he reasoned. "In essence, the mat-trans is a closed loop, and barring a few stray units, is comprised of what were military compounds of the U.S. military.

"We have seen proof that the system is compatible with its counterparts in other countries, such as the Soviet Union," Lakesh went on. "But even they would leave a data trail of some form, some manner in which they could be tracked back."

Farrell ran his eyes over his notes once more. "We can't track her further back than our unit," he confirmed. "It's as if she didn't exist until she arrived here."

"A data glitch, then?" Lakesh mused. "Rogue data, old info somehow generated by the mat-trans?"

Brewster Philboyd adjusted his glasses as he spoke. "I can check into that," he confirmed.

When he broke off, Lakesh encouraged him. "What's on your mind, Mr. Philboyd?"

"Well, it just seems that those sort of things would have been ironed out at the development stage," Philboyd reasoned. "We've not seen such a glitch before. Why now?"

"Could it be that the unit itself is getting older?" Lakesh proposed, deliberately playing devil's advocate.

"I don't see it," Philboyd told him. "We've replaced and upgraded much of the hardware that lets this unit function. At a stretch, it could be something we've added recently."

"While our unit may have been renewed," Farrell pointed out, "what about the others? There are over two hundred of these things on the map. It could be one of them is corrupted and sending us rogue data."

"In which case," Lakesh reminded him, "we would be able to trace the source. And since we can't, it seems reasonable to discount that possibility."

"Which puts us right back where we started," Farrell groused, eyeing his notes with vexation.

"Things don't just appear," Lakesh said. "Nor do people. Our visitor had to have come from somewhere, gentlemen. And if it's an error in our system, I want it tracked and locked before it can happen again."

"And if not?" Philboyd asked in a wary tone.

The question hung in the air unanswered as the three men went back to their investigations.

KANE SAGGED AGAINST the long table as the terrible screech echoed through his ear canal. The Commtact was going haywire in his skull, vibrating his eardrum to a frenzy. It sounded like a hornet trapped behind glass.

As Kane sprawled on the table, the bald head of the accountant came into view, the stubby nose of his revolver swooping down toward Kane's eye.

"Credit's withdrawn, big man," the accountant snarled. His words came to Kane through the shrieking howl of the Commtact. "Time to settle your account."

OUTSIDE THE ROOM, BRIGID found herself staring at the vicious point of a metal nail file as Jerod Pellerito jabbed it at her pretty face, her own Commtact straining with the noise.

"I don't like hurting women," Pellerito admitted. "It will upset my stomach for days doing this."

"Don't...force yourself...on my account," Brigid gasped, struggling to hear her own words through the quagmire of ghost noise.

A LITTLE WAY ALONG THE metal catwalk, Grant had scrambled behind a low stack of boxes, hiding from view as the once-cowed guards renewed their attack.

His head was throbbing, too, the subdermal Commtact vibrating in its hiding place along his mastoid bone. Bullets pelted the other side of the crates as Grant crouched there, clenching his teeth against the awful noise. He was in trouble, he knew, but he couldn't think straight—not well enough to mount a defense, at least.

KANE GROWLED AS THE accountant pulled the trigger, shifting his body even as the bullet left the chamber, dropping from the table in a heap. There was a loud report as the blaster fired, drilling a bullet into the table's wooden surface as Kane slid away.

Finely tuned reactions kicked in, and Kane ducked and rolled as he hit the floor, the shriek in his head obscured by the sound of the bullet being fired. Kane had been so close the bullet had left him temporarily deaf, and that was just what he needed. While he could feel his eardrum vibrating as if it was an itch he couldn't scratch, the static noise from the Commtact had been overwritten by the ringing of the bullet, masking one noise with another.

It gave Kane just enough clarity to think.

The accountant whipped the blaster around, tracking Kane as he rolled away. He snatched at the trigger again, sending another 18 mm shell in the direction of Kane's fleeing figure.

Kane was in continuous motion, letting his highly tuned senses generate a random pattern that kept him just one step ahead of the bald man's gun. Before the accountant realized it, Kane was on him, snapping out with his right fist in a blur of motion, squeezing his Sin Eater's trigger.

There was a burst of propellant as the bullet left the chamber of the Sin Eater, but Kane heard nothing. It was like shooting underwater, the sound obscured into something like a distant, hollow pop. And then the accountant was dropping back, his face and neck erupting in a bloom of blood, its scarlet lashing out across the back wall of the office.

OUTSIDE, GRANT WAS STILL crouched behind the stacked boxes as three guards approached. He peered to his left, seeing their shadows get nearer as they closed in. He had to do something, but he was unarmed and the frenetic buzzing was still running through his skull with the force of a hurricane.

Grant watched the shadows get nearer, then did the only thing he felt able to do—he leaned back hard against the piled boxes, giving them one almighty shove.

KANE IGNORED THE BROKEN figure of the accountant, dismissing the man as he toppled back against the far wall in a splash of blood. Kane's attention was fixed instead on the octagonal box that rested on the window ledge, its strips of light running a triplicate pattern of peaks and troughs. There was a bullet dead center; it had split the casing in two and now rested inside a mess of wires and circuits. Kane glared at it for a moment before reaching for a toggle switch on the side and nudging it to the off position with his thumb.

Kane was still deafened by the gun report, but outside his companions felt a sense of relief as the jamming signal finally abated.

THE STACKED BOXES toppled back, crashing into the guards who had been hunting for Grant. As they did so, the sound in Grant's skull finally cut out, and he breathed a momentary sigh of relief, surprised at the sudden absence.

An instant later, Grant was on his feet, swiftly disarming the guards as they struggled to get free of the toppled stack.

RELYING SOLELY ON HER well-honed battle instincts, Brigid Baptiste had spent the past minute and a half deftly avoiding the jabs of the metal nail file that Jerod Pellerito held, straining to ignore the shriek from her own Commtact. As soon as the awful buzzing stopped, Brigid was moving like a tigress, leaping up and into Pellerito and swiping at the vicious little blade he had attacked her with. In a matter of seconds, the man was disarmed and held in a firm grip.

Down below the struggling figures, the factory was all but abandoned now, almost all of the production-line workers having disappeared once the first shots were exchanged.

Brigid looked up as Kane reappeared from the far end of the catwalk, stepping from the self-contained office. There were still two guards standing there, close to the staircase, unsure of what to do.

Kane leaped over a fallen guard, turning his weapon on the others who remained. Up ahead, Grant was taking potshots at them with a stolen MP-9, and with Kane descending on them from behind, the guards found themselves caught in a pincer movement. As they realized this, the last of them threw their weapons to the ground in surrender, raising their hands in defeat.

"Wise choice," Kane acknowledged as he gathered up the discarded weapons.

For a moment, Pellerito struggled in Brigid's grip, raising one foot and trying to stomp on her toes. She pushed forward with the full weight of her body, driving the arms dealer forward until he was doubled over the safety bars that surrounded the catwalk.

"Do that again and I'll drop you," she warned, "bitch or not."

GRANT GLANCED UP FROM where he was now crouching over the fallen form of Robert Buchs, checking the man for hidden weapons, and he laughed. "Gotta know when the hold 'em…" he reminded the sec man.

Grant's ears were still ringing as Kane disarmed the remaining guards, but the pain was subsiding by the time he joined his companions at the far end of the catwalk.

"I should have recognized a Magistrate sting op." Pellerito cursed as he watched Kane approach. "Didn't expect to see you this far out of the villes, though."

"I told you before, Jerod," Kane said, shaking his head. "We're not Magistrates."

"Then what are you?" Pellerito demanded.

"Something much, much bigger," Kane told him.

Grabbing Pellerito by the collar, Kane brought the Sin Eater up to his nose, shoving it so hard that the gunrunner was forced to tilt his head away.

"Now," Kane growled, "you and I are going to have a chat about where this nuclear material of yours is. And if I don't like your answers, you won't like mine."

IT TRANSPIRED THAT PELLERITO had been bluffing about the nuclear material. All he had was a potential supplier and, as he put it, the ink hadn't dried on the deal. Kane tried to find out more, while Grant and Brigid worked their way through the abandoned factory, setting charges that they had found in the factory's own supplies. Pellerito proved to be of little further help. Wherever the nuclear material was coming from, there were multiple layers of intrigue between here and there. Kane wasn't surprised. This was black market stuff, and he knew from experience that it was the territory of aliases and double agents. In fact, that was one reason that he and his team had been able to infiltrate it with such relative ease.

When Grant and Brigid returned, they came bearing new weapons. Grant had opted for a Sin Eater like Kane's, and he tossed his partner several ammo clips from a bulging box he'd jammed into a workbag strapped over one shoulder. Brigid had chosen something larger, a 12-gauge shotgun based on the old Mossberg design. She held it comfortably by one hand at its rear-mounted grip, its eighteen-and-a-half-inch barrel stretching down to almost scrape the floor beside her heeled boots. The shotgun had no stock and ended abruptly at the grip end. Seeing it, Kane gave Brigid a quizzical look.

"Not your usual choice," he observed.

"Only thing I could find rounds for," Brigid told him, the box of ammunition chinking as she bounced it in her other hand. "Well, other than the Sin Eaters, and I just wouldn't feel right showing you boys up like that."

Having set the charges, Grant led Pellerito, Buchs and the few stragglers from the factory out into the hills. "The whole place is going up," Grant said. "The only thing you're going to find here after is a fire sale."

Pellerito edged closer to Grant, speaking in a low whisper. "You don't want to do that," he said. "Kane's got issues, but you—there's still money to be made here. An ex-Magistrate like Kane can't see that."

Grant fixed the unscrupulous trader with his grim, no-nonsense look. "*I'm* an ex-Magistrate," he said.

Pellerito backed away, cursing both men and the red-haired woman who had accompanied them. Ten minutes later, he and his sec team watched helplessly as Kane's team departed in their Chinook helicopter, the factory burning behind them.

Chapter 7

"They're on the move," Beth Delaney advised as she watched the map update on her monitor screen.

Lakesh peered up from his own desk, putting aside the initial breakdown report that Reba DeFore had handed him just five minutes earlier. Though incomplete, the report gave the first feedback data on the strange visitor who had arrived via the facility's mat-trans less than ninety minutes before. If nothing else, Lakesh was always well served by his efficient staff.

"Who?" he inquired as he caught Delaney's attention.

"Kane's team— CAT Alpha," Delaney told him. "Looks as if they're heading back to their mat-trans. And they're moving at a fast clip."

Delaney was able to confirm this from the real-time updates that were fed to her computer from transponder units worn by each member of Kane's team. The transponder featured global positioning technology that could be tracked via satellite, providing information concerning an operative's current health status. Subcutaneously embedded, the transponders made tracking personnel across the globe an easy and painless task.

"I imagine they're back in the helicopter," Lakesh mused. "Have they been in touch?"

"Not yet," Delaney told him. "Do you want me to raise them?"

After a moment's consideration, Lakesh nodded.

"There may well be good reason they've not contacted us, but in this instance I feel it is prudent to break protocol. We need to warn them about the mat-trans glitch before they access the one in Panamint."

Turning back to her desk, Delaney began hailing Kane and his team. While she did so, Lakesh's eyes flicked over DeFore's report again, checking through the figures she had provided. Besides the nylon and Nomex content in the sample, DeFore had found traces of polytetrafluoroethylene, spandex, Mylar and Kevlar, as well as the expected biological remains. The presence of Nomex and Kevlar worried at Lakesh's sharp mind; it suggested that the mystery woman had been wearing a protective suit of some sort, one designed to survive a harsh environment.

As Lakesh continued to ponder the report, Delaney turned to him and he saw that her brow was furrowed. "No answer," she elaborated, indicating the Commtact.

Stroking his chin in concern, Lakesh placed the report back on his desk. With the Commtact's capacity to pick up subvocalized commands, there was no reason that one of Kane's team could not send a response of some form, even if it was the most basic, veiled acknowledgment.

"Keep trying," Lakesh instructed, but he wasn't looking at the comms op anymore. Instead, his gaze had been drawn back to the mat-trans chamber in the corner of the busy room—the chamber from which the mysterious oil-spill woman had emerged.

"STRANGE," BRIGID MUTTERED as the Chinook dipped low over the Panamint range.

Grant sat at the controls, working the chopper across the snow-dappled mountains toward the hidden military redoubt they had accessed before to reach Pellerito's people.

Strapped in the copilot seat, Kane was peering out the cockpit windows through the cool mist emanating from those mountain peaks when he heard Brigid speak, the word cutting through the regular drumming of the rotor blades. "What's that, Baptiste?" he asked.

Brigid was tilting her head slightly, one hand pressed against her left ear. "I can't seem to raise Cerberus," she elaborated. "Commtact's not responding."

Without further ado, Kane tried his own Commtact, engaging the unit embedded in his skull and calling on the Cerberus monitoring team. The frequency was dead. In fact, all the frequencies were dead.

"Pellerito had that signal scrambler in his office," Kane reminded Brigid. "It took a hit during the firefight, sent a jolt through my head when it went off."

"Mine, too," Brigid said, and Grant added his own agreement with a grunt.

"But I switched the jammer off," Kane said, mystified.

"Could be it shorted our comms," Brigid reasoned. "As soon as we're back at Cerberus we'll run a subroutine to check for a bug. No big deal."

"Yeah," Kane agreed as the chopper skipped over a pocket of turbulence, snow crystals fluttering past its reinforced windows.

A moment later, the hidden military redoubt came into view in a gorge between mountains, its rusting metal door still beautifully camouflaged against the rock-and-soil background.

"Bringing her down in five," Grant advised, raising his voice a moment over the thrumming rotor blades. Then, with marked efficiency, Grant brought the vehi-

cle straight down to the ground in a rapid drop, touching down in a smooth landing.

"Nice touch," Kane complimented him as Grant
powered the chopper down.

"I aim to please," Grant told him

Moments later, the three Cerberus warriors were out
of the helicopter and making their way into the redoubt.
Abandoned for two centuries, the subterranean military
complex smelled of damp, with brownish stains running up its concrete walls. The lights were no longer
operational, their bulbs long since burned out, so Kane
pulled out his xenon-beam flashlight to light their way.
The team had used this redoubt's mat-trans to get here
six hours earlier, and had trekked some distance to the
initial meeting with Buchs and the sec men, keeping
its location hidden.

Their footsteps echoed from the hard walls, sounding like hammer blows in the grim, warrenlike tunnels.
Vast store rooms and living quarters waited beyond the
darkness's edge, their ghostly spaces like half-finished
paintings, empty and forgotten.

It took three minutes for Brigid to lead the team back
to the mat-trans chamber located on a lower level of the
subterranean complex, her eidetic memory more con-
venient and efficient than any map.

The mat-trans chamber took up a dedicated room far
below ground level, the unit itself protected by armaglass tinted cherry-red. With their identical hexagonal
designs, each mat-trans included armaglass of a different color to make identification easier when one traveled
to a new locale. The cherry-colored armaglass shone
for a moment under the powerful beam of Kane's xenon
flashlight, transparent red like a laser wall.

Kane, Grant and Brigid took a few moments to check

around the immediate area until they were happy nothing had been altered since they were last here a few hours earlier. Engaging the mat-trans involved willingly allowing the discorporation of one's physical form; it paid to be certain that nothing had been tampered with.

"All clear," Grant confirmed as his partners returned from their own checks.

Kane tried his Commtact once more before the three of them entered the mat-trans chamber, but still he received no response from Cerberus headquarters. Irritated more than concerned, Kane joined his partners in the teleportation room, mentally preparing himself for the forthcoming journey through the quantum ether as Brigid set things in motion.

"Cerberus, here we come," Brigid said as she confirmed their destination coordinates.

The exterior door locked, and Kane switched off and pocketed the flashlight as the mat-trans powered up. The three Cerberus warriors stood in darkness as hidden mechanisms whirred into action, charging the mat-trans in preparation to send its occupants across a fold in quantum space.

"Kind of scary, ain't it?" Grant joked as the mechanical pitch grew higher in the darkness, a deep vibration shaking their bodies.

Before either Kane or Brigid could answer, the mat-trans chamber came alive with streaks of lightning and an incredible burst of color seemed to overpower their senses.

An instant later, the three warriors found themselves standing in another location. But they did not see the familiar, sleek walls of the mat-trans chamber in the Cerberus redoubt with its brown-tinted armaglass. Instead, the armaglass was honeycombed like an insect's eye, its color a smoky black. And the floor and wall tiles were black, too, with dirty streaks across them the rusty color of dried blood. There was a distinctive smell here, like week-old flowers, their fragrance turned cloying and heavy.

Kane was alert immediately. "Where are we, Baptiste?" he spat, eyes on the chamber door, Sin Eater pistol materializing in his hand.

"I...I don't know," Brigid admitted, raising her shotgun.

Beside them, Grant had brought his own Sin Eater up, watching the door.

The lights of the mat-trans flickered for a moment before fading out, leaving just the burning line of their filaments glowing red in the darkness.

The three of them watched as something moved past the fractured panes of the armaglass, its shadowy silhouette doubling, tripling, quadrupling in a stuttering motion as it filtered past their fractured aspects.

It had taken just a split second to arrive here, to enter the unknown.

Chapter 8

"You brought us here, Baptiste," Kane whispered as the shadow thing passed behind the pebblelike armaglass. "Where did you send us?"

Brigid held her shotgun in a two-handed grip, steadily targeted on the chamber door. Short of breaking through the reinforced armaglass, the door was the only way in and she reasoned that, as such, it was the only entrance an attacker could use. "I programmed the mat-trans for Cerberus," she assured Kane in a harsh whisper. "I'm sure of it."

"Brigid never makes mistakes," Grant reminded Kane, keeping his own voice low as the shape continued to flutter beyond the ridges of the glass, obscured from view. "You know that."

"This ain't Cerberus," Kane stated softly. "So something, somewhere, is out of whack."

Brigid hissed through her teeth with annoyance. "I'd need to check the equipment to find out, run through the logs here. Which means going—out there." She indicated the chamber door.

Warily Kane and his colleagues eyed the dark figured rippling past the armaglass, moving slowly from right to left. They could not hear anything through the soundproof wall of the armaglass; the only noise in the chamber came from the mat-trans unit itself as it ran through its power-down cycle. It didn't sound like the familiar winding down of a mat-trans; instead it sounded rough, like an old smoker clearing his lungs.

Hesitantly, Kane moved closer to the door. Grant and Brigid followed, covering Kane and the door as he reached for it.

"I don't like this," Grant hissed.

Kane turned back to him. "Me, either," he agreed in a whisper. He watched the shadowy form move outside the chamber, trying to make sense of it from the fractured glimpses the pebbled glass offered.

There was no way to know what was out there. All they knew for sure was that nothing had responded to their arrival—so far, at least. Which meant, moving fast may just be the only advantage they had. Getting out of there, getting their backs out of this corner with its lone exit—that was the only option open to them.

Kane held his free hand up, the fingers outstretched. Then he silently counted down from three, closing his hand into a fist that the others could just barely see silhouetted in the faint glow from outside. On zero, Kane reached for the chamber door, tapping the exit code. It opened, not with the usual sigh of compressed air, but with the mournful whine of old metal on runners.

Even before the door had slid back to its full extent, Kane was moving, hurrying out of the mat-trans chamber, gun raised, his head ducked low to his body. It was cold out here, icy wind howling through the room with such force that it buffeted Kane and his companions. A narrow strip of light poured into the room from the far side, where the exterior wall was entirely missing, leaving the room open to the elements, just a few struts of rubble where the brickwork had once stood. The light was silver and gray, and outside Kane could see it was overcast.

The room itself was a shambles, like something a
bomb had struck, just a few pieces of furniture scattered around, all of it worn and broken. A line of beaten-
up locker-style cabinets ran along one wall, and there
were holes in the floor where exposed copper piping
gleamed. The shadow that Kane and his allies had seen
moving across the pebbled glass of the mat-trans chamber was just a sheet, grimy with dirt, streaks of soil
and blood marring its already dark surface. The sheet
clung to a metal strut, flapping around it in the wind.
It dawned on Kane that perhaps it had been cinched
there by someone, like the curtained-off area of Pellerito's factory, better to obscure the fierce outburst of the
mat-trans when it functioned. There were other metal
posts dotted around the twelve-by-ten room, and they
appeared to be riveted in place to hold the ceiling up.
The ceiling was low, and it bowed in the center, black
mold stretching across it.

Kane padded across the room, eyeing everything
with disdain, breathing shallowly to relieve the threat
of nausea that the room's damp stench brought. It was
abandoned, empty, dead. "We're alone," Kane confirmed, trusting his two partners to follow.

Grant joined Kane in his search of the room, while
Brigid spied what she was looking for—a control podium. Hesitantly, she lowered her shotgun as she made
her way to the control terminal at the edge of the mat-
trans chamber. The controls were set in a free-standing
podium a few paces from the mat-trans door, but they
were covered in debris that looked like shingle washed
up by the ocean. Brigid brushed at it with her forearm.
How long had it been since this thing was used? The
controls were unlit and looked dead. Brigid's heart sank
when she saw that, and she searched around the unfa-

miliar design for an on switch of some kind. "Looks foreign," she told Kane and Grant. "No design I've ever seen before."

"Can you work it?" Kane asked. He was walking toward the open gap in the wall, eyeing the room's low ceiling warily where the metal struts held it in place.

"Maybe," Brigid said, "but it will take time."

Kane had reached the end of the room and he peered out through the gap that had once been a wall. They were three stories above street level in the middle of some vast, empty city. "Looks like time may be something we have a lot of," he told Brigid grimly.

Grant had found a door on the far side of the room. It was wide enough for two men, with a thick frame around it. Both door and frame were made of metal, reminding Grant of a bank safe door, and all of it was streaked with black grime. Grant tried the handle, confirming the door was locked. A keypad waited beside the door frame, molded into the wall. Grant flipped open its plastic cover door—cracked with a brittle hinge—revealing the pad itself. It looked something like a pocket calculator that had been mounted to the wall. Grant tapped a few combinations of buttons, but the device gave no response, not even a light.

"Power's down," he muttered, resealing the dust cover. The cover snapped as he closed it, the dried-out plastic breaking at the point where the hinge met the wall.

Brigid rested her shotgun down by her side as she stood before the control podium, tapping the raised keys there to bring up a display. Inset in the podium, the display was horizontal, like a tabletop, forcing Brigid to stoop forward to see it clearly. She ran her fingers over the keys, bringing the system to life. The display ran behind black glass, as if seen through smoke, and for a moment all she could see was a flashing number: 9. It reminded her of the rhyme she had thought of earlier, in Pellerito's factory. "Hell-o, operator, give me number nine…"

Brigid watched as the system reacted lethargically to her prodding, powering up with a stuttering reluctance. Finally the single digit faded and more information came across the screen, garbled and nonsensical.

When the system failed to provide an automatic locator on boot-up, Brigid typed a query on the strangely raised keys on the podium. The keys were oval, and their shape and size reminded Brigid of fingernails. Furthermore, although the letters were recognizable, they were not laid out in the classic QWERTY keyboard style. It took a few seconds for Brigid to find her way around the unfamiliar design so that she could enter her query: "Location?"

The screen flashed for a moment before bringing up a word Brigid didn't recognize: "Quocruft."

Brigid looked at the word flashing there on the dusty screen, her eyes running over it a second time to make sure she had read it correctly. "Either of you ever hear of Quocruft?" she asked aloud.

When neither Grant nor Kane answered, Brigid turned back to the screen with furrowed brow. Quocruft? Was that their location? She couldn't place it. Foreign, maybe? Turkish? It didn't even sound like any place on Earth.

Brigid tapped again at the keys, entering a more complex query. The naillike keys were brittle; two snapped off as Brigid tapped in her question to the database, after that she worked them more gently. With a little effort, she requested a locator map, which the system duly provided. It showed nothing, just a glowing spot in the center—presumably representing the mat-trans chamber. Written across the map in bold letters was that same word again: "Quocruft."

Chapter 9

Brigid tried adjusting the map, striving to find a way to show more detail, but the system remained stubbornly intractable. With a huff of irritation, she attacked the question from a different angle, tapping into the details of the mat-trans unit itself. After a little trial and error, she brought up a settings log and began reading.

Grant, meanwhile, had joined Kane at the broken exterior wall, and the two men stared out across the desolate city. They stood at a sheer drop, the wall torn away by who knew what. The buildings were familiar, towering high into the overcast sky like the old structures of Cobaltville where both of them had been raised. The buildings were soot-dark, and the roadways looked cracked and broken, abandoned. The streets were arranged in a spiderweb pattern, expanding outward to the horizon. It was possible, Grant realized, that streets would always expand in that manner, no matter where one stood, a trick of architecture. The punishing wind channeled through those streets to create an awful groaning that ebbed louder and softer but never ceased, a terrible banshee wail.

"See anyone down there?" Grant asked.

"No one," Kane confirmed. He was statue-still as he watched the streets, scanning every road, every window, hoping to find a sign of life.

"Strange," Grant muttered, taking a step closer to

that vertiginous drop. Down there, thirty feet below them, were road vehicles. Some were overturned, others burned out and some just parked, a thick layer of grime obscuring their paintwork and blackening their windows. Not one of them was moving.

Brigid came striding across the messed-up room, peering out at the abandoned city for a moment before speaking. "Bad news," she said. "I think this is a receiver unit, but I'm not sure it can send."

Kane looked at her quizzically. "That's not normal," he stated.

Brigid shook her head. "It's like nothing I've ever seen," she said. "The tech is similar to a mat-trans, but the deeper I explore the less like ours it is."

"Maybe it's foreign," Grant suggested. "Where was it you said we were? Quod—?"

"Quocruft," Brigid corrected. "At least, that's where I think we are."

"And where is that?" Kane asked.

"I can't tell you," Brigid admitted. "I haven't heard of it. The computer's running in English, but the place name doesn't sound like anywhere I know of."

"Places change their names," Kane reasoned. "Happens all the time. Look at Luikkerville out in the west. Used to be called Snakefishville."

Brigid looked less sure. "Quocruft. It doesn't even sound like a word we'd use. I don't know, Kane, something about it doesn't sit right with me. All of this feels wrong."

But Kane had turned back to the open chunk of wall space, his gaze attracted by something. "You see something down there?" he asked. "Something moving?"

Grant and Brigid followed where he was pointing, trying to make out what he had seen. The streets looked empty, the dark buildings looming over them like tightly packed gravestones.

"Missed it. What did you see?" Grant asked after a moment. He had known Kane a long time, trusted the man's keen eyesight as well as his instinct.

"Looked like…" Kane started, then shook his head. "I'm not sure. Could have been a person, could be a dog or just a bag blowing in the wind. Can't say for certain."

Brigid was staring, not at the streets now but at Kane. "I know that look," she said. "You want to investigate, don't you?"

Kane smiled, still watching the street below. "We're in a strange part of a strange town with no backup. I want to find out what's happened, and I figure the answer's down there somewhere. Especially if there *is* someone down there."

"Curiosity can get you killed," Brigid warned him.

"So can not knowing. And a hell of a lot quicker," Kane replied.

"Door's locked," Grant reminded them both. "I checked it."

"The wall isn't," Kane said with that brutal pragmatism he sometimes displayed in the face of the unknown. "Let's find some rope and see what Quocruft has to offer the tourist."

"I'll go along with it," Brigid agreed reluctantly, "but let me go on the record now as saying I don't like it."

"Objection noted," Kane assured her. "Don't get your panties in a twist."

WITH PROFESSIONAL SWIFTNESS, the three Cerberus warriors split up to search the room for some rope. They worked well together thanks to years of familiarity, like a well-oiled machine.

Other than the mat-trans chamber and its control podium, there was little in the way of furniture, certainly not in a state that might contain climbing rope. The desks had been smashed to firewood, and—if there had been any in the first place—there were no chairs left in the room now. However, there was a single line of cupboards running along one wall, six in all, their metal paneling bent out of shape and scuffed with bullet holes. The cupboards were tall, like gym lockers, but the locks were of poor quality, disintegrating with rust. Grant, the strongest of the group, walked the length of metal cupboards and pulled the first open while Kane kept watch on the open external wall, wary. While he could not be certain that there was anyone out there, he was conscious that making an undue amount of noise could attract anyone who was—even over the sound of those howling winds.

Brigid worked speedily through the contents of each cupboard while Grant made his way along the line to open the next. An archivist by trade, Brigid was best suited to sort through the contents for anything useful. However, what she found as she pulled the first door open made her rear back with a shocked gasp. Crouching there, arms clutched around its legs and head bowed beneath the higher shelf, was a skeleton wearing a set of rags.

"You okay, Brigid?" Grant asked as he snapped the lock from the second set of doors.

Brigid swallowed, eyes fixed on the skeleton crammed between the thin metal walls. It looked small, as if its originator was not yet fully grown. But it was hard to tell, Brigid knew, with the flesh wasted away. The loss of flesh made everything seem smaller.

"I'm fine," Brigid said finally, eyes still fixed on the figure in the cupboard.

Grant was beside Brigid now, and he saw the skeleton crouching there in the gloom. "Sorry, I should have checked first," he said.

Brigid shook her head. "No need to mollycoddle me, Grant," she assured him. "Just surprised me for a second.

"I wonder how she got there," Brigid mused. "Did she hide there or was she locked inside?"

"Maybe someone just put the bones in afterwards," Grant said, "as a joke or something."

"Not in that position," Brigid said with grim certainty. "She was alive when she entered the cupboard."

"'Nother mystery," Grant muttered. "Just what we need."

With that, Grant continued on down the line of cupboards, taking a little more care to eyeball their contents before letting Brigid check for anything they could use. Mostly the cupboards contained desk supplies, rotted away with age. Two of them included bottles, including a whole host of medicine vials, but the labels had long since faded and the liquids had either been used up or had evaporated.

While his colleagues searched the cupboards, Kane was assessing the broken wall itself, wondering if there might be another way down. By the time Grant and Brigid came over to give him the bad news, Kane had already stretched himself flat on his belly, well out beyond the edge, and was dangling upside down searching for handholds.

"Kane, we've come up empty," Grant explained. "There's nothing here we can use to climb with."

"Forget it. New plan," Kane explained. "We can

climb down. Just got to be careful where we find our grips."

Grant peered over the edge once more, eyeing the sheer thirty-foot drop to solid paving slabs below. "You sure about this?" he asked uncertainly.

Kane pulled himself back from the edge, bounding back to a sitting position and offering his companions a broad smile. "Sure I'm sure," he said with false bravado.

Before anyone could argue, Kane drew himself over to the edge, scooting across on his buttocks, and turned, dropping his legs over the side so that he still faced the wall. "Follow me," he told his companions. "And, Baptiste—bring your blaster."

Brigid hurried back to the control podium where she had left her shotgun. Since the Mossberg replica had no safety, Brigid unloaded the shells from the breech and dropped them in her pocket before snapping it back together. Her best option was to climb down with it tucked into her shirt—empty wasn't ideal, but it was better than blowing her own legs off through a false jolt of the trigger. While she was readying herself for the descent, Brigid removed her glasses and tucked them into a protective case in her inside pocket. While she needed the glasses for reading, she could manage without them for most other operations.

Grant was already clambering over the side by the time Brigid returned to the edge of the room. "Watch that first step," he warned jovially.

Brigid smiled grimly as she knelt down. A moment later, she too was over the edge, following the path Grant took, which in turn followed the route Kane was taking down the rough side of the building.

The wall felt like dried plaster, and Brigid felt her heart skip a beat as a great chunk of it crumbled away in her hand. She reached forward automatically, fingers clawing at the wall until they locked into another crevice above a line of windows. Her red-gold hair whipped around her face in the wind, billowing like a flame. She ignored it, scrambling onward down the wall.

Kane reached ground level first, letting go of the wall and dropping the last six feet to land in a semicrouch. The sidewalk seemed to crumble on impact, the slabs of stone cracking underfoot, dusty powder spilling from their edges. Kane looked down in irritation as the cloud of dust brushed over his boots.

He was so intent on the dust that he almost missed the movement. But his ears detected it, the subtle change in the howling winds as something passed through them. Kane was suddenly very conscious that his partners were still above him, sitting targets as they clambered down the wall.

"Get down here," Kane called, the echoing words sounding out of place in the abandoned city. "Hurry it up— we have company."

As he spoke, his eyes twitched left and right, scanning the fan of roads that stretched away. There were automobile wrecks all around, one street playing host to a whole traffic jam of burned-out vehicles, all of them skeletal, just frames of blackened metal. There was no movement now, not that he could see.

Kane was out in the open here, too; he needed to correct that. The building was at his back, and he kept it there, moving across a little until he was closer to one of the hollowed-out wrecks of an automobile. It had high sides and a five-door design, but the windows had been smashed and the whole frame was blackened with fire damage, the wheel rims collapsed to the road.

Grant joined Kane seconds later, the Sin Eater materializing in his hand. He kept silent, recognizing what Kane was doing. Grant knew the man's body language well enough to identify it—Kane was drawing on his fabled point-man sense, an uncanny combination of his normal senses that made him almost prophetic in a hot zone.

"There's someone out there," Kane said. "I'm certain of it." He kept his voice low, aware of how close Grant was.

"Where?" Grant asked.

Brigid joined them, hurrying from her descent of the wall and ducking behind the edge of the automobile. "What's happening?" she whispered.

"Company," Kane said.

As he said it, he spotted the movement down one of the streets. Four figures were moving from behind a burned-out truck and trailer. They strode in step, walking side by side, shoulder to shoulder. Each was dressed in dark clothes, faces hidden behind the brutal lines of their matching helmets, eyes obscured behind tinted visors.

"Magistrates...?" Grant muttered, not quite believing what he was seeing.

Before anyone could say anything else, the distant figures raised their right arms, tensing their trigger fingers as sleek blasters appeared in their hands. And as the bullets left the chambers, there came a screaming like dying children. The agonized shrieks grew louder as the bullets closed in.

Chapter 10

Four bullets came spiraling toward Kane and his companions, screeching like living things as they cut through the air.

The Cerberus warriors were highly trained, and all of them ducked down behind the cover of the burned-out automobile as the bullets struck, cutting chunks out of the blackened metalwork, abruptly ending their loud screams.

"The hell?" Grant spit. "Don't these guys even ask questions first? What did we do wrong?"

"Probably not the time to ask, partner," Kane said, scanning the nearby buildings for better cover.

Grant stretched his Sin Eater out before him, eyeing down its sights. "You want to return fire?" he asked.

Kane watched the approaching figures from behind cover, automatically ducking as another cluster of screaming bullets came hurtling across the distance between them. There could be no mistaking the phenomenon now—the bullets really did let out a shriek like a child's scream as they were expelled from their foe's blasters. "Once we do, it sets a precedent we may never be able to go back from," Kane pointed out. "They're Magistrates. Hold fire—for now."

Crouched beside the two ex-Magistrates, Brigid was reloading her shotgun. She peered over the hood of the auto, watching the approaching figures with morbid interest as they strode down the street. There were four in all, each of them dressed in the familiar black-leather garb of a Magistrate, just like the uniforms that Kane and Grant had once worn. Though they were each dressed in the Magistrate uniform, they were not matching. The one to the right wore a heavy black duster over his regulation uniform, with bloodred piping that highlighted its neat pleats. The third from the left had a subtly different helmet; a motif was emblazoned across its center in a putrid green script.

Brigid narrowed her eyes a moment, focusing on the man's helmet. From this distance, the motif looked like a child's skeleton, curled in on itself. But as he took another step closer, she saw something else there—the humanoid skeleton had a curling tail of bones, reaching up from the base of its spine to wrap around its own neck.

"Hideous…" Brigid muttered, feeling sickened by the image.

But as she spoke, the figures stepped more clearly into the sunlight—what little of it there was—and Brigid's words seemed to catch in her throat, her mouth suddenly dry as bone.

Beneath his visor, the leftmost figure had putrid sores spreading across his skin, and black pus oozed from them. His flesh was red, like cooked meat, the skin flayed away, leaving the muscles exposed.

To his right, the second figure had a crack running through his tinted visor. Beneath it the skin seemed to rupture, the lidless eyes swiveling as he hunted for prey.

The face of the third Magistrate, the one with the demon child's skull decorating his helmet, seemed to be oozing away, teeth and bone visible through the torn flesh of his chin, his lipless mouth drawn back in a cruel snarl.

And if the third had been like something from a nightmare, the fourth was infinitely worse. This one's face was nothing more than blackness, a shining pool of dark in the shape of a skull.

The weapons of these Dark Magistrates blasted again, firing another burst of screaming bullets at the Cerberus exiles. As they came closer, the Cerberus warriors could hear a strange shrieking noise emanating through the streets, screeches and hums that seemed to cut off abruptly like badly edited audio tape.

"Are they...human?" Grant spit, still eyeing the eerie-looking Mags along the length of his Sin Eater.

"They're...Magistrates," Kane said in disbelief. "But they can't be."

"They are," Brigid insisted, "and they're getting closer."

"You're nuts, Baptiste," Kane growled. "If they're Magistrates, then where the hell are we?"

"'Hell' may be closer than you think, Kane," Brigid chided ominously.

Beyond the blackened car chassis, the fearsome-looking Magistrates took another pace closer to their prey, their Soul Eater pistols bucking in their hands as they blasted in tandem.

"THEY'RE OFF THE MAP," Beth Delaney blurted as Lakesh stood over her, staring at the computer screen.

Lakesh scanned the screen for a long moment, studying the map that was projected there. The map featured an overlay grid identifying the largest and most significant locations. That grid should also be showing the glowing report from the transponders of Kane, Grant and Brigid, three shining dots that could be tapped for additional data. But, as Delaney had stated, they were not there.

"What happened, exactly?" Lakesh asked, his gentle tone belying the rising fear he felt at the sudden disappearance of his colleagues. "Track back for me."

Delaney shook her head, her blond hair brushing her shoulders. "I don't know exactly," she said, regretfully. "One moment, we were getting a strong transponder signal from each operative. The next time I looked—they'd gone."

"So, where are they?" Lakesh demanded.

"I ran a systems check," Delaney assured him. "It showed everything was intact. We can track our other transponder implants. It's just Kane's team that has disappeared."

"That's impossible," Brewster Philboyd chipped in from where he had overheard the conversation from his own workstation just a few desks along. "Even if Kane and company were killed, we would still get a location signal. Their life signs would just be flat."

Lakesh nodded, welcoming the talented astrophysicist's opinion. Philboyd was a logical thinker and good with a mystery, he knew. "Unless their bodies were completely obliterated," Lakesh suggested grimly.

"In that case, you should still be able to track back to the moment of death," Philboyd insisted. "It would stand out as a sudden peak in the transponder signals, all three going at once."

Considering this for a moment, Lakesh nodded, accepting Philboyd's hypothesis. "Most likely. Then, what would you suggest has happened, Mr. Philboyd?" Lakesh encouraged.

"The transponders can be switched off," the astrophysicist proposed, "but they are very hard to find. One would have to know what one was looking for to do that. Alternatively, the signal could be jammed somehow, but that would likely create a trace echo—a null zone that would be as obvious as if the transponders were still functioning."

"What if it was a very wide null zone?" Lakesh asked.

Deep in thought now, Philboyd shook his head. "We might have more trouble spotting it, but I don't see it myself," he reasoned. "That would take a lot of equipment to boost the jamming signal. It's too elaborate for gun runners."

"An outside party, then?" Lakesh proposed.

"Again, same notation," Philboyd said. "And it's too specific. It could not be by chance alone—it would take a targeted attack on our specific transponder frequencies to hide them."

"What about the Original Tribe?" Lakesh suggested. The Original Tribe were a group of technological shamen who operated from a hidden location in the Australian outback. They had clashed with the Cerberus organization one year ago during a mission to recover a reactivated doomsday device, and had subsequently marked the Cerberus operatives—and specifically Lakesh himself—for death. With their advanced technology, the Original Tribe had shown incredible ingenuity in infiltrating computer systems, and had even managed to remotely tap into the mat-trans.

Philboyd looked uncertain. "They've been quiet for so long," he said. "It just doesn't feel right."

"Then what else could have happened?" Beth asked.

"The transponder signals are bounced to us via satellite..." Lakesh began, still forming a working theory. "Could there be a problem there, Beth?"

Delaney tapped her computer keys, engaging a systems check of the satellite uplink. "We're still getting a strong signal in other respects," she said doubtfully. "It's only the CAT Alpha team that has dropped from sight."

"Well, if the satellites are still operational," Philboyd realized, "then either the signal's been blocked by a screen, or Kane and his team are somewhere beyond their reach."

"Off planet?" Lakesh said doubtfully. While Cerberus had mounted off-planet excursions before now, including battling with an alien mothership outside of Earth's atmosphere and visiting the Moon and Mars, the abruptness with which Kane's team had disappeared did not seem consistent with such a journey. For one thing, they should have reported in. "Recheck the data and replay the signals with an echo trace," Lakesh decided. "Try to pinpoint exactly when and where they were when they disappeared. Brewster, backtrack on the satellite footage. Let's see if we can eyeball our team from above and learn where they went to."

Brewster Philboyd nodded, removing his glasses for a moment to clean them on his tunic before he got to work on this new problem. It seemed that the mysteries were piling up today, one upon another.

As he wondered what had happened to CAT Alpha, there was something else nagging at Lakesh as he made his way back to his desk. The report that Reba DeFore had provided concerning the components of their mysterious visitor, most specifically those nongenetic components that suggested protective clothing of some sort. Could that possibly be a space suit, the kind man had designed to walk on the Moon? If Kane's team had been spirited off planet, was it possible that an astronaut had

come to visit Cerberus via the mat-trans? And if that
was the case, were the two things linked?

Lakesh sighed heavily as he plucked up DeFore's report for another check. There were just too many questions right now, and he couldn't shake the feeling that
the one thing they didn't have enough of was time.

KANE DUCKED DOWN AS another bullet clipped the burnt-
out car close to his ear, shrieking like a delirious child
as it cut through the air.

Crouched beside him, Grant and Brigid were both
awaiting his decision.

"Fight or flight, Kane?" Grant pressed. "Which is
it?"

He didn't want to fight Magistrates, but if it was
necessary, they needed somewhere they could defend,
where they would be less out in the open. Kane's eyes
darted to the building behind him, the one from which
they had emerged, its ruined wall showing the guts of
four floors like some cutaway diagram.

"Follow me," Kane instructed, his body already in
motion.

Grant and Brigid followed as Kane dashed across
the cracked sidewalk and darted through the wide gap
in the first-floor wall. As they ran out into the open,
the corpselike Magistrates picked up their pace, their
determined strides turning into a sprint as they hurried after the disappearing Cerberus warriors. Another
cluster of screaming bullets struck the ruins, several
finding their path through the holed wall and into the
shadowy rooms beyond.

In the lead, Kane was first to see the ground-level
room. Ill-lit by the cloud-obscured sun, it appeared to be
a waiting room with vast banks of fixed chairs molded

from plastic and scattered coffee tables at regular intervals. While the metal-bar structure that held the rows of chairs remained intact, the vacuum-molded chairs had melted in a radial pattern, its center somewhere in the street behind them. The room stank of smoke damage, its cloying scent had seeped into the walls and what remained of the furniture, saturating the air throughout.

Kane ran through the decimated room, using instinct to navigate through the ruined chairs and tables in semidarkness, leaping over the knee-high metal bars that had once held more of the chairs. Grant and Brigid followed, their arms pumping as they ran for cover, screaming bullets clipping the furniture all around them.

There was an entrance up ahead, Kane saw in the gloom, twin doors with circular glass panels in their upper levels. He ran for the doors, ducking his head as another burst of bullets came dangerously close to him.

Kane took just a moment to glance over his shoulder. Grant and Brigid were paces behind him, and beyond them he saw the deathly Magistrates just beginning to make their way into the waiting room through the missing wall.

"Heads down," Kane shouted as he saw the Magistrates' weapons glow, unleashing another burst of those nightmarish bullets.

Kane's partners did not need more warning than that. Both of them brought their heads low to their chests, ducking down behind whatever remained of the ruined chairs.

Kane brought his Sin Eater around, firing a warning shot for the first time. He had hoped to avoid it, but the Mags were making good ground, getting closer with each step, relentless in their pursuit. The Sin Eater fired high, 9 mm parabelium bullets striking the ceiling in a shower of sparks.

Incredibly the dark-clad figures kept coming as the sparks lit the room, not even so much as flinching, let alone slowing down.

"You're making a mistake," Kane warned. "We're not your enemy. Stay back and we can discuss this like reasonable…"

The rest was cut off by the sound of the Magistrates' matching weapons firing and another burst of screaming bullets zipping across the room as Kane and his partners sought cover.

Kane was at the double doors now, his back pressed to them as the Magistrates approached like wraiths through the darkness. Kane watched their weapons discharge, noticing something for the first time in that gloom. The weapons kicked out a white residue that glowed in the darkness, swirling through the air like smoke. The smoke seemed to contain faces, mouths taut in screams.

Chapter 11

"Get down," Grant shouted, grabbing Kane by the belt and pulling him to the floor.

Kane looked startled as another swarm of the howling bullets drilled into the wall above his head.

"What's got into you?" Grant demanded. "You were just standing there."

"There's something in the bullets," Kane said, shaking his head to clear it. "Faces."

"Worry about that later," Brigid said, sliding across the floor to join them. "We need to get out of here."

Before Kane or Grant could reply, Brigid pulled her shotgun around, bringing herself up on one knee and firing. The loud cough of the shotgun pounded at their eardrums as the weapon discharged.

"She's right," Grant agreed, and Kane nodded.

"Sorry, I just…zoned out," Kane explained, the confusion evident in his voice.

The shotgun's discharge lit the room as Brigid fired again, blasting another shell at the oncoming Magistrates. They returned fire, their bullets screeching through the air as they hurtled toward the Cerberus teammates.

Then Kane was through the double doors, Grant's hand between his shoulder blades as he shoved his disoriented partner through. Brigid followed a second later, reloading the shotgun as she crashed through the doors.

"What got into you, Kane?" she demanded.

"I...don't know," Kane said, bewildered. "I saw something...in their blasts."

They were in a wide corridor that ran to a junction at one end and an abrupt stop at the other where the rubble of the wall had collapsed to block it. Light crept through the gaps in the rubble, illuminating the corridor. The whole atmosphere was heavy with that same burned stench. It had a tiled floor, but the tiles were blackened and stained with the rust color of long-dried blood in sweeping streaks, as if a painter had gone mad. Long light fixtures hung from chains, all of them dead, and there were gurneys shoved against the walls here and there. There were at least a dozen doors emerging from this corridor, along with a bank of three elevators, their thick metal doors cratered with impacts, one set wrenched entirely free and strewed across the floor.

"Don't know about you, but I'm guessing it's a hospital," Brigid said, looking around. "Maybe a military one. The waiting room, the stretchers..."

Kane nodded, still struggling to organize his thoughts. The things he had seen in the expulsion of the bullets, the faces frozen in screaming agony, played again and again across his mind's eye, hideous and terrifying all at once.

Grant peered through the ruined glass portal of the left-hand door. "They're still coming," he reported over the sounds of impacting bullets. "We're gonna have to return fire."

Kane shook his head. "Not yet. Let's find cover and keep hidden."

"Better find it fast," Grant warned, turning away from the doors as a burst of fire rattled them on their hinges.

Taking the lead, Kane headed down the unlit corridor at a sprint, ignoring the doors leading from it in
favor of the distant junction. "We'll try to get to the far
side of the building," he instructed, his voice coming
rapidly between breaths. "Keep moving away from the
Magistrates."

Together, the three Cerberus warriors sprinted toward the junction, heading to the right on Kane's instructions. Behind them, the sickly looking Magistrates
had just broken through the double doors of the wrecked
waiting room, and their guns whipped up as they spotted their prey. The weapons fired, spouting eerie puffs
of whiteness that hung in the air for a moment, shimmering in the shafts of light creeping through the rubble behind them, ghostly faces drawn in agony amid
the smoke.

A moment later, screaming bullets peppered the far
end of the corridor, but Kane and his two companions
had disappeared, passing around the junction corner
and sprinting through the ruined corridors of the hospital building.

At the rear of the group, Grant peered over his shoulder as the bullets lashed against the wall, their screams
dying with each impact. "That was close," he hissed,
redoubling his pace.

The corridor here was narrow in parts, where a great
hunk of ceiling had collapsed, and Kane had to weave
past it, his pace seldom slowing. Above him, one half of
the ceiling still held, but just barely, its lowest surface
scraping above the hair on his head. Brigid followed,
hefting the shotgun one-handed as she zipped through
the narrow gap. In the rear, the wide-shouldered Grant
was forced to go sideways past the collapse, but it gave
him an idea.

"Brigid," he called, and both she and Kane slowed their pace momentarily to see what Grant needed. Grant was standing on the near side of the ceiling collapse, pointing at it with his Sin Eater. "I don't have any charges. Use your shotgun to blast this thing shut."

Brigid needed no further encouragement. As Kane scouted ahead, she brought the 12-gauge around and targeted the partly collapsed ceiling. "Get back," she warned.

As Grant stepped aside, Brigid squeezed the trigger, and the old Mossberg design unleashed a burst of deadly fire, striking the drooping ceiling with a crash of splintering wood and plaster. Grant ran as the rest of the ceiling collapsed behind him, his arms pumping as he hurried to join Brigid.

Up ahead, Kane had found a possible exit. His head appeared from a side room, calling his companions over as they raced along the corridor. They followed him inside, entering another waiting area of fixed seats and low tables. This one, however, had specially low seats in one section, and the scarred walls showed the remnants of a cheery mural, a cartoon version of a field with smiling flowers and cheerful bunny rabbits hopping across it. Like the rest of the rooms, this one was blackened with unidentified debris, rusty brown streaks smeared all over the floors and painted walls.

"Looks like a children's ward," Brigid observed as she followed Kane through the upturned tables and chairs.

"Which scratches your idea that it was a military hospital," Kane pointed out.

"Not really," Brigid reasoned as he led the way. "Military brats get sick, too. I think with the mat-trans upstairs—"

"Think later," Grant growled from behind them both. "I don't reckon that little trick back there is going to hold our playmates for long."

BARELY THIRTY FEET AWAY, the four Dark Magistrates hurried in pursuit of their quarry as the ceiling fell down before them. Lined up, the four dark figures halted before the collapsed ceiling, eyeing it through rotted and putrescent orbs. Magistrate North, whose flesh was black with infection, skin rotted away from muscle, held his Soul Eater pistol up and blasted a burst of rapid fire at the barricade before him, sending a dozen shots screaming at the fallen ceiling in the space of two seconds.

The rubble kicked and spit as the screaming bullets struck it, slugs vibrating across its surface in an angry tarantella, chunks of plaster and wood ripping from it in angry spits. But when he was done, the barricade remained intact, only the slightest damage showing across its rough surface, more dislodged pieces falling in place.

The Dark Magistrates did not say a word, as the capacity for speech had departed them long ago. Instead, they conversed in a series of abrupt shrieks and hums, identifying the problem and settling on a solution with rapidity.

A moment later, two of them turned back, returning the way they had come in search of another path through the ruined hospital. The others—North and West—remained at the collapsed ceiling, clawing at it with gloved hands as they searched for a way to lever the debris out of their path.

They would catch these living perpetrators—catch them for their crimes against Baron Trevelyan.

Chapter 12

In the darkened wing of the children's ward, Kane led
the way through two rooms and into a third. Open plan
in style, the rooms opened one into the next like Russian dolls, a waiting area leading into a smaller waiting room and that into a cluster of joined consultation
rooms. The whole wing was constructed in an oblong,
but there was wreckage all over, with holed walls and
collapsed chunks of ceiling to be navigated around.

As Kane led the way through the ruined area, Brigid
realized why he had brought them in here. She could
see tantalizing glimpses of a bank of windows off to
the left, obscured by the piled debris. An inviting lake
glistened beyond.

"There are no gaps large enough," Kane growled,
clawing at a handful of the rubble.

"Then we'll make one," Grant suggested, pulling
a large hunk of masonry aside. But as he pulled the
stonework free it began to crumble, turning to sifting
flecks as he moved it away. It was like trying to move
shifting sand.

"We don't have time," Brigid observed, voicing what
they all realized. "Without tools, it'll just keep dropping
on us, filling in any progress we make."

"Dammit," Kane cursed, searching around for another way through. "Come on, Kane," he admonished
himself. "Think—think!"

Before Brigid or Grant could say a word, Kane was in motion again, hurrying back the way they had just come, launching himself toward a closed door that was partly hidden behind a fallen I beam. The door stood between two others, a narrow room lying beyond.

BACK AT THE ENTRY TO THE children's wing, two dark figures were just entering, their shining Magistrate badges glinting like spilled blood in what little light infiltrated the waiting room. Magistrate North and Magistrate West had clawed through the fallen rubble in the corridor beyond, ripping piece after piece out of their way in a mess of dust and plaster. Their clothes were caked with dust, hunks of plaster falling from the creases as they moved and their helmets smeared with chalky residue.

The two Magistrates strode into the children's wing, twitching with alertness, searching for their prey by sound and smell. They moved through the room like prowling sharks, following some inherent instinct that drove them to their prey while, elsewhere in the abandoned hospital complex, their companions did likewise, seeking another route.

KANE TRIED THE DOOR AND found it locked. The handle turned but the door wouldn't budge. Taking a step back, he kicked out, driving the cushioned sole of his foot into the door, heel first, just beneath the handle. There was a splintering of wood and then the door gave, the metal handle breaking off and falling away to the floor, the wooden frame splintering.

Kane gave the door a brutal shove as he barged inside while Grant and Brigid waited, weapons at the ready. Within, Kane found himself in a small pharmacy storeroom, ten-by-eight feet, the shelves stocked with bottles of pills and serums, all of it covered with plaster dust. Here, too, the ceiling bowed, causing several of the shelves to tip. Their contents had spilled to the floor long ago. Kane kicked his way through the mess, searching for the room's window. It had to have one; he felt sure of it.

Outside the storeroom, Grant and Brigid waited in the semidarkness of the ward, watching for any sign of their wraithlike pursuers.

Suddenly Grant flinched and Brigid followed, both of them spying the shadow moving through the darkness at the same time. It was a Magistrate—no, *two* of them, moving stealthily into the waiting area at the far end of the room.

Grant began to say something but Brigid stopped him with a raise of her hand.

"I see them," she said quietly. "Two."

"Make that four," Grant whispered, his eyes fixing on the other side of the room where an open doorway led into some kind of playroom.

Without saying a word, Brigid and Grant stepped back, merging into the shadows amid the upturned furniture.

INSIDE THE STORAGE ROOM, Kane was staring at the farthest wall. He could make out a window there, or at least a sliver of one, light streaming in from outside, but it was obscured by a high shelving unit laden with bottles. Kane reached forward, pressing his hand to the window, feeling the coolness of the glass. It was an outside window, he was certain of it—the light could be artificial, but that feeling of a draft snaking around the window's edge was something you couldn't fake.

Kane worked his hand around, reaching behind the shelves as far as he was able until he found a catch. He manipulated it, feeling for how loose it was. He could work it—maybe not from this angle, but if he got the shelf out of the way, then maybe.

Kane drew his hand back and rested it against the side of the shelves. Then, using both hands, he shunted the shelving unit, gritting his teeth as he pushed it across the floor. The unit's metal feet whined as they scraped against the floor tiles, tearing chunks out of them as it moved two inches. It was enough for Kane to reach behind. He pulled at the back of the shelving unit and clambered up it to add his full body weight. It began to rock unsteadily.

Kane leaped free as the shelving unit tumbled from the wall, its contents spilling across the floor, bottles shattering as they smashed against the blackened tiles. Midway through its tumble, the shelving unit slammed into the next closest unit and stopped with a crunch, poised at a thirty-degree angle. The jarred contents of the second unit went toppling from those shelves, too, further littering the floor in a carpet of pills and serums.

THE DARK MAGISTRATES all turned at the cacophony that emanated from the storeroom as Kane yanked the shelving unit free from the wall. They descended from opposite ends of the ward, their blasters raised as they sought their prey.

"What the hell is he doing in there?" Grant muttered from his hiding place just outside the storeroom's door. He was watching both sets of Magistrates as they came closer, their eerie squawks and hums cutting through the air like a poorly tuned radio.

Across the door from him, Brigid held her shotgun ready, watching those dark silhouettes get closer. "Come on, Kane, get it together."

INSIDE THE STOREROOM, Kane stood before the window, staring in frustration at the twin vertical bars that had been placed on the outside—presumably to stop anyone breaking in to steal drugs. "Trust the luck," he muttered to himself. Even if he did get this window open, there was no way that any of them could squeeze through that gap between the bars, not even Brigid.

He was trapped; they all were. Trapped like rats.

Chapter 13

The Magistrates moved through the wreckage of the waiting room like sharks scenting blood, running toward the open door of the storeroom. Grant and Brigid watched as they came from two different directions, leaping the upturned furniture as they searched for the Cerberus warriors hiding in the darkness.

They had maybe five seconds before they arrived, Grant guessed—that was all. He analyzed the situation in a heartbeat. There was a wide archway at the far end of the room, precisely between the two sets of Magistrates, leading to an adjoining room. If he could head toward that, through it, the Dark Magistrates would be caught in a crossfire, unable to shoot at him for fear that a rogue bullet would strike one of their colleagues.

Thrusting one arm in front of Brigid, Grant pushed her back into the open doorway of the storeroom. "Help Kane," he directed. "I'll distract them."

Brigid was about to argue, but Grant was already in motion, pelting across the children's waiting area, shouting at the top of his voice. "Come on, you psychopathic fuck-wits. I'm right here."

As one, the Dark Magistrates turned toward the sound, their eerie weapons blasting. The bullets screamed as they left the gun muzzles, caroming through the air with strained shrieks.

Grant ran as fast as he could, head ducked low as he

weaved through the smattering of blackened tables and charred chairs. The screaming bullets cut chunks from the furniture all about him, drilling into the scarred plasterwork of the walls behind him. As he reached the wide arch, Grant felt something strike his arm just below his right shoulder and swerved his body automatically away from the pain. Then he was through the arch, dropping almost to his knees as shots blasted overhead.

Behind him, the Magistrates had realized their mistake, twittering to one another in those abbreviated shrieks and hums as they stopped firing. Grant hurried through the next room in a semicrouch, teeth gritted against the pain throbbing through his arm. He had taken a glancing blow, he realized, not a bullet but a hunk of ruined masonry or furniture that had been caught by the crossfire. His shadow suit had taken most of the impact, redistributing it to lessen the blow. It still hurt like the devil, though.

He was in a room filled with weighing scales and height charts, the torn remains of graphs on the walls showing growth patterns. Grant glanced behind him, checking that the shadowy Magistrates were still following, and picked up his pace as he saw them warily approach the archway.

BEHIND THEM, WHERE GRANT had started his desperate run, Brigid was watching from the doorway of the storeroom, urging Grant to escape. "He's through the arch," she whispered, "but I think he got hit."

"Grant can take a hit," Kane dismissed her concern. If he was worried about his partner, he didn't show it. "But we're all dead if we don't find some way out of this rabbit hole."

Brigid skipped backward across the wet floor of the

storeroom, joining Kane at the barred window. The sunlight seemed fierce after the gloom of the hospital, and Brigid could see a grass verge out there leading down to a decorative, manmade lake. From here, the lake's waters looked dark. The vertical bars that masked the window were secured on both the inside and the outside; even if they broke the glass, there was no way they would be able to get out.

"Any ideas?" Kane asked, fixing Brigid with his laser-sharp stare.

Brigid eyed the metal bars a moment longer, then turned her head, rapidly assessing the contents of the room.

"Medicines," Kane told her helpfully.

"Good," Brigid said. "Find me anything combustible. Lots of it, if you can." As she spoke she was already on her knees, sifting through the fallen bottles, checking those that remained intact. The floor was wet with spilled liquids and it reeked of medical spirits, rubbing alcohol and cleaning product.

"What are you planning to do?" Kane asked as he searched the remaining shelves. "Blow up the wall?"

Brigid looked up for a moment and smiled mischievously. "Why? You got a better idea?"

GRANT DUCKED AND RAN, weaving through the discarded furniture of a small waiting area, the four diseased Magistrates in hot pursuit. As they spotted him, the lead Magistrate shot, blasting another of those howling bullets from his Soul Eater. The weapon glowed for a moment with the discharge, a belch of smoke exuding from its muzzle as the screeching bullet was launched.

Grant kept running, diving through the glass panel of a doorway as the bullet struck the wall behind him.

The panel shattered on impact, and Grant ducked his head as he went crashing through, shards of glass skittering all about him.

He was in an even smaller room now. This one was dominated by a wide desk whose wooden top was blackened with fire damage. The walls, too, were tar-black, a lopsided metal filing cabinet crouched against one wall, genuflecting where it had been melted by incredible heat. More importantly, there was no obvious way out.

Grant turned, surveying the whole room in a heartbeat, scanning the walls. There were no windows, no doors, no way out of the consultation room except the way he had come in. The Russian-doll rooms had come to their end. Outside, Grant could hear the Magistrates screeching at one another in those sharp, abbreviated cuts of noise, following his trail.

"No way out, no way back," Grant muttered.

He stepped behind the desk, where the melted filing cabinet sagged, and rapped his knuckles against the wall. It was board, a partition wall that had been added to create the office space from a bigger room. Whatever had hit this place, it had generated incredible heat, enough to turn metal to liquid. Grant guessed it must have been something brief and sudden, the effect short-lived. But it was possibly enough to weaken the back wall of the office. He just had to move quickly.

The Sin Eater was in his hand with just a thought, reappearing from the hidden holster he had attached beneath his coat sleeve. Grant squeezed the trigger, blasting a line of bullets across the back wall, sweeping the gun left to right in a tight arc. The bullets pierced the wall, kicking back chunks of plasterboard with drumbeat precision. When he stopped firing, a neat line of bullet holes was visible across the walls—enough, he hoped, to weaken it.

As the four Magistrates appeared at the door, Grant ran for the wall, shoulder down, striking it with all his might. The wall crumbled, dropping away with the impact, and then Grant was running through. He turned, bringing the Sin Eater around and stroking the trigger, laying down cover fire to force the hostile Magistrates back. As he did so, he heard—and felt—the shudder of an explosion vibrate through the building.

"That had better be Kane," he told himself as he ran through the next room and out into a corridor, sending the Sin Eater back into its hidden rig. Already he was working out a map in his head, figuring which direction he needed to take to get back to his partners.

IN THE AFTERMATH OF THE explosion, Brigid was doubled over, coughing as the dust caught in her throat. Before her, the window and a small chunk of the wall that surrounded it had been obliterated, leaving a hole that was roughly fourteen inches square.

"Come on, Baptiste," Kane urged, placing an arm around her midriff.

Brigid had caught the worst of the explosion when she lit the flammable liquids she had doused the wall in, but Kane had caught a lungful of plaster dust, too. He spluttered as he sucked in breath, trying to clear it from the back of his throat as he guided Brigid and himself through the debris. They were covered in white plaster, as if they had been frosted.

Brigid clambered through the windowlike cavity, spitting out dust as she pulled herself through the hole she had made. Kane followed, narrowing his eyes against the particles of dust that swirled in the air.

Once outside, they were immediately buffeted by those howling winds once more, playing all around them and rippling across the surface of the lake. Kane and Brigid stood beneath the overcast sky on a grass verge that rolled down to the decorative lake. The grass was overgrown in great clumps that brushed the tops of Kane's boots, scraping and bowing with each billow of the gusting wind.

"Kane, they must have heard that," Brigid rasped. "They'll come back to check."

"Then we'd better keep moving," Kane said.

"But Grant's still…"

Kane silenced her with a look. "He's still out there," Kane finished. They had no Commtacts, no way to speak to Grant or track him. For now, their partner was on his own.

GRANT WAS THROUGH THE office wall but they were still chasing, following him down the corridor. It was another smoke-damaged tunnel, its ceiling and walls exuding the unmistakable stench of fire. There were doors all along it, consultation rooms and offices and who knew what else.

Behind him, two of the Dark Magistrates came striding through the hole he had made in the wall, stepping into the corridor like twin visions of Death. They stopped there, searching left and right with their weapons before them as if those guns were sniffer dogs. Spotting Grant running away, they began to follow while their colleagues turned back to check on the explosion that had rocked the children's ward.

The Dark Mags raised their blasters, firing another burst of those dreadful, screaming bullets that zipped down the corridor. Hearing the weapons' discharge, Grant turned, ducking into the next doorway and through to the room beyond.

Grant slammed the door behind him, wincing as the screaming bullets drummed against the walls outside. They were close…damn, but they were close. His breath was coming faster now, yearning for more oxygen to drive his muscles. He was in a small office much like the one he had left moments earlier. This one had two desks face-to-face so that their occupants could talk across them to each other. The room was fire damaged, dark curling streaks running up the walls and across the ceiling, the paint blistered where it had not melted away. There was a sash window on the wall opposite the door, and Grant ran to it, wrenching it up with both hands, knowing it was the only place left to run.

When he looked, he saw a tiny square courtyard out there, surrounded on all sides by offices. The courtyard was designed solely to give air and light. Nowhere to run once more, and no false walls to demolish.

Chapter 14

Grant turned back as he heard the Magistrates reach the office door. His only option was to wound them. He commanded the Sin Eater back into his hand, brought it up to target the door as it swung open, aiming low. He would shoot their legs out from under them—painful, but survivable, at least.

The Sin Eater bucked in Grant's hand, firing almost without conscious thought, sending three quick bursts of lead at the bottom panel of the door as it swung toward him. The Magistrates had played it safe, opening the door from the side, keeping themselves out of any potential line of fire. Grant cursed, knowing it was just the thing he would have done. Like him, his pursuers had gone through that same Magistrate training.

"All right, fellas," Grant called out as his Sin Eater stopped firing. "We've got us a Mexican stand-off here. We all need to back off, talk about it, or someone's going to end up shot to hell."

He waited, but the only response he heard were the strange screeches and burps that he had heard before. It was like interference bursting through on a radio, cutting into the signal; snatches of it popped in and out without any discernible beginning or end.

Then, without warning, one of the Magistrates appeared in the doorway, his own weapon raised. This one had a flaw running across his tinted visor beneath which

his skin seemed to rupture. His lidless eyes drilled mer-
cilessly into Grant's gaze. Grant fired without thinking,
blasting a 9 mm bullet straight into the figure's lower
leg. There was a hiss like escaping steam, and the Magistrate spun on his heel, his own weapon discharging
as he toppled toward the wall. Something was pouring
out of his leg, Grant saw, a stream of greenish-gray gas
spurting out into the air.

The Magistrate continued to fire as he fell, a trio of
those screaming bullets exploding from the barrel of his
blaster in a straight line toward Grant. The first bullet
whipped past Grant's flank, driving into the wall behind
him with a strained screech. The second came closer,
whizzing past his ear like a whisper before meeting with
the topmost windowpane and shattering it. The third
bullet came lower, and its scream stopped as it slapped
against Grant's sternum, pushing him backward with
a pained, outburst of breath.

Grant stumbled back against the exterior wall, his
limbs suddenly heavy, a terrible coldness radiating outward from where the bullet had struck. After that, it was
just black, absolute darkness replacing any thoughts or
actions. Replacing any notion of escape.

TOGETHER, KANE AND BRIGID had hurried down to the
edge of the lake, and they crouched there, watching the
abandoned hospital. The grass here was tall enough that,
if they lay down, it would hide them from prying eyes.

"You see any sign of him?" Brigid asked quietly.

"No," Kane answered slowly.

The hospital had been quiet for a few minutes now,
but the wailing banshee winds continued to howl all
about the lifeless building. From outside, parts of the
building were ruined, as if some cancer had attacked the

masonry. There was a great strip of wall facade missing from the far left edge, stretching around the corner.
The upper windows were shattered. Hints of decorative
coving budded along the stonework, but most of it had
been blasted away by some powerful force, leaving a
gravellike surface.

"You want to go back in?" Brigid asked.

Kane's eyes flicked to the opening they had made in
the wall, something catching his gaze. A shadow moved
within. Kane held his breath, watching it move. Then
the shadow came to the hole, poking its head out, and
Kane saw it was one of the mysterious Magistrates,
blistered skin oozing black pus over his chin.

"Down," Kane ordered, reaching over to push Brigid
into the dirt.

Kane and Brigid watched, their breaths held, as the
dark figure sniffed about at the opening, poking at it
with the stubby barrel of his blaster. They could hear
nothing over the angry sound of the howling winds;
if the Magistrate made any noise at all it would not
carry this far. The dark-clad figure looked up, eyeing
the verge that led down to the lake, searching the overgrown vegetation there. Kane waited, still holding his
breath.

For thirty seconds, the Magistrate stood there, peering through the hole in the wall, scanning the commu-
nal area beyond. Then, satisfied, he turned away, and
Kane and Brigid watched as his shadow flickered from
the hole they had blasted in the wall and disappeared.

"That was close," Brigid said with a sense of relief,
breaking the tension they both felt.

Kane pulled himself up, his head peeking over the
long grass once more.

"No sign of Grant," Brigid stated, downcast.

Kane ignored her, surveying the building and its surrounds. "What happened here?" he asked.

"What do you mean?" Brigid asked.

"The rooms, the furniture," Kane said. "It was all melted. And the streets—like a bomb went off."

"And where are all the people?" Brigid asked. "Other than the Magistrates, it's as if the whole ville is dead. I didn't see a single person out there, did you?"

Kane shook his head. "Not just that, there was something else. People have a feel to them. It's subtle, but you know it by its absence. This ville, its buildings—they all feel like they were abandoned a long time ago. Years."

Brigid considered this, nodding her head in agreement. "You're right. It's as if they all just up and left."

"So what happened?" Kane asked, pulling himself up from the grass. "Where did they all go?" He offered Brigid his hand as she got up off the dirt.

"A bomb would make sense," Brigid said, checking her shotgun. "Maybe a biological weapon. That would engender a mass evacuation."

"You mean some kind of plague?" Kane queried.

"Anthrax, smallpox—the list of germ weapons is inexhaustible," Brigid said solemnly. "Some of the old, lab-created weapons just have file numbers, they never got to the point of naming them."

"What about the burning?" Kane said. "It's hard to ignore the evidence on those walls."

"Twin attack," Brigid suggested, her bright hair catching in the wind. "Why kill 'em once when you can kill 'em twice over?"

"Hmm," Kane growled. "Why didn't we hear about it? This didn't just happen, not damage like this. We stepped into the mat-trans to gate back to Cerberus, and suddenly we're in an abandoned ville none of us had heard of, being chased by Magistrates. Something's not right about that scenario."

"Maybe we missed it," Brigid reasoned as they walked away from the hospital, stepping up to the lake's edge.

"Cerberus's satellite feeds would have picked up some evidence of a bomb being set off," Kane assured her.

"Even satellites can't see everything, Kane," Brigid told him. "Maybe Brewster or whoever looked away from the monitor screen at the crucial moment."

"We'd still see the fallout," Kane told her with a shake of his head. "Something like this, a whole city abandoned, we'd see repercussions. A change in the radiation levels, a mass exodus—*something.*"

Brigid was inclined to agree. What Kane said made sense; Cerberus should have picked up some evidence during one of its routine global scans. And yet the name of the settlement remained a mystery, too—Quocruft. There was no Baron Quocruft, that was for sure. Where exactly were they?

Standing at the edge of the lake, Brigid watched the surface ripple as the relentless wind played across it. She stared down at her feet, where her reflection shimmered beside Kane's on the rippling surface, and for just a second she thought she saw something in Kane's reflection. "Daryl?" she said, almost without thinking.

"What did you say?" Kane asked, staring at his red-haired partner.

"D— Kane, I'm sorry," Brigid said. "I thought I saw..." She paused, uncertain, distracted.

"Thought you saw what?" Kane asked, his brow furrowing. "Baptiste?"

Brigid was staring at the water again, looking at

Kane's reflection. Only it wasn't Kane—the man in the water was of average build, with brown hair and brown eyes. It was Daryl Morganstern, the Cerberus mathematician who had died defending Brigid during a devastating attack on the redoubt.

But he was dead—wasn't he?

Chapter 15

In the water, Brigid appeared to be standing beside Daryl Morganstern, Cerberus's theoretical mathematician with whom she had briefly become romantically involved. Less forthright than most of the men in her life, Morganstern had appealed to Brigid on an intellectual level, his inquiring mind challenging hers. But he had died after a stone had been hurled at his skull, the blood cascading down his face. She remembered it, every red drop.

In the water he looked perfect, with his tousled brown hair and those deep brown eyes looking up at Brigid expectantly. The water around him was black, a black so absolute that it seemed like paint. Brigid didn't think it strange.

"Daryl," she said, the word coming as a whisper, tripping over her lips fearfully.

Daryl spread his arms wide, reaching up for her. He was naked, or at least shirtless– –it was hard to tell. His body was still in the water, hidden in the inky dark. "Come, Brigid," he crooned. "I've missed your touch so much. It's cold here, so cold without you."

Her eyes fixed on the rippling surface of the lake, Brigid took a pace forward, one step closer to the lapping edge. "I'm so sorry," Brigid said, her voice choked. "I left you to die. I had to."

"I died alone," he told her, but there was no malice

in his voice, just sadness. "Now I'm so cold. Join me, Brigid, and we can keep warm together."

Brigid took another step toward the lake, her eyes fixed on the vision within. Daryl spread his arms wider, reaching out to pull her in, his smile as perfect as she remembered, just the way it had always been.

"I shouldn't have left you to die like that," Brigid declared, her words little more than a whisper. "I should have done something, should have found a way."

"There was nothing you could have done then," Daryl reassured her. "But you can change all that now. You can make things right if only you'll join me. We'll be happy, oh so happy. My Brigid, my love."

Brigid took another step, the black waters of the lake lapping at the toes of her boots.

"Daryl," Brigid said, "I can help you. I want to."

"Just another step, my dove," Daryl said. "Just one more."

Brigid took another step, and the waters covered her toes now, lapping around her boot heels like liquid onyx. If she just held Daryl's hand again, she knew she could make everything right, could fix everything.

But as she went to take another step, she felt something tugging at her sleeve, pulling her back.

KANE REACHED OUT, grabbing Brigid's arm and shaking her. "Baptiste?" he called. "Look at me. Look at me."

Lethargically Brigid turned, looking away from the water where she stood and staring at Kane. Her eyes were wide, their emerald-green nothing but a sliver where the pupils had dilated. She seemed mystified, as if unable to comprehend what she was seeing.

"D-Daryl?" she asked slowly.

"No," Kane told her. "It's me. It's Kane."

"Kane? Is that you…?"

"Come on, librarian," Kane said, shaking her by the shoulders. "Get your files in order."

It took a few more seconds until Brigid saw him properly, and even then the daylight seemed to hurt her eyes. "Kane? What happened to me?" she finally asked, breathless.

"I don't know," he admitted. "You sort of zoned out."

"Like you back in the waiting room when the Mags first fired," Brigid realized, her senses coming back to her slowly, like lights in a circuit.

"Yeah, I guess," Kane said. "You were looking at the lake. You kept saying Daryl's name."

"Daryl…Morganstern," Brigid concluded after a moment's thought. "He's dead. But I saw him, there in the water. He called to me. Kane, I wanted to join him."

Still holding her by the shoulders, Kane looked Brigid directly in the eye. "Join me. It's a lot drier."

Kane and Brigid shared a bond like no other, something that pulled them through situations that others could scarcely imagine. It was referred to as *anam chara,* a friendship of the souls that reached through eternity, outside of time and space. Some had mistaken this for a romance, but it was far deeper than that; it was a trust, a guardianship, akin to the link a man has with his own heartbeat.

"Let's get out of here," Kane said, pulling Brigid back from the dark waters. "I don't like being here, not out in the open like this." What he failed to tell her was that he had seen something, too, lying there by the lake in the long grass. A glimpse of something he had all but forgotten, something capable of haunting even an ex-Magistrate.

THEY RAN, WORKING their way westward where the sun's rays stretched through the clouds like white fingers. Whatever it was that Brigid had seen in the water, Kane chose not to discuss it. They could do that later, once they had found shelter, well away from the dogged Magistrates and their screaming guns. Grant would have to look after himself for now, as there was no sense in all three of them being in danger.

They were in a business district, all office blocks featuring characterless atriums with benches and unobtrusive sculptures at the front, a place where the workers could relax and eat lunch.

The two Cerberus warriors checked some of the buildings, finding their doors broken or unsecured. All were largely the same; abandoned with that same radial pattern of fire damage, as if some incredible heat blast had hit them from the street.

Some of the buildings included clothing boutiques or food vendors at street level, there to serve the people who worked above them. The boutiques were a testament to the power of fire, burned rags clinging to melted metal hangers on melted metal rails. The food vendors had been ransacked or destroyed, and all of them had that same sickening smell of overripe fruit and stale bread, of coffee left too long on the boil.

Kane kept looking. He told Brigid that he wanted to find somewhere they could defend, but there was more to it than that. He was searching for a clue, for evidence of what had happened here to cause the whole ville to be abandoned. But so much had been burned, whatever records may once have existed were likely sacrificed to fire, man's most ancient god who took everything in return for heat and light.

"Kane, we have to stop," Brigid said as they entered

the sixth office building. Its brutal lines moved away from the street in steps, each level added like the tiers of a wedding cake, the glass front shattered and its paint-work blistered from heat.

In the lobby, Kane half turned, not giving Brigid his full attention. He was scanning the office directory as he had the others, reading the raised characters there through the smoke damage that had obscured them. "You tired?"

"Yes, but it's not just that," Brigid said. "We're getting farther away from the hospital where we left Grant. Without operational Commtacts, we could lose him entirely—he'd have no way of tracking us down."

Kane looked up at her then, and Brigid noted his unsettled expression. "There are no insects around, you notice that?"

"What?" Brigid asked.

"No matter where we've been, there aren't any insects," Kane said. "Not any that I've seen. Not even when we were crouched in the grass. That tell you anything?"

Brigid pondered this for a moment. "Something hit this ville," she said. "Something big."

"Big enough to kill a bug?" Kane asked doubtfully. "I thought the roaches survived even a nuke."

"They would," Brigid agreed. It was a generally accepted truism that cockroaches would survive just about any bomb.

"Makes it all the stranger, doesn't it?" Kane suggested. "These buildings are open, that hospital was missing a whole wall. It's not as if there's anything keeping the insects out. So where are they? And the birds, the dogs, anything?"

"If there's nothing to feed on…" Brigid began.

"Then they'd feed on each other," Kane told her. "But there's still food here, nutrition enough for a bug, at least."

Brigid glared at him with frustration. "Do you have a point?"

Kane stood by the reception desk of the lobby, its faux-marble facade pulled away by what appeared to be incredible heat. "What did you see in the lake?" he asked.

"I told you—Daryl Morganstern," Brigid said, irritation clear in her tone.

"A dead man," Kane murmured, talking now to himself.

"A hallucination," Brigid reasoned. "I'd thought about him earlier, I must have just…I don't know, mistaken your reflection."

"No, you didn't," Kane told her. "I saw it, too."

"What? Daryl?" Brigid asked, stepping closer to him in the abandoned lobby.

"No, someone else," Kane said with a shake of his head. "In the water there. Someone who died."

For a moment, just one name came to Brigid's mind, and she hated herself for thinking it. But she knew she had to ask. "Was it Grant?"

Chapter 16

Kane had a faraway look in his eye, as if reliving whatever he had seen there in the black waters of the lake.

"Kane?" Brigid probed. "Was it Grant?"

"No," he said. "It was someone from a long time ago, from before I met you."

Brigid looked at Kane, this noble warrior who had regained his humanity by defying the very system he had been indoctrinated to protect, trying to read his expression. He was struggling with this, trying to comprehend it. "You think it means something?" she asked finally.

"I looked in the water and I saw her face, but I knew it couldn't be," Kane explained. "She was dead the first time I saw her, just a kid. Helena Vaughn. She couldn't be here. The only place she still exists is in my head."

Brigid ran one hand through her hair, trying to understand. It did not make sense, not yet, at least.

"We should keep moving," Kane said after a moment. "It wasn't just dumb luck that we ran into that patrol. There'll be more Mags out there, and we have to assume that if they see us they'll try to hunt us down."

Brigid nodded. "Agreed."

Together the two of them left the lobby and its ruined glass front, returning to the street of howling wind but keeping to the shadows of the buildings' forecourts.

"What are you looking for, anyway?" Brigid asked as they trekked along the street.

"Someplace high," Kane told her, eying the skyline. "I'll let you know when I spot it."

THE DARK MAGISTRATES had reconvened outside the hospital with Grant's body in tow. One of the dark figures—Magistrate South—held a pair of glasses in his hand, turning them over and over as he examined them. Magistrate North had patched up the bullet wound to his leg, wrapping a roll of gauze around it.

The four of them stood over the slumped figure of the Cerberus warrior, speaking in their jagged, screaming language, each fractured syllable like a bird's caw.

There had been two others, besides this one with the mahogany skin. They had seen them, sensed them, smelled their bloody scents. They were alive against the baron's wishes, a crime punishable by death. But this one, whom North had shot with his Soul Eater, needed to be taken back to base, where the baron would decide what to do with him. It had been so long since the living had walked the streets of Quocruft.

The dialogue continued for a few seconds, stopping as unexpectedly as it had started. A decision had been reached.

Two Magistrates lifted Grant's limp body by the arms and legs, marching him to the nearest access point for the Hall of Justice where he would be picked up. The other two returned to their patrol, scouting the abandoned streets for the other living shells, checking for more. Magistrate South shoved the spectacles in the pants pocket of his uniform—evidence.

Around them, the winds howled, banshee cries from the ghost city of Quocruft.

KANE FOUND THE KIND OF building he was looking for two blocks later. But as Brigid went to cross the ghostly, abandoned street, Kane stopped her with a gesture.

She eyed him questioningly, worried. He was standing in the shadows, watching something in the distance. When she looked she saw nothing there at first, but after a moment she spotted the movement. It was distant, at least five blocks away, and looked to be two figures carrying another, but it was difficult to tell from this distance. Without Kane, Brigid might not have noticed it from this far out; once again, his point-man sense proved its worth.

"We'll cross the street on my command," Kane told Brigid.

"Can't we find another…?" she began.

"No, look," Kane told her, pointing up to the roof.

The building was over a dozen stories tall and it was taller than any of the buildings around it. Much of the window glass was missing, a great trail of broken glass lining the forecourt like a barricade where it had fallen. Up on the roof, Brigid could see metallic spines sticking up into the air. It was a radio array, designed to converse with satellites.

"What are you thinking?" Brigid asked in an urgent whisper. "That they're still receiving transmissions?"

Kane nodded. "And that we could send them," he told her, raising his eyebrows.

Before Brigid could query that, Kane gestured her to cross the road, and the two of them scurried across the cracked surface and into the forecourt with its glass carpet. Brigid picked her way through the shards until she reached the shadow cast by the awning, while Kane was more direct, keeping pace with her and crushing the glass underfoot, the popping tinkles, barely audible over the incessant howl of the winds.

When they stopped, Brigid looked at Kane quizzically as he stared back down the street, watching for the figures he had spotted there.

"You want to send a broadcast?" she asked. "What, to Cerberus?"

"Yeah," Kane said. "Unless you're up for rebooting our Commtacts. I know you're a dab hand at most stuff, but microwiring, coupled with the respective surgical procedure... Well, under normal circumstances, I'm sure you'd manage, but out in the field...?"

"Thanks for the vote of confidence," Brigid said, hefting the shotgun so that it rested on her shoulders. "Are we going inside, then?"

"You go," Kane instructed. "I'm going to wait here, see what John Ghost there is up to."

Brigid nodded and made her way into the tall building. She knew better than to argue with Kane when he was in a mood like this. He was in hunter mode now; something had piqued his curiosity.

The doors to the tower block were warped and buckled where something powerful had struck them. It looked like the result of a hurricane. Inside, Brigid found a typical office lobby, one long reception desk coupled with a small waiting area that featured a low table for magazines. Everything was blackened with smoke damage and the fabric coverings of the chairs had burned entirely away, leaving the stuffing, melted and congealed, hanging within their skeletal metal frameworks.

After a quick scan of what remained of the office directory behind a sheet of melted plastic, Brigid found what she was after; a monitoring station attached to a media group, likely the owner of the equipment on the roof. The group would have disseminated official information, a mouthpiece for the ville's baron.

Brigid pushed open a couple of doors—one for a store cupboard, the next for a cloakroom with a long metal rail—before she located the stairwell behind the dead elevators. Like the lobby, the stairwell smelled of fire damage and damp, and Brigid winced as its pungency struck her, making tears stream from her eyes. The stairway door had been closed a long time, so the stench had had nowhere to escape to. Drawing a breath, Brigid began the long trek up eight flights of stairs to the office in question.

OUTSIDE, KANE HAD MOVED away from the forecourt and was making his way down the street toward a lone figure he could see moving there. The others had disappeared, but Kane had been watching this one for two minutes now. The winds continued to howl through the streets, wailing like a creature in pain and making it hard to distinguish if the figure was making any noise.

Kane continued toward the figure, sticking close to the shadows as he made his way to the end of the block. He could see clearly now that it was another Magistrate, dressed in dark leathers with the bloodred badge of office pinned to the left breast of his tunic. He wore the outer coat of the Magistrate Division over his uniform, and this, too, featured the red symbol of the Magistrates along with scarlet piping. The Mag seemed to be picking through the wreckage that was strewed on the street, discarding great chunks of melted metal as he searched.

Ducked down in the shadows, Kane watched for almost five minutes, conscious of the weight of the Sin Eater pistol pressing against his wrist. The Magistrate moved normally, but each time he looked up Kane could see the bulging flesh beneath the helmet, distended and colored an angry red, the veins running like dark fingers through it, the skin split here and there. Kane had seen enough corpses to recognize the look. He appeared to be in the second stage after death, the stage known as bloat, when a body's gases accumulate. And yet the man still walked, going about his business as if nothing was wrong. Kane felt a shiver down his spine as he watched, hoping he was mistaken. There was only one way to find out for sure.

"Hey, Magistrate!" Kane shouted as he stepped out of the shadows. "I heard there was a happening at the big house—you think you could maybe point me the way?"

The Magistrate flinched, his blaster emerging from his sleeve as he looked up to see who dared taunt him. Kane started to run.

THE STAIRWELL WAS DANK, dark and it had a smell like burned toast. Brigid climbed the stairs, passing floor after floor as she made her way to the ninth floor. Water was pooled everywhere, its dampness clinging to the walls opposite a line of shattered windows. Kane had the right idea about radio communications, she knew. They just needed the right equipment and she could tap the Cerberus network and alert them to their dilemma.

There was a presence on the staircase. Brigid could feel it, sense it, but when she looked it wasn't there. It was just out of sight, waiting around the next turn or following behind her. Her mind playing tricks.

From the staircase the floors seemed characterless, just smooth gray concrete with a floor number plated to the wall beside each dull-painted door. The paint of the doors had blistered with heat, a sign that something had

struck the building. This was designed as a fire staircase, and it featured heavy doors to every floor. Any
fire would not have penetrated that barricade easily, yet
the well still stank of burning and the doors showed the
evidence of suffering a dose of extreme heat. Maybe it
wasn't fire, Brigid wondered—maybe it was just heat
of such intensity it had melted everything in a flash.

Brigid stopped at floor nine. She waited a moment
at the closed door that led onto the floor itself, gathering her thoughts and calming her breath. She was in the
peak of physical fitness, but hurrying up this stinking
staircase still took effort. And there was the thing behind her, the lurking presence with the familiar face.
It wouldn't do to get caught unprepared now, after she
had come this far.

Raising the shotgun one-handed, Brigid pulled at
the heavy fire door and peered into the floor beyond.

The door opened up straight into an office, open-
plan design with low screens that boxed in each section,
standing a little over four feet in height. The desks were
mostly arranged in blocks of four, with one or two lone
desks at the end of each row. They reminded Brigid of
cages in a zoo. Two entire walls of windows cast light
into the room, painting it in a charmless gloom that
would force its occupants to rely on the fluorescent
strip lights overhead. The window glass had broken in
places, and Brigid could feel and hear the breeze blowing through those holes, fluttering coasters and address
cards across the floor like tumbleweed.

Taking a step from the fire door, the shotgun ready
in her grip, Brigid called out, "Hello? Anyone here?"

No one answered, which didn't surprise Brigid in the
slightest. She had hoped that perhaps she was wrong,

but sadly, like every other building they had checked here in Quocruft, the office was emphatically empty.

Brigid stepped to her left, gazing out of the nearest bank of windows, the breeze tousling her hair. She was at the side of the building, as far from the forecourt as one could get. Her own reflection played across the glass. The reflection was translucent, and it took just a slight adjustment of Brigid's focus to see through herself and down to the access road beyond, where garbage and delivery wags might have come to service the building. No one down there.

As Brigid turned away, she saw something standing beside her, reflected in the smooth surface of the glass. It was a man, seen only in shadow, his proportions familiar. She turned, looking behind her at where the man—Daryl Morganstern—should have been, but he wasn't there.

Shaking her head, Brigid turned back to the window for just a moment, searching its reflective edge. He was still there. She couldn't quite see *him,* only his absence, but she could feel him, watching her. A resentful guardian angel.

Warily Brigid paced the long aisle that ran between desks, seeing more signs of the great heat that seemed to have incinerated so much. Devoid of life, the room had been left to rot, computer units and comm devices spread untidily on the desks, some tipped on the floor. Besides the computers, there was a monitor screen on almost every desk, enough to make Brigid conclude that they had all featured such a device once. She took a few moments to test one of these, trying its switches. They were television sets, a built-in playback device attached to their bases. Nothing worked.

She moved on, spying the seared artifacts on the

walls, two dust-drenched coats that had been left on a coat stand between desks. There was a smoke-streaked comm array, designed for taking satellite feeds. Brigid eyed it for a moment, recognizing the setup. Hypothetically, she could use this to contact the Cerberus base, tuning into the Commtacts' frequency and bouncing a signal off the Keyhole satellite. But of course, that would require power, which was something that this building did not have.

Over to the right, away from the bank of windows, was a long wall that had been used to store recordings. They ran almost the whole length of the wall, double-stacked in places, with occasional gaps where items had been removed. At first Brigid took them to be books, but on closer inspection she saw they were reel-to-reel magnetic tapes: video recordings. The tapes nearest the windows had been melted, their plastic covers liquefied and solidified in new and interesting shapes, like hot toffee sticking to a cooking ladle, but most had survived intact. She pulled one from the shelf at random, reading the identifying label that had been slapped on the box. The label was handwritten over a formatted printout, and it gave the date of the recording, along with the story and the reporter's name. It was a news recording of some sort, Brigid realized, this one celebrating the opening of a new school.

Brigid checked a few of the tapes, finding stories concerning food deliveries, recycling and one about the declining radiation levels. It was the kind of information she had regularly processed as a junior archivist in Cobaltville, before she had been given more important responsibilities in the Historical Division.

Archived news reports. Of course, without power she had no way to play them.

Brigid pushed the tapes back onto their shelves, returning them to their correct places with the ingrained meticulousness of an archivist. The shelving units were split in the center to reveal a door that Brigid guessed led into an editing suite or similar. She strolled over, tested the handle and let herself in.

There, Brigid found herself staring straight down the barrel of a gun pointed right between her eyes.

Chapter 17

Automatically, Brigid skipped back, dodging out of the firing line with a movement born of honed reflex. The shining revolver did not fire but simply remained there, pointed at the door.

It was dark in the room, the only light spilling in from the office outside, where Brigid had left the door open. The blaster was held in a bone hand that was attached to a skeleton draped in stained clothes. The skeleton was balanced in a swivel chair that had been placed between two tight shelving units filled with videotapes. There was barely enough room for the chair, though its long-dead occupant scarcely cared now. The room itself was windowless.

The first thing Brigid did was disarm the skeleton and check over the revolver in the office outside, where the light was better. It was a .38 with five bullets still in the chamber and the safety off. She flipped the safety on and shoved the weapon in her waistband at the small of her back.

"Don't think you'll be needing it anymore, friend," she told her grisly discovery.

After that, Brigid returned to the room, reached for the light switch on the wall and flipped it once, twice, only proving what she had already suspected—that it didn't work. There was no power; nothing worked here any longer. When night fell, she and Kane would likely see the whole city plunged into darkness.

Swiftly she pushed the swivel chair and its gruesome occupant out of the storeroom before returning. Then, leaving the door open behind her, Brigid checked the room. If there was a communications device, she might be able to use an emergency backup generator to get it running. But she needed to find both, and here seemed as good a place to start looking as any. Things like that ended up forgotten in dusty storerooms like this.

There was no comm array. Little more than a storeroom, the tiny office featured a reinforced metal door—the one Brigid had entered by—twelve shelves containing video tapes, two further shelves that contained a dismantled editing box designed for editing in the field and a one-man desk at the far end on which there was a lamp that no longer worked, a television and a bulky, handheld video camera. Brigid looked at the camera for a moment, turning it over in her hands as she thought. The camera ran on battery power and could take a full-size videocassette. She flipped open the side-mounted screen and watched as, to her surprise, it illuminated with life.

"Batteries still working," she said. Standing behind her, the shadowy figure of Daryl Morganstern smiled at Brigid's discovery, his silhouette visible in the reflection of the dark television screen. Brigid ignored him, knowing he couldn't be real.

With the camera's video player and power, she could watch the tapes, at least until the battery ran down. Brigid took a minute to familiarize herself with the camera's operation, bringing up a user's menu on-

screen. The camera had two hours and eighteen minutes of battery power left.

Brigid scanned the shelves. "So, what are we going to watch?" she muttered.

KANE RAN THROUGH the ghost streets of Quocruft, his arms pumping at his sides, feet splashing into the puddles that littered the broken tarmac. Behind him, the imposing figure of the Magistrate sidestepped as he followed, weapon raised, trying to get a bead on his zigzagging prey.

Kane flinched as a clutch of bullets came howling toward him, cutting the air with their ghastly shrieks. Kane's pursuer shrieked, too, his strained voice echoing through the empty buildings like a whale song. All around Kane, the Magistrate's screaming bullets clipped into the ground and the charred street furniture, whipping into it with an abrupt curtailment of their screams.

Kane needed to finish this, and quickly. The noise of gunfire, the screaming call of the Dark Magistrate, even his own running footsteps on the hard ground—all of this would attract others, he felt certain. Kane leaped as more bullets clipped the road at his feet, spitting up chunks of broken tarmac.

There was a car up ahead, a burned-out wreck, its tires flattened husks that clung to the road like the tendrils of a creeping plant. As more of the Mag's screaming bullets blistered the air all around him, Kane leaped onto the hood of the parked car with a loud thump, rolling across it in a second before dropping below, out of sight of those vicious bullets.

Crouched down in the puddles behind the automobile, Kane checked his right hand. He could bring his own Sin Eater into play, either execute this Magistrate

or wound him. But he needed to find a way to catch the man so that he could question him, perhaps even reason with him.

Kane scanned the area, searching the immediate vicinity with his eyes as his opponent stalked closer. There was water here, pooled on the cracking road surface, shimmering silver as it reflected the cloud cover from overhead. Kane's eyes were drawn to that water as ripples ran across its surface where the breeze brushed against it. *Vaughn.*

Her face was there, the face of the schoolgirl who had died on his watch. Her blond hair swirled about her face, cutting across her eyes for a moment, tangling around her narrow stem of a neck. *Helena Vaughn.*

Kane looked at the face in the water, the clouds overhead drifting past her. She looked beautiful in her innocence, a beauty that he knew had been stolen away by Pellerito and his drugs. He should have saved her. But how could he? He had only been called to the scene once the girl had died; he could not possibly have—

Something exploded close to Kane, a shriek of terror as the bullet cut the air and struck the side of the burned-out automobile. Kane jumped, instinct driving his body, pumping him with adrenaline. He was away from the car even before he quite realized, charging across the street toward an open concrete quadrangle framed by the jutting struts of an office block. The concrete had been pounded by some great force, dark, cracked lines running across it as if an earthquake had struck. In the center, a statue stood atop a plinth, mother and child captured in embrace, the woman's head crumbled away with damage.

Kane ran at the statue, still seeing the innocent face of Helena Vaughn in his mind's eye, still smelling her

girl perfume, pencil shavings, hairspray. Behind him, the Dark Magistrate tracked his prey, screaming bullets blasting from his hand cannon, his fixed expression stern behind the cracked mask of his visor.

His mind whirling, Kane tripped, the toe of his boot catching on one of the ruined paving slabs. Suddenly he was falling headfirst at the ground as another burst of bullets lunged through the air toward him.

THERE WAS NO CHOICE, not for an archivist like Brigid. Most of the tapes in the store cupboard were labelled with dates and identifier numbers, but Brigid didn't pay that much attention. She simply looked around the room until she found the lowest number, took that tape from the shelf and pushed it into the open tray of the camera. Then, sitting on the floor of the storeroom with the video camera between her knees and its flip screen open, she pressed Play.

The screen lit up immediately, coming in midway through a news report. A dour-faced man in a raincoat stared into the lens as a parade marched past behind him, the familiar lines of the ville buildings to his rear. He was speaking to the viewer in that mock-urgent tone reserved for television news reports.

"…with this, Baron Trevelyan promises a new era of prosperity, tapping the sun's resources to provide a near-infinite stream of power into our residences."

The image cut to the marching figures as the report continued in voice-over. A marching band of uniformed schoolchildren passed the camera, alternately grinning and concentrating hard, followed by the grim figures of Magistrates walking five abreast, their expressions hidden beneath their helmets.

"The process has been over a decade in development,

we are told, with last summer's prototype launch conducted in secret. Now the baron feels ready to share his triumph with his grateful people."

The scene changed once more, cutting to a pale-faced figure flanked by two Magistrates standing on a balcony, a vivid red banner draped beneath it in a long vertical that continued past the bottom of the screen. Brigid gasped as she saw the figure, recognized what it was: a hybrid, one of the quasi-human monsters who had ruled the nine villes until they finally revealed themselves to be the major players in a millennia-long alien conspiracy to subjugate and conquer humankind.

The hybrid baron spoke in an effeminate, weaselly voice, an echo coming from the speakers set up around him. "My people, today is a proud day. With the launch of our first sun shield, we are now able to tap the energy of the sun itself, utilising solar power to achieve our dreams. With this near-infinite power source, we are able to dream bigger than we ever have before. The world is ours."

Brigid swallowed, her mouth suddenly dry, as the reporter wrapped up the news story. A sun shield that could provide infinite power? Into what world had the mat-trans unit thrown them?

KANE WAS SPRAWLED BY the statue, his jaw throbbing, head spinning. He pulled himself back from semiconsciousness, rolling his body back to a sitting position.

Across the street, the Magistrate moved like a wraith, the dark lines of his uniform weaving between the burned-out automobiles and ruined benches like a beetle's glistening shell as he strode toward Kane in the quadrangle.

I'm trapped, Kane realized.

There were walls on all sides, holding him in a pincer between the office blocks. Tucked behind the mother-and-child statue, Kane raised his right arm—his gun arm—and thought about the Sin Eater, about what it would cost him to shoot this Magistrate. No, he decided. There had to be some other way. Killing the patrolman would achieve nothing. He needed a witness, someone to interrogate, so he could figure out what was going on and where they had materialized.

Kane's eyes flashed around the area where he found himself trapped, searching the pooling water and the broken office furniture that had found its way to this enclosed concrete square. The furniture gave Kane an idea.

Behind him, the Dark Magistrate loomed closer, seeking his prey amid the ruins of the sprawling avenue. He called, mouth wide, a shriek like nails down a chalkboard bursting forth, becoming louder with each ululation. Abruptly the sound stopped, cut off in midstream when the Magistrate closed his lips. His prey had gone, was no longer hidden behind the statue.

The Magistrate turned, searching the area with his hidden eyes. And as he turned, Kane ran at him from his hiding place under a pockmarked desk, wielding the broken leg of a chair like a baseball bat.

"MY NAME IS BRYAN BAUBIER, and I'm a journalist," the man on the videotape said without preamble.

This recording looked washed-out, the colors muted, and there was a fuzzy white blur at the top of the screen where the playback head needed cleaning, but Brigid watched without complaint. The man was sitting in what looked like this very storeroom, the wall visible right behind him with a shelf full of videotapes. The room was so small there was barely enough room to set up the camera, lending almost a fish-eye effect to his face. He looked young, still in his twenties, a mop of curly blond hair hanging partway over his eyes. In a different set of circumstances, Brigid might have described him as cute. He spoke in a whisper, his eyes furtive throughout the brief recording.

"This isn't going on the record," Baubier said. "They won't let it.

"There was a protest in the town square today," he continued, his eyes darting back and forth, "and it turned ugly. The people are rioting over food because so much has been reassigned for the baron's grand project. Without any freight vehicles available, food's no longer reaching the ville, and even the black market is struggling now where once it flourished.

"They sent Magistrates to quell the rioters. They were the new breed of Magistrates, ones I had heard about but not seen before. They walk like men but there is something wrong with them. They smell like they don't wash, and they never speak. They simply lash out, attacking anyone who comes within arm's reach. I saw a woman shot in cold blood as she tried to get free. She had been there to protest about the lack of food—she hadn't been a part of the riot. She had been trying to calm everyone down when the Magistrates shot her in the head."

Despite the low quality of the recording, Brigid could hear the fear in the man's trembling tone, see it in his eyes.

"People are starving, but all the baron does is command his Magistrates to shoot them," the man concluded. "One less mouth to feed. Or to complain."

Brigid watched as Bryan Baubier leaned forward

and switched off the camera, at which point the recording cut to static.

Brigid's eyes returned to the shelf of video recordings, scanning their spines. The tapes to the left had
dates on them, but as she got farther across the shelf
she saw the dates turn to day numbers, and then tapes
with simple blank labels where no one had taken the
time to fill them in. She picked one of the undated ones,
identified as Day 461, and slapped it in the video player.

KANE SWUNG THE HUNK of wood like a bat, driving it
into the back of the Magistrate's helmet with a loud
crack. The wood struck so hard that it snapped, breaking along its central line, one half flipping over before
crashing into the street.

The Magistrate fell, too, tumbling forward as the
wood struck his helmet. The Magistrate's helmet toppled from his head, rolling three feet across the sidewalk as he sagged to the ground. Kane stood behind
him, the hunk of wood still clutched in his hand, watching for any sign of consciousness. He hadn't killed him;
he was sure of that. He just wanted the Magistrate unconscious so he could drag him somewhere secure to
interrogate him.

The Magistrate lay before Kane, utterly still, sprawled
across the tarmac, his arms stretched out before him. But
as Kane watched, a weapon materialized in the Magistrate's right hand, some curious adaptation of the Sin
Eater pistol. Kane stepped away even as the dark-clad
figure began rolling, bringing the blaster up and snapping the trigger. A trio of those shrieking bullets burst
from the muzzle in quick succession, piercing the air
with their haunting sound.

Kane was already in motion, diving for cover as the

bullets clipped by overhead. In that moment, the Magistrate caught Kane's eye, skewering Kane with his sinister stare. Beneath the helmet, his eyes were bulging, like two fried eggs sizzling in the pan, and his skin was an angry red, shredded and splitting, dark wounds oozing all across his bloated face.

Kane tossed the useless hunk of wood aside, scrabbling in the street debris for a better weapon. He did not want to use his Sin Eater, that was a last resort against a fellow Magistrate, even one in such a state of physical decay. The Magistrate, however, had no such compulsions, and he snapped off another burst of fire from his retractable blaster as Kane rolled away.

THE FACE ON THE VIDEO screen was talking again. Same face, same room, but the voice sounded flatter somehow, as if the man called Bryan Baubier had been stripped of his emotions.

"...see my mother," Baubier said, beginning in the middle of his sentence. "When I go to shave, I see her there, looking out of the water."

His tone reminded Brigid of the way people sound after a loved one has died, that week-later sound, when they have cried as much as any person can and simply don't have anything left to give to the world.

"Hadn't seen her in three years, since she...the home." His head dipped, and Brigid found herself looking into the crown of his hair for a few seconds as he muttered something that the microphone did not properly pick up. "I thought I'd stopped missing her. My sister always took it worse. But here it is, I'm mourning her all over again. When I do the dishes, even though there's barely anything to eat. Why I'm coming into work still I don't know, it's…people need to know what happened, how it all went down."

Brigid watched the face on the screen as the man sat there, staring into the lens—or through it. He seemed to be gathering his thoughts, less scripted than the earlier entry she had seen. Ninety seconds passed before Bryan Baubier reached forward and the screen finally went blank.

Brigid ejected the tape, took another from the shelf. This one had no date on it, no indicators at all, other than a number that had been peeled from a sticker sheet and placed in the center of the spine. It was tape number 9.

"Hell-o, operator," Brigid muttered as she pushed the tape into the player. Behind her, the other figure watched, too.

KANE SNATCHED UP A LENGTH of metal piping as he rolled, the Dark Magistrate's pistol bucking in his hand. The pistol fired, rattling off another burst of those howling slugs as the Cerberus man plucked up the metal pipe and doubled back. The screaming bullets were lost somewhere in the street, while Kane regained his footing and began to lunge toward the Mag.

His arms pumping, Kane ran at the Magistrate, swinging the metal piping like a baseball bat. The Magistrate's blaster rushed up at him even as Kane swung, and the two weapons met in a clang of metal on metal. The pistol spat another shrieking bullet from its muzzle as Kane knocked it aside, and the bullet raced past Kane's ear so close that he felt it brush his hair.

The Magistrate glared at Kane with huge yellow-white eyes, bloody streaks coloring them at the outer edges. He tried to bring his weapon around again, but

Kane kept the length of piping against the blaster, holding it firmly away from his body. Kane's other hand shot forward in a cross, punching the Magistrate with a powerful blow across the jaw. The Mag stumbled a half step, his finger still pressed against the trigger of his screeching weapon.

Kane pressed his advantage, driving his right knee up into the Magistrate's gut, forcing him backward with weight alone. Kane suspected that the longer they spent out here, the more noise they made, the more chance there was that someone else would come to investigate. That would most likely be another Magistrate, and Kane didn't want that. So he needed to finish this quickly and decisively, whether or not his foe was actually alive.

The Dark Magistrate scooted backward, letting out an abbreviated screamlike noise close to Kane's ear before dropping to the ground. Kane drew his hand back and swept it, arrowlike, at the Magistrate's exposed throat to silence him.

"Zip it," Kane snarled.

ON SCREEN, BRYAN BAUBIER had grown a beard, though it did little to disguise how gaunt he had become. It took Brigid a moment to realize why he had grown the beard—it was most probably to avoid looking at the reflection in the water basin, the one that looked like his mother.

"Mags are all over now," he explained in a hoarse voice, "more of them than us. They use those blasters on anyone who moves—Soul Eaters, they're called. The Mags don't speak, they just arrest people who break curfew, and those people never appear again.

"It's three in the morning, and I'm still at work because I'm scared of going out there. If the Magistrates see me…

"A bomb went off, near the center of the ville. They're saying it was an experiment, that's the official line. I don't know what kind of experiment would do that. People died, burned up in the blowback.

"Teresa's gone."

Brigid watched the haunted face of the man on the screen as he sat in this same claustrophobic, metal-walled room, talking into the camera.

"Baron Trevelyan put out a statement promising us that everything was okay," the man on the screen continued. "But it's not. People are disappearing day by day, and there's little enough food for those who remain. I've hardly eaten in ten days."

For a moment the mop-haired journalist reached forward, and the picture jumped as it cut to a new recording—the same face, some indeterminate time later. He looked tired, had dark circles under his eyes.

"My mother's here," Baubier said. "She was in the men's restroom—I saw her out of the corner of my eye. I couldn't go. I wanted to piss myself when I caught sight of her, but the irony is I couldn't go. She looks sick, like how I remembered the last time, only worse."

There was a noise from somewhere off camera, and the journalist turned away from the lens, peering off toward where Brigid realized the door would be. Then he turned back, reaching for the switch on the camera once more.

"Security's here," Bryan Baubier explained in a hushed voice. "Maybe they can figure out what my dead mother's doing here."

The image winked out.

LYING ON THE SIDEWALK, the Magistrate rocked, his Soul Eater firing again as Kane held it back from his face. The bullet screeched as it left the chamber, screaming like a child in pain as it shot away from the two figures wrestling on the ground.

The Magistrate was well-trained—Kane expected no less—and he shifted his muscles to gain leverage, flipping Kane back. Kane let his body go limp as he was thrown, knowing better than to struggle. He was tossed away by the Magistrate, tumbling over and over on the sidewalk before regaining his balance.

Glass tinkled under his hands and knees as Kane drew himself up on all fours, a bloody red line drawing a path down from his left nostril to his mouth. As he looked up, the Magistrate was pulling himself to a standing position, bringing his blaster around to execute this human irritation.

"This can't be good," Kane muttered as the Magistrate targeted him once more.

Kane winced as the Magistrate's trigger finger tensed.

BRIGID TOOK THE last tape from the shelf and she inserted it into the player with a sense of foreboding.

Static ran on the screen for a few seconds, then was replaced by the face of Bryan Baubier. He looked tired, haunted, with an unkempt beard and uncombed hair.

"I just wanted to let you know that I didn't kill my mother," he began. "Even if that's what she's saying. Yes, I should have visited her more in the home, but I…" He stopped, drew a heavy breath before he went on. "A part of me knows that something is happening, this rational part of me, the journalist part. Everyone is so heartsick but they can't express it. Like we're all being followed by the people in our lives who have died. As if there isn't enough death out there already."

Brigid turned away from the screen for a few seconds, her eyes on the closed door. Daryl Morganstern was there, watching her from the shadows. She saw him, shook her head, willed him to go away.

On screen, Bryan Baubier was still talking. "They did something, the baron, the Magistrates. They did something to us. I don't know what it is, can't get a grip on it, but I know it's something. Like we're all out of true."

Brigid was watching the screen again, trying to ignore the figure poised in the darkness behind Bryan's head, a refection of the figure whom she knew was waiting behind her. *Daryl.*

"We were people with lives," Baubier muttered, shaking his head. "Now…" He stopped again, brushing at the tears that had formed in his eyes, tears that the camera's resolution could not even pick up in the dimly lit store cupboard. Then, sniffing loudly, Baubier stared into the camera, his face close to the lens, and spoke in a defiant tone. "We're not living anymore— we're just spaces filled with sorrow. Sorrow spaces."

Brigid watched as the man reached forward and switched off the recording again. The screen reverted to static. There were no further tapes on the shelf; the only possibility now was to go backward and watch what had come before.

Brigid let the tape turn in the player, watching the snowstorm patterns that the static made on the screen, looking past it at the reflection of the figure who was standing over her shoulder, so close she could reach out and touch him. Daryl Morganstern was not there, she told herself. But his reflection continued to wait, a statue in the darkness, infinitely patient.

"Are you just going to ignore me?" Daryl Morganstern wanted to know. His voice sounded colder than Brigid remembered, harsher.

STRUGGLING ON THE SIDEWALK, Kane winced as the Magistrate pulled the trigger on his blaster. But nothing happened. No bullet, screaming or otherwise. The weapon simply clicked on empty.

The Magistrate stared at the blaster in disbelief, his finger curling again and again on the trigger as if that would somehow resolve the problem of running out of ammo.

Kane meanwhile drew himself up and charged toward the Magistrate, head low, driving himself with a growl of determination. The Mag looked up at the last moment, just as Kane slammed against his chest using the crown of his head as a battering ram.

The rotted Magistrate went down, crashing into another office forecourt, where everything was strewed with glass. Both figures slid, Kane's momentum driving them back. Then they were at the edge of the building, where a revolving door stood, its glass panels missing, just steel bars poised in a dance of vertical lines. The Magistrate struck one of those steel lines headfirst, with a sickeningly hollow sound.

Kane pulled away, staring at the Magistrate as he lay on the paving slabs, head lolling at an angle. Without hesitation, he kicked away the Magistrate's weapon— that strangely altered Sin Eater that shot screaming bullets in curling facelike smoke—and shook his head. "What the hell have we stumbled onto here?" Kane asked himself.

Helmetless, the Magistrate was no longer moving, and he certainly was not answering. Kane leaned down and hoisted the man onto his shoulders, hefting him off the street. It wouldn't do to be caught out here. Besides, he wanted to interrogate this Magistrate when he woke up—if that was possible.

"I hope you're the chatty type," Kane said as he stepped into the lobby with the man on his shoulders, "or this bastard-long afternoon is going to turn into an even longer evening."

BRIGID SAT STILL IN THE unlit storeroom, the camera's television monitor burbling with silent static before her. Her hand reached forward, ejecting the video cassette and plucking it from its tray.

"Pretend I'm not here? Is that what you're going to do, Brigid?"

With a sigh, Brigid pulled the cassette free, turning it over in her hands. She refused to turn to where the voice came from, where *his* voice came from, refused to look.

"Like you did when you left me to die? That's the way you do things isn't it? Out of sight, out of mind."

"It wasn't like that…" Brigid began, murmuring the words without turning.

"You killed me. There, I said it. Now we can stop pretending."

Brigid turned in her chair, glaring at the other figure in the darkness. "I didn't kill you," she told Daryl Morganstern.

Morganstern waited in the shadows, his face obscured from the sliver of light slicing from the room beyond. *"I'm dead, aren't I?"* he said with the logic of a mathematician.

"A lot of people were killed in the attack," Brigid told

him, feeling the hot tears plucking at her eyes. "I didn't have a choice. What do you want me to say?"

She could smell him now, that subtle blend of soap and aftershave that he had had at their second meeting. He stood there in the shadows just an arm's reach away. "What could I possibly do to make this right?"

"Complete the equation," Daryl said. *"Kill yourself."*

Chapter 18

His head was pounding and his eyes were closed. And it was cold, really cold. Like the Arctic.

Wherever Grant was, he could hear voices talking.

"...thought the recruitment was over..."

No, not voices—just one voice, talking to itself. A man's voice, clear in its enunciation but with a weasel kind of whine that made Grant want to hit the speaker.

"...where could this one have been hiding for so long?"

Grant struggled to open his eyes. He was awake but he felt numb, his body unresponsive. He tried again as the voice droned on, willing his eyelids to open.

"It beggar's belief."

He felt nauseous just listening to that rodent voice with its penetrating nasal twang.

"Am I to understand the converters are almost at capacity?" the weasel voice demanded. It waited a moment as if listening for a response, before speaking once more. The only response was a stuttered shriek that sounded more like an electronic data feed than a voice. "In which case, we shall send another test subject. Today."

More of the strange whining, stopping and starting abruptly as if it were the recorded result of a man flicking through television channels. Beneath it, ever-present like a drumbeat, Grant heard the dripping of water. *Plop. Plop. Plop.*

"Yes, today," the whiner replied hotly. "Now. Set things in motion now. We don't need to wait. Tonight will suffice. Look..."

Tuning out the irritating voice, Grant finally opened his eyes, but it felt as if he had clawed his way up from beneath some great weight. His eyelids opened heavily, as if they had been gummed shut, and he narrowed them almost immediately against any light. It hurt. He had been shot by something, he remembered. When it struck, it had felt like his very core was being ripped from him, as if his organs themselves were being yanked out of his body. It had hurt like hell, whatever it was, but evidently it hadn't killed him.

The weasel voice was droning on, speaking the kind of techno-babble that Grant had happily left to Lakesh and his desk jockeys.

He was sitting down with his arms secured behind his back. He appeared to be in a long room like an aircraft hangar, with strips of pale green light running its length, painting everything in a putrid glow. Despite the size of the room, it was almost entirely empty apart from a few tables arrayed along the walls, each of them piled with paperwork, folders and printouts. The dripping noise came from close to his right where a basin, its white porcelain cracked, stood against the wall. A single splitter faucet arched over it like a swan's neck, a steady leak of water dripping from its nozzle.

There was something else, too, at the far end of the room. It was circular and made of metal tubing, looking like a gigantic hula hoop standing on its edge. There were people buzzing about the hoop, men dressed in the dark uniforms of Magistrates, and they gave Grant an indication of the hoop's size. It was taller than a man, perhaps ten feet in diameter. Behind the hoop sat a stack of machinery, wired together in a hexagonal pattern, and above it a window through which Grant could see the cloudy sky. A way out, then…?

Grant eyed the figures, trying for a moment to identify what it was that they were doing. A strange figure strolled among the Magistrates, with stooped shoulders and a gait that suggested he had trouble walking. He wore a long gray robe and was at least a head shorter than the shortest of the Magistrates. His cranium was larger than a normal man's, and he appeared so thin that one might presume he was emaciated. Grant's stomach seemed to drop as he registered exactly what the figure was—a baron, one of the human-hybrid creatures who had ruled the nine villes that dominated the post nuke-caust United States of America. But each of the barons had been artificially evolved via a personality download from the alien starship *Tiamat*, physically transforming into towering reptilian creatures known as the overlords. The barons were no more. As the Annunaki, they had enslaved mankind during prehistory and appeared as gods in mankind's myths and legends. When they returned, they had done so to enslave humanity once more, and only through the efforts of the Cerberus organization had they been stopped. Grant had gone toe-to-toe with several of those would-be gods, barely holding his own against their incredible, superhuman stamina. So how could one of them have missed the download? How was it that this baron remained in his chrysalis state?

"Ah good, it's awake," the hybrid said as he shuffled toward Grant, long gray robes brushing against the floor. He was flanked by two pairs of Magistrates, an honor guard for this ethereal creature.

Grant stared up at him from his seat, saying nothing.

"Now, you pose some interesting questions," the hybrid said in his weasel voice. "Such as where you have been hiding all this time, and just how many of you there are?"

Grant stared at him defiantly.

"It's been almost a year since the patrols last picked up a straggler," the baron explained. "Eleven months, six days and nine hours. I thought they had all rotted by now. Apparently I was wrong."

Grant said nothing, watching as the baron's face took on an ugly sneer.

"I vehemently dislike being wrong," the baron told him. "It is a sensation I experience rarely, and it does not agree with my constitution." He leaned close to Grant, glaring at him. "You can speak, can't you?" he demanded.

Grant nodded. "When I've got something to say," he admitted with a smirk.

The hybrid figure laughed at that, a trilling sound that reminded Grant of breaking glass. "Oh, very droll," the baron said after drawing a great breath to curtail his laughter. "You would know me as Baron Trevelyan. Do you have a name?"

"Grant," Grant told him, his dark eyes scanning the area behind the baron where the black-clad figures continued to work at the metal ring.

The baron noticed where Grant was looking. "You are intrigued, yes?" he said. "By what you see here, by my pathway. I wonder if perhaps you know more about it than you let on."

"I don't know what the fuck it is you're talking about," Grant admitted.

"Typical human," the hybrid baron said with a sigh, turning away from Grant. As he did so, Grant began hurriedly working at his bonds. His hands were tied behind his back, cinched tightly at the wrists with some kind of plastic cable. The cable tightened as he tugged against it, and Grant stifled a grunt as Baron Trevelyan twittered on.

"Afraid of what you don't understand," the baron was saying, "channeling your fear into anger at the slightest provocation. I must admit that I have not missed their company. The silence has been…magnificent.

"You primitives make such an incessant racket that one can hardly hear oneself thing. It's been bliss without your kind cluttering up my ville." Baron Trevelyan turned back to Grant, his eyes like two wells, water washing in the inky darkness of their fathomless pits. "Which brings us back to my original question— Where have you been hiding all this time? And are there any more of you?"

Grant set his jaw, glaring at the baron. "You really think I'm going to answer that?" he demanded.

The hybrid baron nodded very slowly, a ghastly smile like a reptile appearing on his lips. "Of course," he said.

As Trevelyan spoke, two of the quartet of guards who flanked him stepped forward, dragging Grant—chair and all—along the hard metal decking of the room toward the cracked basin. The faucet was still dripping, a steady, hollow echo that had played against Grant's ears throughout the conversation with Baron Trevelyan. Poised before the basin, Grant could see the grimy water within, swirling with eddies as one of the silent Magistrates began filling it with water, stopper in place.

"Sooner or later, you must comply with your baron's wishes. I would recommend sooner," the baron said as Grant was set down in his chair before the filling basin.

Grant took a deep breath as the cruel hands of the Magistrates grabbed him behind his neck. Then they yanked him up from the chair, his hands still tied, and forced him forward, plunging his head beneath the swirling waters in the basin. The water felt like ice, and Grant got a new insight into how cold *cold* could be.

IT WAS LIKE DRAGGING A corpse, Kane thought. He was hefting the unconscious Magistrate over his shoulder through the battered doors of the office block. They were wide double doors, designed to impress with their opulence. But the glass had been broken from both, and one hung on its frame, the lower hinge wrenched away at an angle. Despite the damage, the doors had some muffling effect on the high winds that shot through the streets, turning their scream into a dull roar.

"Come on, pal," Kane muttered, his breath coming in forceful puffs through his nostrils. "Almost there now."

In the street outside, Kane spotted several dark figures moving, more of the sinister Magistrates conversing in their strained and abbreviated tones. He rolled the Mag from his shoulders, ducking down behind the reception desk as the other Mags passed by. They strode down the center aisle of the street, where a raised concrete line marked the delineation between traffic going one way and the other. Kane watched them walk past the shattered glass facade of the office block, four abreast, their steps in sync. They were searching the area, searching for him and Baptiste, alerted by their colleague who now lay unconscious at Kane's side. Kane held his breath until the Mags moved on.

Kane stared down at the figure he had dragged in from outside. He was still unconscious, those putrid yellow eyes hidden behind now-closed lids. Kane triggered his Commtact to advise Brigid of their situation before remembering that the Commtacts were out of commission. "Damn."

Swiftly, Kane checked the desk, pulling free an inoperative telephone and a computer and monitor, snapping their leads off so that he could use them to restrain his quarry. There was a potted plant behind the desk, too, the pot twelve inches in diameter. The plant itself had withered and died, just twigs and dry brown leaves remaining. "Don't want you running out on me," Kane explained to the dozing figure as he tied his arms and legs with the cables.

Kane felt tense as he tied the Magistrate up, goose bumps running along his flesh where he touched the man's raw skin. The skin was cold, like fresh meat retrieved from the refrigerator, and it was colored as red as a ladybug.

Once the man was properly tied, Kane dragged him farther into the office, stashing him in a small side room that had once been used to store coats; an upright vacuum cleaner was propped behind the door. The vacuum cleaner wore a coating of dust.

With swiftness borne of practice, Kane checked the Magistrate for other weapons. He had already lost his Soul Eater pistol somewhere on the street. Kane found a knife strapped to the inside leg, by his boot, and took it. Once he was certain that the Magistrate was disarmed, Kane shoved him to the back of the cloakroom, pulling several discarded coats from their hooks and laying them over the unconscious figure. If anyone were to look they would see nothing out of the ordinary, just a couple of coats fallen from their hooks.

Then Kane was back at the door, pulling it open. "Let me check on Baptiste before I get into this with you. That okay?" he asked as he closed the door on the strange Magistrate.

The Mag offered no response.

AFTER A QUICK SCAN OF THE building directory, Kane figured that Brigid would be up on the ninth floor where a media business operated. They should have some kind of comm set-up there, through which Brigid might reach Cerberus, either by boosting or replacing the output of her Commtact.

With the elevators out of commission, he located the fire stairs at the back of the building. The stairwell was cold, wind billowing in through missing windowpanes, striking Kane as he hurried up the concrete steps. The light was limited in this stairwell, leaking through the ruined windows in patches, marred where some of them had been stained with smoke.

Kane's boots splashed through the water pooling on the stairs, blown in through the open windows. The far wall was damp, the concrete dark with water where the sun never reached to dry it. There was no mold, just dampness and the chill that damp generates. Kane could feel that coldness even through the self-regulating environment of the shadow suit he wore beneath his clothes, a deep cold biting at his bones. The power of suggestion. He hurried on, ignoring it.

Two stories up, he heard a girl's sigh. It sounded wistful, sad. Surprised, Kane stopped, spinning in place, searching for its source. The water on the stairs rippled beneath his boots as he turned, but there was no one behind him.

He pressed on, taking the next flight of stairs at a run, shifting his center of balance by holding his body low. As he turned the stairs at the midflight corner, Kane saw the girl. She was waiting at the next doorway, nude, skin pale with the cold, blond hair dark and heavy with damp.

Surprised, Kane commanded the Sin Eater into his hand, retrieving the weapon from its hidden wrist holster in an instant. He held the gun on the naked girl, eyeing her as she stood in place.

The indifferent light left her partially in shadow, her face hidden in a pool of blackness. Still, Kane recognized her instantly, she looked just as she had the last time he had seen her when she lay on the coroner's slab in the Cobaltville Hall of Justice.

"Helena," Kane whispered, the Sin Eater wavering where he had trained it on the teenager in the shadows.

She stepped out into the light then, her bare feet crossing over each other as she took the first of the steps, descending toward Kane. Her face was drawn and pale, the blue eyes wide, yet vacant, as if she were looking through Kane, into his soul. Water ran down her cheeks—tears? Her skin was pocked with gooseflesh where the cold breeze struck it, playing across her naked form.

"Stay where you are," Kane ordered, bringing the Sin Eater up in a firmer grip.

Chapter 19

Kane knew she was dead, he had even examined the body.

Helena Vaughn ignored Kane's warning, took another step down the staircase toward him, and another wistful sigh emanated from her pursed lips.

"Stay. Where. You. Are," Kane instructed, gesturing with the muzzle of his Sin Eater. "Don't make me shoot you."

Helena Vaughn continued to approach, her jaw dropping open. She was five steps above Kane, and he could smell her breath from here, the stench of something rotten, of death.

"I won't tell you again," Kane said. "Stop where you are."

Bare feet sinking into the pooling water, bare arm brushing against the damp of the wall, the naked figure of Helena Vaughn took another step toward Kane down the enclosed staircase.

SEVERAL FLOORS UP FROM KANE, Brigid Baptiste was crying. "'Yesterday, upon the stair, I met a man who wasn't there,'" she whispered. "'He wasn't there again today. I wish, I wish he'd go away.'" It was an old rhyme, something her eidetic memory had stored.

Looming over her, the figure of Daryl Morganstern was a dark presence, his breathing heavy, his aroma close—coffee and sweat and cologne. Brigid saw him out of the corner of her eye, through the salty tears that plucked at her tear ducts, washing against the nose clips of her spectacles. "I didn't have a choice," she said, her voice barely a whisper. "You have to understand…"

"Oh, I understand just fine, my dove, my love, my precious flower," Morganstern assured Brigid. *"I'm a mathematician, logic is my arena, my playground. I died so that you could live."*

"No," Brigid whispered, but Morganstern ignored her.

"Just like so many others have. I'll bet that if we add it up here and now, you could name dozens of people who gave their lives so that you and your little team of do-gooders could continue running around playing your silly 'save the world' game."

"It's not like that," Brigid insisted, but her head was already racing, calling to mind the faces of others who had been hurt and killed over the past few years: Skylar Hitch, Henny Johnson, Clem Bryant and others in the Cerberus ranks, and numerous more beyond the walls of the redoubt who had appeared in Brigid's life for just a few days or simply a few hours. Her life, along with that of her field teammates, Grant and Kane, had taken so many casualties, people whose names she had barely had time to learn, some for whom she had never even done that.

"Do the math, Brigid," Morganstern insisted. *"How many lives does it make? How many lives equal just one Brigid Baptiste? I don't think the equation is balanced, do you?"*

"Please," Brigid pleaded. "I don't know…"

"Wouldn't you say it's time to make sure both sides of the equation balance?" Morganstern pressed, loom-

ing over Brigid's shoulder, so near that she could almost touch him. *"The operator requires that the equation be balanced. We'll do it together."*

"Operator," Brigid whispered, shaking her head.

Hell-o operator, give me number nine.

She tried to ignore the figure looming at the edge of her vision, tried to dismiss his accusing words. But he was right, wasn't he? She had left him there, had made the choice whether he lived or died. And she had chosen death, chosen to leave Daryl Morganstern to bleed out on the floor of the laboratory in the heart of the Cerberus redoubt as their enemies swarmed on him. She had killed him, hadn't she?

IN THE HANGARLIKE ROOM, Grant felt the cold water against his face as the Magistrates held his head under. The Magistrates pushed hard against his back, forcing him down into the basin, where the dark waters swirled. The faucet still blurted out more icy water across the back of his shaved head. Grant felt that water trail across his nape like icy fingers running down his spine, felt the freezing water in the basin press against his face like a punch.

Almost immediately, his face began to feel numb, the frigid water like a wall pushing against his skin. His eyes felt hard, two steel balls against the pressure of the water. He could feel the edges of his skull where the eyes threatened to pop free of their sockets.

Before his open eyes, the water was dark, almost black. Patterns brushed across his retinas, shapes forming and unforming, dark shadows conjured from the imagination.

It took two Magistrates to hold him there, bent over almost double to dunk his head in the grim water. Grant was a big man, and even tied as he was, he struggled, fighting against the Mags who held him in place. But it was no use, he could not get any leverage, not while they had him like this. He would just have to tough it out, endure this dunking until the sadistic baron called time on the punishment.

Grant had almost drowned once before, back when he had been caught up in a tidal wave in the fishing settlement of Hope. He had survived that and he would survive this. It was just a matter of holding his breath, that was all.

The water pressed against him like a living thing clawing at his face. For a moment, something seemed to whisper to Grant from the water, reaching out from the dark pool that pressed against his eyes. He watched, eyes drawn to the darkness. Despite knowing that the water was only a few inches in depth, it appeared bottomless to Grant's eyes—a dark, cold, bottomless pit of terrors.

He expelled the breath at last, feeling the stream of bubbles blurt from his nostrils, running across his face beneath the water like living things. In a moment they were gone, popping close to his ears, but their sounds were muffled by a sort of numbness that was overcoming his sense of hearing. The bursting bubbles sounded distant, scratchy, like an old recording from a wax cylinder.

He stared into the water, hearing the whispers plucking at his ears, seeing the dark faces that waited beneath the water's surface. His chest felt hot, a balloon expanding inside its cavity, pressing against his ribs.

The shadow things swirled about the water, like crows taking flight. He needed to breathe, heaven help him, he needed to breathe.

Underwater, Grant's mouth opened, the jaw slackening. His eyes were losing focus, the black shapes blipping in and out of his vision. He could taste the water; it tasted of dirt. He felt it wash against his teeth, his tongue, felt it lapping against his throat. He began to cough, sputtering out into the water, and then it was in his throat, sucked down, the cold so powerful it felt as if it were burning him.

There were things in the darkness of the water. Dark things. He saw them, dancing there, swimming closer.

"Enough!" Baron Trevelyan's voice boomed through the sound of splashing water as Grant was pulled from the basin. The word ran around Grant's head like an echo chamber.

Grant sucked at the air, coughing as it mixed with the water in his throat, a stream of water pouring from his mouth like so much drool.

Grant was manhandled, his head streaming wet, his goatee and eyebrows pouring with water. He blinked it back from his eyelashes. The room seemed bright now and for a moment his eyes struggled to focus. He felt himself slung against the hard back of the chair, his hands still bound, stabbing pains in his wrists and forearms where they had been held so tightly. He slammed into the chair, lolling there as water poured from his face, his head feeling terribly heavy.

Trevelyan was standing before him, a dark silhouette in the brightness of the room. Grant remembered Baron Cobalt and his brethren as mystical creatures far above human considerations of beauty.

"—speak now?" Trevelyan was saying, the sentence not quite making sense to Grant. Water sloshed in his ears, bubbling and popping against his eardrums, a feeling as much as a sound.

Two deathly Magistrates flanking him, Trevelyan looked at Grant, fixing him with his dark, inky eyes. Grant looked at the Mags, his vision swimming, seeing the way their faces were tarnished, their skin ruptured.

The baron spoke again, sneering, "Tell me where your friends are. How many."

"Go t' hell," Grant muttered, water washing between his teeth and down his chin.

"Stubborn, aren't you?" Trevelyan trilled in his weasel voice. "So be it. Put him under again. Make it longer this time. Let's see what Grant is made of."

With that, Grant was yanked up from his seat and dragged over to the basin again, thrust against it so that the cold enamel thudded against his chest. He tried to fight as two Magistrates shoved him headfirst into the swirling water again, the faucet gushing above him. He did not even know what he was fighting about; it was just instinct to never trust a baron. Just instinct, like breathing.

As THE SYLPHLIKE FIGURE OF Helena Vaughn took another step down the stairwell toward him, Kane squeezed the trigger on his Sin Eater, unleashing a stuttered burst of 9 mm lead up the stairs. The shots sounded loud in the enclosed space of the stairwell, and bullets rattled as they spanged off the concrete walls and steps beside and behind the naked girl. She seemed unaware of them, letting them drill into and through her unclothed body.

Kane gritted his teeth as his discharge passed through the girl's pale, ethereal flesh.

"You aren't real," he spit. "You can't be."

Helena Vaughn just stood there, shaking amid the barrage of bullets that pummelled her body, the dark shadows of the stairwell obscuring her sad expression, turning it into something much more haunting than Kane remembered.

Kane eased his index finger from the blaster's trigger, bringing his weapon's violent monologue to an end. The girl still stood there before him, the skin taut across her naked torso, clinging to her ribs in a mottled, pale sheet. She looked up at Kane through the curtain of her bangs, the blond tresses tangled and in disarray. Kane watched as her mouth opened and she let loose a soft sigh before drawing a tiny, stutter of breath as if in pain.

"I never heard you speak," Kane realized, still training his weapon on the teen.

The girl stood there in darkness, watching him, her expression accusing.

"You never had a voice to me," Kane told her. "That's why I can't hear you now. I was your voice. As a Magistrate, I had to be your voice seeking the justice you demanded. The justice your murder demanded."

The girl was still watching him, her thin body like a skeleton in the darkness of the wet stairwell. Kane could hear her breathing.

"I don't know what you are," Kane told her, "but you're not real. Something is happening here, something I don't properly comprehend. But whatever it is you think I've done, I can assure you it wasn't me."

Kane stood, breathing hard, eyes fixed on the shade in the darkness. His gun felt suddenly heavy in his grip. "Magistrate psych warned us that sometimes the job, the pressures, might get to us," he recalled, almost reciting the speech he had been given on graduation. "They warned us not to let it, to keep our distance, to remember what our job was. I brought your killer to justice, and just because that didn't save you doesn't mean I did wrong."

The girl—Helena Vaughn—continued to watch Kane from the darkness, bullet holes visible in the wall behind her. Kane marched up the stairs past the girl, striding defiantly to the next flight without looking back. She watched him go, watched as he ascended toward the ninth floor and Brigid Baptiste. He knew she was watching, could sense her eyes on his back, hear her labored breathing. With an enormous effort of will, he ignored her.

"WE CAN BE TOGETHER in the infinite embrace," Morganstern told Brigid as she sat alone in the storeroom. *"Finish this. Complete the equation. Kill yourself."* He spoke from just behind her now, his voice a solicitous whisper, tickling against her ear.

Slowly, reluctantly, Brigid reached for the shotgun she had rested on the narrow desk beside the television monitor. Picking it up, she turned it over in her hands and brought the barrel up so that it rested beneath her chin. "I'm so sorry, Daryl," she sobbed. "I never meant for you to die."

"Make things right," Morganstern urged. *"Kill yourself."*

The gun felt cold against the underside of Brigid's jaw, the metal of the muzzle like ice on the soft spot beneath her chin. Brigid reached down, pushing her thumb blindly behind the trigger guard as tears rolled down her cheeks, jamming the digit against the trigger, preparing to squeeze it. She had left Daryl to die in one of the labs of the Cerberus redoubt, where he had always been at home. It had been as good as signing his execution papers. She could have stayed, fought for him, sought the medical attention that he needed. But she had not. He was right, she had been too busy looking out for herself to worry about this man who lay wounded at the hands of the base's infiltrators.

"Kill yourself," Morganstern repeated as Brigid grasped at the trigger.

She closed her eyes, forcing the hot tears from them in a cascade of salt water, willing the pain of the guilt to end. In the distance, someone was calling her name, as if they knew what she had done to Daryl, how she had killed him.

Brigid felt the cool metal of the gun brushing the underside of her chin, secured it to be sure she would blow her own brains out through the top of her skull. Then Brigid's thumb stroked against the trigger.

Suddenly a loud crash seemed to fill the tiny storeroom.

Chapter 20

"Baptiste—don't!"

It was Kane, standing by the open doorway of the storeroom. He had shoved the door open, some instinct guiding him to Brigid when he had failed to find her in the main open-plan area.

What he saw when he shoved open the door with a crash was Brigid Baptiste hunched in a swivel chair in the cramped little storeroom, her shotgun rammed under her jaw as she prepared to blow her brains out. She was alone, and tears glistened on her cheeks as the light spilled in from the main office.

"Baptiste," Kane repeated, more softly this time. "Move the gun away. You can do this."

"K-Kane?" she asked. It was like waking from a dream. She could not quite tell what was real and what was still the dream. "What happ— Where?"

"The gun," Kane urged. "Let it go. Move your hand very carefully and let the blaster go. Okay?"

Brigid saw Kane through the shimmering glaze of her own tears, felt relief and joy surge through her. "Kane, what am I doing here?"

"The gun," Kane repeated for the third time. "Let it go."

Confused, Brigid looked down at her hands, saw the shotgun poised between her own jaw and the floor. Swiftly, reacting as if she had touched something dirty, she moved her hands away, tilting her head back and allowing the gun to fall from her grip. Kane was there instantly, plucking up the weapon and breaking it open so that it wouldn't—couldn't—go off. Then he was at her side, one arm reaching around her shoulder. She felt his warmth against her, and it was a relief in the coldness of the room, the cold that had been plucking at her mind like a harp string.

"You're okay now, Baptiste," Kane reassured, "you're okay."

"What happened?" Brigid asked. "Daryl said…" She stopped, feeling confused and silly.

Kane stepped back, stood by the door checking the office beyond for any signs of movement. The skeleton remained in its chair. He did not want them to be surprised by any of those rogue Magistrates.

"Something's screwy about this place," Kane told her, still watching the office. "Don't ask me what it is, but it preys on the mind. You said it was Daryl you saw, right?"

"Daryl Morganstern, yes," Brigid confirmed, removing her glasses and swiping at the tears. "He told me to…to kill myself. It all seemed to make sense at the time. But now I think about it…"

"It taps into our unresolved feelings of guilt," Kane told her. "Don't ask me how, but it manifests them as visions, hallucinations, maybe. I saw someone, too, a girl I knew."

"Anyone I…?" Brigid began to ask.

Kane shook his head. "No. Old business, something I thought was long dead. Seeing Pellerito today must have churned it all up again, that's all."

Kane stopped talking, and he made it clear by his silence that he was not going to explain any further.

Brigid took that moment to check the storeroom, scanning the shadows, looking for Daryl Morganstern, that dead man who had called to her from beyond the grave. Besides the videotapes, the room was empty, and yet his presence lingered, the scent in her nostrils, as if he were standing there just out of sight.

"He wanted me to kill myself," Brigid said solemnly.

Swivelling his head, Kane looked at her, penetrating her with his steel-gray stare. "No, he didn't," Kane told her. "I knew Daryl Morganstern. Not well, I'll grant you, but I knew him. He didn't want anyone dead."

"But I…" Brigid began, the feelings churning inside her breast. "He said that I'd killed him because I left him to die."

"That true?" Kane asked.

Brigid looked at him helplessly, her mouth open, unable to answer. "I should have done something maybe…" she admitted cagily.

"And then what, more people would have died?" Kane challenged. "You go back over the past and it's all different and you have all the time in the world to do everything right. But that's just in your head. You were there and you would have made the best decision you could based on the information available. I know you, and I know that's what you did. Because it's what you always do."

Brigid nodded her head with a heavy reluctance. "I'm that predictable, am I?" she teased.

"Sucks, doesn't it?" Kane said. "Now, come on, let's get out of here. I have something downstairs I want to show you."

Wiping away the last of her tears, Brigid raised herself from her seat and joined Kane at the doorway, taking back the shotgun that he held out for her.

"Careful with that this time, all right?" Kane advised with mock seriousness as he watched her snap its breech closed.

Brigid nodded solemnly. Guilt had haunted the reporter, Bryan Baubier, she remembered from the video recordings. Guilt about his mother. Guilt that seemed to plague the ville, destroying people by turning their own darkness against them.

"He said we were sorrow spaces," Brigid said as she plucked up a hunk of radio equipment and strode with Kane toward the fire door leading to the stairs.

"Who did?" Kane asked, perplexed.

Brigid told him about the recordings and the history of Quocruft.

THEY HAD DUNKED GRANT under the water five times in total, each time holding his head for a longer period until he blacked out. He awoke in a cell, his hands still tied, delirium touching at the edges of his mind. There had been something in the water, a dark something that looked at him with accusing eyes that shone like moonlight on a lake.

He was lying on his side upon a simple cot, just a plain board bolted to the wall, with a coarse blanket draped over him. The blanket smelled of human sweat. Grant shrugged, struggling to get the blanket off as he woke properly from his daze. It was not easy with his hands still bound behind him.

"Gently now," a voice instructed, well-spoken, the words sharp as cut glass.

"Who...?" Grant muttered, searching the room with eyes that did not want to remain open.

The room was drab, ill-lit with peeling paint on the walls. There was a workbench with a wooden chair to one side of the room. The bench was piled with mechanical debris from a child's construction kit along with a notebook and pencils. Across from this, a gray bucket sat in the corner, a soiled rag draped over it. A man was hurrying over to check on Grant, skin the same ebony as Grant's own, his dark gray hair in wild disarray around his head and clothes frayed at the edges, a dirty bow tie cinching in his collar. He moved with a limp, his teeth showing as he sneered through the pain. As he did so, Grant saw that something attached the man to the ceiling, a long, flexible hose that connected directly into the back of his skull. The hose looked dirty with oil and grease, but the man seemed to pay it no mind, as if it had been attached to him for a very long time.

The stranger set Grant back down on his side, rearranging the blanket over him. "You're still cuffed," the man explained in his resonant voice. "Careful now, or you'll roll right off this bed and do yourself a mischief."

Grant stared at the older man in confusion. "Where... am...I?" he muttered through thick lips.

"You're quite safe, my friend," the man replied. "For now. Name's Roger Burton. You'll accept my apologies for my appearance. Been a long while since I did any entertaining."

"Grant," Grant told the man. "How long?"

"What?"

"Since you did any entertaining?"

Sucking at his teeth, Burton shook his head. "Months. Maybe a year," he admitted. "Hard to keep track of time around here."

Warily and with the gray-haired man's help, Grant pushed himself to a sitting position on the cot and peered around the room. His head felt woozy and his throat was sore, as if he had vomited. The room seemed to pulse a little in his vision, swaying slightly as he looked at it. In the dark corners, he could still see those accusing eyes staring at him from the water basin. The air within the room was fetid, and Grant realized after a moment that the pail in the corner served as the latrine.

Grant tried to stand, but he stumbled back to the cot, sagging against Burton as the man caught him.

"Steady there, Grant," Burton instructed. "Take it slow."

Grant thanked the man for his assistance, struggling to piece together everything that had happened to lead him here, of how he had lost Kane and Brigid.

Burton spoke up, intruding on Grant's thoughts. "You came as quite a surprise," he exclaimed. "Baron Trevelyan told me everyone was dead."

Grant looked at the man quizzically.

"I guess his counting was a little off," Burton added with an amused smile.

"Everyone's dead?" Grant repeated, the words only now sinking in. "Where is here, exactly? Where are we?"

"You really are lost, aren't you?" Burton said with genuine amusement. "I shouldn't be surprised. You must have been hiding for a long time to escape the authorities like this."

"The what?"

"The Magistrates," Burton elaborated. "Grant, I wouldn't wish to presume, but it seems to me that you're a little more than just confused. Perhaps you'd care to explain just where it is you've been hiding out."

"I haven't," Grant told him. Something about this man made Grant feel he could trust him, something in his manner, a rather understated poise that Grant associated with men of good standing. "I traveled to this ville via a quantum inducer unit," he explained, keeping the exact details and the fact he had been with his teammates secret.

"A mat-shifter," Burton said, nodding.

"I've never seen this place before, didn't even know it existed."

"You must have traveled a heck of a long way," Burton exclaimed, bemused. "Quocruft has been established for almost eighty years."

"You said you thought everyone was dead," Grant pressed. "What made you say that?"

"Because I killed them," Burton told him. "I'm responsible. For the weapon that destroyed humankind."

Chapter 21

"You ever hear of a Baron Trevelyan?" Brigid asked as she and Kane descended the stairwell of the office block. She was holding a small radio communications unit, something like a car radio with a microphone hookup.

"Me?" Kane responded, boots splashing in the pooled water on the concrete steps. "No. Why?"

"The footage in that media suite included a newscast featuring a speech from him," Brigid explained. "I never heard of him, either. Nor this Quocruft ville."

"He a hybrid?" Kane asked, taking the radio unit.

Brigid nodded. "Yes, looks just like Baron Cobalt or any one of the others," she explained.

Kane slowed and turned to face Brigid. "You're figuring something out," he said. "Want to clue me in?"

"It's hard to rationalize," Brigid admitted, "but I don't think we're on Earth. Or at least not our Earth."

"We got here via mat-trans," Kane pointed out. "Some kind of glitch sent us to the wrong destination. Could be we skipped a planet."

Brigid shook her head. "People speaking English, a recognizable ville structure—it doesn't add up."

"The Annunaki came from outer space," Kane reminded her. "Could be they colonized more than one planet, seeding them with hybrids just like the barons we knew."

Brigid's hand ran along the metal bar that served as a banister, the dark paint there feeling cold against her palm. "Same gravity, same atmosphere, same…paint on the banisters. No, this is Earth-—I'd stake my life on that."

"Then what?" Kane asked.

They were seven flights down now, almost to the first floor, where Kane had left his prisoner.

"What if we skipped dimensions when we entered the mat-trans?" Brigid proposed.

"Is that possible?"

"The mat-trans is simply a transportation system, Kane," Brigid explained. "At its heart, it's no different from an automobile or an aircraft. We just took a wrong turn, landed in the wrong place."

"Right off the map," Kane said sourly. "If that is the case, and I'm not saying you're right, then we can use the same process to get back to Cerberus, right?"

Brigid was silent as she thought this over. They had reached the bottom of the staircase, and she was doing her utmost to ignore the shade of Daryl Morganstern who had reappeared at the edge of her vision and was beckoning her.

Reaching for the heavy fire door, Kane prompted again, "Right, Baptiste?"

"We don't know why we jumped the way we did," Brigid replied, her cool emerald eyes meeting Kane's stare. "If something's tapping into the quantum ether, utilizing a similar process or sending a pulse through it, then that would potentially disrupt the mat-trans flow."

Kane glared at her. "Wait a minute. You think someone's tapping into the mat-trans? *Our* mat-trans?"

"Might not be intentional," Brigid told him. "It would take an enormous amount of energy to bridge between dimensional planes. A release of such energy—like a nuclear reactor going into meltdown—might have that effect. I stress *might*."

Depressing the safety bar on the fire door, Kane pushed through it and back into the lobby of the office building. The lobby was as he had left it: charred marks across the ceiling, walls and furniture, much of the equipment damaged or melted. The same as every other building they had seen in this strange, abandoned city. He gestured to the despoiled lobby area. "Seems to me, we've been staring at the result of some almighty outpouring of energy ever since we got here," he said. "What do you think?"

Brigid gasped. "The sun shield," she said, shaking her head. "He's utilized solar energy to generate the power to…"

"To what?" Kane asked.

"Bridge dimensions," Brigid told him gravely. "But if he's done that deliberately, then…"

"Cerberus is in trouble," Kane finished.

"Not just Cerberus," Brigid told him. "Earth and everyone on it."

"I'M THE MAN WHO KILLED Earth," Roger Burton told Grant earnestly.

They sat together on the bare cot in the grim cell, its light fixture buzzing in a cage above their heads. Grant watched the way the light played along the hose that was attached to Burton's head, studying the attachment without touching it.

"I always had a talent for making things, even when I was very young," Burton continued. "Even here, he's given me a rudimentary lab so I can keep working, as if I'm something other than his prisoner. After I graduated, I was placed in the research labs doing design work, engineering mostly, with some applied physics, a little chemistry. While I was there, I kept tinkering with things, improving them, coming up with new ways of doing stuff. Guess it drew someone's interest." He smiled in a self-deprecating manner. "One day I got called into the super's office and she told me I would be working on a special project, something to harness energy in new ways. So I did, worked diligently and without question. Why would I question anything?"

Grant nodded in agreement. "Easy to get caught up in the system when you're stuck inside it," he said, speaking from his own experience as an ex-Magistrate.

"One day the baron came to visit," Roger Burton said. "Heck of an honor that, like meeting something from one of them old 'ligious books. You read any of those?"

Grant nodded, encouraging the man to continue. He was still looking at the tube pipe. It seemed to be permanently attached to the back of the older man's skull, pressed through his messy hair and into his skin. The tube was three inches in diameter and made of some kind of flexible metal links, stained with the grease and oil that kept them mobile. The tube was attached to the base of Burton's skull, where it bulged out from the stem of his neck, connected via a sturdy metal band. The flesh around the circular attachment was an angry red, with old scar tissue around its edges that had never completely healed. The skin and hair had grown over parts of the metal attachment, tying it more fully to the man.

"Baron Trevelyan spoke to me, said he was aware of my work," Burton said. "Wanted me to head up a special project, funding no issue. He wanted to explore the limits of knowledge, he said, and that appealed to me. I'm a scientist. I'd been trying to figure new ways to apply engineering my whole life. Now my baron commanded and I obeyed." He paused, looking around the room as if for inspiration.

"I didn't invent stuff because there was a need for it," Burton explained sadly. "They didn't give me these projects and say 'There, make this better,' you understand? I just came up with ideas, ways of doing things, new applications for old processes.

"You know, it's been so long since I actually spoke to someone like this," Burton lamented. "It's almost hard to believe I'm doing it. Maybe the baron thought it would be ironic, putting us together. The last two men on Earth."

Grant watched as the scientist shifted restlessly on the cot, pulling the tube that fed into the back of his skull around to get it more comfortable. Grant knew the body language from his days as a Magistrate, knew to recognize the man's movements. He was regretful, ashamed, guilty.

"What did you make?" Grant asked gently.

"The regen suits," Burton explained. "They're what keep the Magistrates active."

BRIGID FOLLOWED KANE through the lobby and into the cloak room behind the reception desk where he had hidden the tied body of the Magistrate, leaving the little radio unit on the desk. The figure still lay there amid the fallen coats, hands and legs bound, helmet missing.

"While you were busy upstairs, I picked us up someone to question," Kane explained. "Get some answers."

Brigid took another step into the room, examining the figure lying there in the darkness. Finally she looked up at Kane and her brow furrowed. "Was he alive when you brought him in?" she asked gently.

"Sure he was al—" Kane began angrily, hurrying forward to check.

Just as Brigid had implied, the Magistrate was dead. He lay completely still, his chest unmoving, and when Kane held his hand beneath the man's nose no breath came out. "What the hell? He was alive—I swear it. I wouldn't kill a fellow Mag, unless I had no choice."

"I believe you," Brigid said to placate him. Crouched over the Magistrate's supine form, she rolled his body and checked for any evidence of tampering. The face looked ghastly, the skin rotten and the bulging eyes staring out into the darkness of the cupboard. But it was a level of rot that should have taken several days to reach, longer still in a cold climate. "Kane, did he look like this when you brought him in?"

Kane nodded. "Ugly mother. Helmet came loose during the scuffle. I figure he was a carrier for something nasty, plague or some shit. You'd said something about a virus maybe doing this to the ville, right?"

Brigid stared up at Kane in wonder. "And that doesn't bother you?"

"Back when we were in Cobaltville we were regularly vaccinated against everything from radiation sickness to the black death," Kane replied nonchalantly. "If what he's got is catching, and if I'm not immunized, then—one—I've got it and—two—we're still stuck here with no way home."

Brigid shrugged, accepting Kane's explanation without too much bother, aware they had bigger problems right now. "On the physical evidence alone I'd say this man's been dead four days minimum," she explained.

"Impossible," Kane spit. "He was up and walking a

half hour ago. I was fighting with him. He fought back. He shot at me."

"Well, he isn't shooting now," Brigid told him.

"THE REGEN SUITS ARE WHAT keep the Mags active," Burton told Grant. "I almost said 'alive,' but it's not that. 'Active' is the polite term for it, you get me?"

"You mean they're dead?" Grant asked. He thought back to the Dark Magistrates he had seen since he emerged from the mat-trans, the ones who had chased him through the hospital, the ones who had dunked his head in the basin of water until he could no longer hold his breath.

"I didn't invent it for that, if that's what you're thinking," Burton blurted. "The design was intended to prolong life for the terminally ill. Baron Trevelyan insisted it be tested to the limit. He wanted to see whether you could take a fresh corpse, bring it back and make it remain alive, on the verge of death. I saw the Magistrates kill test subjects on the baron's instructions, just so that they could test it."

"It worked," Grant said sourly. "But why would anyone want to animate the dead like that?"

"Nearest I can figure," Burton told him, "Baron Trevelyan is what they call a control freak. He wants absolute loyalty—demands it."

"Sounds like a baron," Grant lamented.

"The dead don't answer back," Burton reasoned.

Grant nodded, accepting this without cheer. "Why are you hooked up like that?" he asked, indicating the hose going up to the ceiling.

"This? Little of my own medicine. I got exposed," Burton explained, "to one of my own inventions. Now

I have to keep being fed with it or I start…well, the re-action isn't good."

"What's the invention?" Grant asked.

"The Guilt Bomb," Burton said.

"Guilt Bomb?"

"Yes, well, that's what they called it anyhow," Burton explained, embarrassed. "Not my name, you under-stand. For one thing, it wasn't a bomb. It was a chemical agent that required a dispersal method, but there was no explosive involved. It went in the water, that's how they transmitted it."

"Doesn't sound like engineering," Grant pointed out.

"Chemistry plus a little applied physics," Burton agreed. "How it worked didn't matter so much as how they spread it. The Magistrates needed a docile popula-tion, baron's orders. People were becoming restless. He wanted us to submit, to give ourselves to him."

"But you said it wasn't a bomb," Grant prompted in a querying tone.

"No," Burton agreed, "it was disseminated through water, like I said. In small quantities it works like a tranquilizer."

"What about larger quantities?" Grant asked.

"Repeated exposure brings about morose paranoia. More than that and…" Burton paused, jabbing his thumb in the direction of the hose in his skull.

"It's addictive?" Grant queried.

"The constant supply keeps my head clear," Burton told him. "Relatively. Sin is a knowledge that we can-not lose, Mr. Grant."

Chapter 22

Brewster Philboyd came to Lakesh's desk in the Cerberus operations room with a sheaf of notes in his hand.

"Mr. Philboyd?" Lakesh said encouragingly, peering up from the data screen he had been analyzing.

All around them, the operations room was buzzing with activity. Personnel were checking the rolling data from the satellites; Donald Bry and his programming team were strengthening the security protocols of the computer aspect of the mat-trans; physician Reba De-Fore had accompanied Farrell as they checked the interior of the mat-trans chamber itself. She was looking for biological residue, while he searched for any physical weak points that may have been created with the arrival and rapid demise of their mysterious visitor. Domi, meanwhile, had joined Edwards at a group of desks arranged before the mat-trans entrance, where they discussed possible response to any further infiltrators.

"Kane's squad definitely reached the mat-trans outside of Panamint," Philboyd confirmed solemnly as Lakesh listened. "Accessing the records remotely, the mat-trans there shows activation at 14.07, which tabulates perfectly with their arrival time, factoring in the additional time it would have taken them to reach the mat-trans itself. We can assume they used the mat-trans."

"I don't like this word—assume," Lakesh said. "It suggests a margin of error."

"There are no visual recordings, but the mat-trans data log shows a transferral jump sufficient for three bodies," Brewster explained. "Their transponder signals are logged as reaching the redoubt at that time, and our live satellite imagery shows the chopper they traveled in is still there, close to the redoubt entrance. Short of a time machine to check on them, this is as close as we can get to a categorical confirmation that they used the mat-trans."

"Short of Kane and his team telling us themselves, of course," Lakesh pointed out and Philboyd inclined his head, accepting the man's point.

"Of course," Philboyd agreed.

"What about this redoubt?" Lakesh asked. "What do we know about it? Could someone else have been there?"

Checking through his notes, Philboyd shook his head. "Security seals were still in place when Kane, Grant and Brigid arrived early this morning," he said. "Pulling up the data log, the locks had not been tampered with in the past six months. I can take the log back further if we need to, but I'm confident in saying no one was there. Or, if they were, they've been drinking their own urine for the past six months."

"Redoubts were designed to be self-sustaining," Lakesh reminded him.

"I take your point," the astrophysicist said, "but the nukecaust is a distant memory. There's no reason for anyone to still be hiding in this one."

Lakesh nodded in sage agreement. "So what else do we have?"

"Kane's team reached their initial destination intact

at 11:59," Philboyd read from his sheet. "Their Commtacts died at 12:03. We can backtrack the data and show that no signal was being broadcast from then. Looks like a jammer of some kind was in operation."

"Weapons dealers," Lakesh said witheringly. "Always so wretchedly cautious. So, could the jammed signal be a part of our mystery?"

"Hard to say," Philboyd said, adjusting his glasses on the bridge of his nose. "The mat-trans seems to be where the problems really start. Up until then we simply have a communications fail."

"Fine," Lakesh accepted. "What else do you have?"

"I did a system-wide check," Philboyd told his boss, thumbing through several sheets of data to a page showing a graph. "There's something odd in the mat-trans records. A power spike that runs through everything at 14:07. That's the exact same time that Kane's team was preparing to jump."

"The system was designed to accommodate fluctuations in power," Lakesh stated.

"Maybe not this one," Brewster argued. "It looks to be external, but I can't locate a source."

"And it affected the mat-trans in the redoubt in Panamint?" Lakesh asked, looking for clarification.

"No, Dr. Singh," Brewster said. "It touched the whole network. If we trace back through our records here, we can see our own feed spikes for just a few seconds. The same is true of six others I checked at random. It's line wide."

Lakesh stroked his chin in thought. "With no source," he mused.

"I had to go into a quantum analysis to even locate it," Brewster told him. "This is on the scale of a solar flare or a change in the magnetic fields."

"Natural…?" Lakesh asked.

Brewster pushed back his hair uncomfortably. "You're really putting me on the spot with that, Doctor," he said. "It's hard for me to confirm or deny. I simply can't find an obvious source for it."

Lakesh nodded his appreciation. "So we have a power spike in the mat-trans system at the same exact moment that CAT Alpha team began their jump home," he concluded. "External source, powerful enough to affect the whole network. And our team disappeared during this spike."

"It lasted just four seconds," Philboyd added.

"One obvious conclusion is that the power spike killed them," Lakesh said. "Though it's a conclusion I am reluctant to entertain. If the power spike came from a source, then we need to find the source."

"Data's all over the place," Philboyd told him, flipping another page and showing Lakesh the printout there. The printed sheet showed a lined grid within which was a smattering of specks with no discernable pattern. Lakesh pondered it for a moment.

"This looks like a rift," Lakesh said gravely. "We're only seeing the peaks of the waves, which gives a false impression of the data. And that means that the source is hidden from us even on a quantum level, like something hidden beneath the surface of the ocean."

"Assuming these are the peaks or troughs," Philboyd said, catching on, "we could plot the basic pattern of the waves, which would reveal the source."

Lakesh nodded. "Or we could sit here discussing it further, Mr. Philboyd," he prompted with significant irony.

Philboyd nodded. "Understood, Doctor. I'll get to it

right away." With that, the astrophysicist hurried back to his desk. Lakesh called after him.

"Send the data over to my computer," Lakesh told him. "I'll run through it, as well, and we'll see if we come up with the same result."

"Yes, sir," Philboyd acknowledged with a smile.

"And, Brewster?" Lakesh called across the ops room. "Good work. Truly exemplary."

"THE BARON WANTED A KNIFE," Roger Burton said as he sat with Grant in the cold, dark cell. Across the room, a faucet dripped.

The engineer's eyes were downcast, staring at the scuffed toes of his brown shoes. The shoes were dirty and worn through, and Grant could see the man's sock through a tear above the left shoe's heel where the stitching had come free. The discussion was accompanied by the drip-drip of water into the basin, but Grant was finally becoming used to the stench that emanated from the bucket.

"A knife?" Grant asked gently. "What kind of knife?"

Burton looked at him, and Grant could see the terror in the older man's eyes. "One day, Baron Trevelyan came to my laboratory—that was before he incarcerated me here." He indicated the room. "He told me about his 'sight.' If he looked really intensely, he told me, he could see into other worlds. Worlds like ours, only different."

"Mars, Venus? Something like that?" Grant asked.

Burton was already shaking his head. "He told me they were the Earth," he said. "That's how he explained it to me. He wanted me to design a knife that could reach those other Earths. A way to carve through dimensions."

Grant realized what the man was talking about. He

had some experience of alternate Earths. Balam, a long-time ally of the Cerberus organization, had referred to these other worlds as casements, Earths contained on different dimensional frequencies, each one an altered vision of the one before. They were different realities, each one as complete and viable as the one Grant called home.

It was said that the Annunaki were multidimensional beings, that they could peer into the separate realities and even function in all of them simultaneously. Grant knew that Kane had gained some firsthand experience of that, when he had battled with these pseudo-gods on their own terms. Grant did not presume to fully understand the concept, but what he did understand was that, as a hybrid, Baron Trevelyan had dormant Annunaki DNA twisted into his genetic make-up. The hybrids had been designed to house the genetic outline of the Annunaki for when they were reborn on Earth. As such, the hybrids were nothing short of biological time bombs, containing the DNA sequencing for a superior race of aliens. All of which meant it seemed very credible to Grant that the baron could peer through the quantum veil into other dimensions and hence see other casements, other Earths.

Which led to the obvious question—what Earth had Grant and his companions landed on when they had stepped into that mat-trans unit in the Panamint Mountains? Had they somehow slipped casements? Because, assuming they had, things began to make a whole lot more sense. That would explain the abandoned ville they arrived in, a ville that none of them had ever heard of. And it also explained the presence of a hybrid baron who had never evolved into an overlord; presumably the final part of the genetic catalyst had never been employed, leaving Trevelyan as one biological time bomb that had never been detonated.

But even as he considered this, another question—one far more pressing—became paramount in Grant's mind.

"Did Trevelyan tell you why he wanted to reach out to these other Earths?" he asked.

Burton struggled to meet Grant's gaze. "Why does our baron do anything?" he asked rhetorically. "To own it entire. The way he owns all of us. The way he owns me."

Grant swallowed hard as the inevitable conclusion began to dawn on him.

"I KIND OF HOPED WE'D BE able to interrogate him," Kane growled, staring at the dead body in the cloakroom. "Guess I shouldn't have left him like this."

"You weren't to know," Brigid told him.

Kane glared at the body of the expired Magistrate. "Damned inconvenient is what this is," he muttered with a shake of his head.

As she got up to leave, Brigid noticed something bulging from the Mag's coat pocket that caught the light. It was the arm of a pair of spectacles, poking up where the zipper had come loose in the earlier scuffle. She reached for it, unzipping the Magistrate's pocket fully and pulling the glasses free. "Kane, look," Brigid said, holding them up.

"Didn't look like the kind of guy to wear—" Kane began jovially.

"They weren't his," Brigid said. "They're Grant's. I'm pretty sure they are, anyway."

"Where did you find these?" Kane asked, recalling that Grant had been wearing eyeglasses as a part of his disguise while they infiltrated Pellerito's weapons operation. "Which pocket?"

Brigid showed him. "Here."

"Zip-up pocket," Kane said knowingly. "Evidence from a case. Standard Mag protocol. Shit."

"Why 'shit'?"

"Means Grant got caught," Kane said.

"He wasn't wearing these when he left us," Brigid reminded him. "Could have dropped them."

Kane took the glasses, turned them over in his hand for a moment as he thought. To Brigid, her friend looked just the way she felt—exhausted.

"We need to find Grant," Brigid said, rubbing at her tired eyes with the heel of one hand. "Then find us a way out of here."

"Yeah," Kane agreed, peering up from the dead Magistrate as he pocketed the glasses. "How did that go? Anything?"

"The media operation has a communications rig," Brigid confirmed, stepping out of the cloakroom. "So in theory we could route a message to Cerberus if we had power. But that plan falls down if it turns out we really have jumped to another dimensional plane."

"How so?" Kane asked, following her out of the room. He pulled the door closed behind him, leaving the decomposing Magistrate in the darkness. "If we can move between these dimensions, then why can't your signal?"

Walking out into the lobby, Brigid began to answer but she stopped herself. "I…"

"Baptiste?"

"We could send a beacon signal," Brigid theorized. "By rewiring through a quantum capacitor we could effectively create a quantum radio that transmits its signal via tachyon waves."

"A quantum capacitor?" Kane queried.

"The internal device that self-maps our interphasers, for example," Brigid told him. "Whatever called us here would have one—it has to."

"And where are we going to find that?" Kane wondered. "Back at the hospital?"

"That was the receiver unit, yes," Brigid confirmed, though she sounded unsure.

"Problem?" Kane prompted.

"No problem," Brigid said. "That unit had a power source of some sort, too. We'd need to go back there. I'm just figuring out the logistics."

Kane watched the street beyond the shattered windows of the lobby while Brigid considered the problem. The bansheelike winds continued to churn through the street, but there was no sign of movement now. The patrolling Dark Magistrates were nowhere to be seen, not that that was reassuring.

"We need to split up, use our time more effectively," Brigid announced. "I'll return to the hospital and scavenge the parts we need from the mat-trans receiver. The radio could run through that. You go find Grant, then come find me at the hospital. I'll meet you there."

"I'm going with you," Kane said firmly.

Brigid shook her head. "No. Find Grant."

Before Kane could argue, Brigid plucked up the radio unit from the desk and strode toward the main doors of the reception.

"Okay," Kane muttered to himself, alone in the lobby. "Find Grant. Sounds easy."

He paced across the lobby, eyeing the empty street.

Brigid was gone already, just her red hair showing occasionally, a shadow among shadows.

"Magistrates," Kane muttered, pulling Grant's glasses from his pocket and staring at them. Idly, he worked the arms on their hinges. The glass of one lens had scratched, and the plastic coating of one arm was scuffed. "No, this is good," he announced. "Magistrate takes the glasses as evidence. Which means he's taking it somewhere. Mag Hall, that's the protocol."

Kane strode over to the ruined glass frontage of the building, looking down the street. "Take the evidence, you also take the prisoner," he said with a cocky smile. "Yeah, that's it."

Swiftly, Kane stepped out of the building and made his way across the courtyard, sticking close to the walls where the shadows were deepest. A moment later he was out on the street, where burned-out automobiles creaked in the wind. He may not know this ville but he knew the ville design—which meant he knew just where the Magistrate Hall of Justice should be. And if he found that, Kane felt sure he would fine Grant, too—alive or dead.

Chapter 23

The sun was beginning its slow descent to the horizon, and Brigid could feel the temperature dropping.

The streets were ghost boulevards stretching through the ville, the only movements created by the raging winds that soared through the streets, licking against the buildings with an anger only Mother Nature herself could conjure. Brigid trudged back toward the hospital where all of this had started, Mossberg shotgun in one hand, radio set in the other.

It was six blocks to the hospital. Even in the dwindling sunlight, the ville was a mess. Whatever had struck had done immeasurable damage. Much of that damage was cosmetic, but it gave the overall effect of an environment that had rotted, like a moldy orange left in the fruit bowl too long.

Brigid sought out the shadows to hide her from the predatory Magistrates who patrolled the city. On the one hand, she yearned to cling to the shadows that sat at the edge of the tall buildings lining the streets. On the other, she was fearful of getting too close in case the punishing winds tore something loose—a hunk of masonry or a windowpane—and flung it into her. Quietly she was also afraid of something else—that someone might be waiting in one of those silent monoliths, that Daryl Morganstern might once more materialize in the shadows, demanding his pound of flesh.

By the time she reached the hospital, the sunlight had diminished to almost nothing, painting the streets a bloody shade of red as the sun set. The hospital was just as she had left it, the wreck of an automobile parked out front, the exterior wall ravaged so its floors were visible through the ruins, open to view like some giant's doll house.

Brigid needed to get to the third floor, where the mattrans—or whatever it was—was located. Getting out had been easier, clambering over the ledge and down to the street. To get up again she either needed a fixed line of some sort or she would have to find a staircase.

The reason they had climbed down, of course, was because the doors to the room had been sealed. Brigid was confident that if she could get up there, she could find a way in. With that thought, Brigid strode determinedly into the hospital, shotgun and radio clutched in her hands.

She didn't realize that she was being watched. Two eyes, pale like boiled eggs, peered through the tinted visor of the Magistrate's helmet where he hid in the burned-out wreck outside the hospital, watching as Brigid picked her way inside, her red-gold hair disappearing into the shadows. His helmet had a terrifying motif—a skeletal demon baby strangling itself with its own tail. Magistrate East had been certain that the rogues would return here, to the place of their incursion, in due course. It was simply a matter of time, and Magistrate East had the infinite patience of a dead man.

Once he was sure that the redhead was inside, East pushed at the driver's door of the car, shoving it open with a shudder of warped metal. Then he stepped from the vehicle, Soul Eater pistol ready in his hand, and he squawked into the hidden microphone pickup in his helmet. His shrieking voice sounded like radio static as he reported in, the sound muffled by the howling of the winds as he strode toward the holed wall of the building where the woman had just disappeared.

A moment later, East was inside the hospital, blaster ready, searching for the living.

KANE FOUND THE HALL OF JUSTICE without difficulty. On his Earth, the villes followed the same basic blueprint, with only minor deviations from ville to ville. Brigid had explained it to him recently, discovering a hidden pattern to the construction of man's cities. It was an Annunaki design, tooled to affect an occupant's thinking processes. Variations on the same design could be found throughout history, each one a secret monument to man's slavery and his subservience to the Annunaki will.

Kane approached with the setting sun at his rear, hiding in the shadows it cast. The sunset painted the silver-gray clouds a peachy red as it dwindled in the sky. Carved from stone, the building was several stories high. A stylized representation of Justice stood on a plinth that was inset on a central balcony, presiding over its upper levels in blindfold with scales descending from her outstretched hand. Kane smiled with ironic amusement when he realized that Justice was not a woman, but rather a representation of a hybrid, like Baron Cobalt or any one of the other barons he had encountered in his life since leaving Cobaltville. Like so much of this ville, the exterior stone walls of the Hall of Justice had turned dark as charcoal where they had been burned, streaks of black running across the paler stone like a tiger's stripes. The windows were dark, too, caked with debris.

The Hall of Justice was built on an incline with steps leading up to its impressive main doors. Beneath these, twin roads led to its lowest level, which sank to either side of the steps, where matching rollback doors were located, flush to the walls of the building, adorned with the Magistrates Division shield. An underground garage, Kane knew.

There were several patrolmen about, their faces obscured by the masklike helmets they wore. One pair trudged together down the stone steps, their gait slow and determined. Another waited by the double doors into the Hall of Justice itself, his weapon holstered in a bulging sleeve.

Kane began to walk around the building, looking for a side entrance. As he did so, one of the wide doors at the base of the structure opened, and Kane was surprised to see three vehicles come speeding out of it. They were two large personnel carriers led by a two-man patrol vehicle that hurried past him. Kane ducked back into the shadows as they sped past on the cracked pavement of the roadway. There were two Magistrates in the patrol car, their faces set grimly beneath their helmets. The twin personnel carriers followed, their design reminding Kane of the Sandcats he and Grant had once used, tank treads over their rear-most sets of wheels. The driving pod contained two figures, driver and passenger, both of them in Magistrate uniform. Behind this, the walls of the personnel carriers were solid armor, with a thin strip of tinted armaglass that Kane's eyes could not penetrate. He watched as they sped by, bumping a little over the damaged road surface.

Kane watched them depart from his hiding place in the shadow of an abandoned café's awning, hurrying away from him in the direction he had come from.

Beneath the steps at the front of the Magistrate Hall, the garage door shimmered closed, shuffling down on its greased treads. Once Kane was certain that no one else was nearby, he scrambled across the road, keeping himself low to the ground in a semicrouch. The Magistrate at the top of the stairs took no notice as Kane crept past the front of the building on the opposite side of the street. Kane spotted the service road running to the left-hand side of the Hall of Justice and he headed toward it, scurrying along as swiftly as he could. All around, the winds continued to howl, whipping up flecks of ash and loose gravel from the pitted surface of the road. In the distance, Kane could hear the tinkling sound of broken glass, another busted windowpane being danced across the hard surface of the road.

Then Kane was opposite the side street, head ducked low to his shoulders, arms pumping as he weaved between patches of shadow. There was a barrier there, operating on a hinge assembly and painted with red-and-white chevrons. The barrier could be raised to allow vehicles through and had a sentry post beside it where the operator would sit. From across the street, Kane could see that the sentry box was empty; this whole ville appeared to be lifeless, Kane realized, so there would be little cause to keep the post manned.

A swift look around him, then Kane was dashing across the crosswalk, feet pounding on the cracked road surface. Kane didn't slow as he reached the waist-high barricade, simply hurdled it, one leg kicking out in front of him, the other behind like a pair of scissors.

Past the barrier, Kane kept running, darting into the shadows cast by the building as a pair of patrolling Magistrates came striding obliviously around the street corner. Kane held his breath as he watched them, their

hands pushed deep into the pockets of their black greatcoats. Neither glanced at him. They simply marched
past in silence, the fearsome wind catching at the tails
of the long coats they wore.

Swiftly Kane brought himself tight to the far wall,
the one that sat opposite the Hall of Justice. This was a
service road, the kind used by refuse collectors, he realized. Rainwater streaked across the cracked surface
of the road, pooling in little ovals where the road's surface was uneven. Up ahead there was a fenced-in area
where the trash bins would be stored. The fencing was
made of tightly placed struts of wood, each standing
almost nine feet in height with a sharpened point at
its apex. The fenced-in section ran seven feet square,
enough to hold maybe ten bins. Beyond that was a door
with a step up, set back in a recess in the wall. Kane
eyed the door—it was bolted and riveted in place, and
the paintwork was scarred and flaking. It looked like
a fire exit and, at a glance, Kane would guess that the
door was alarmed.

He turned back to the trash area, analyzing it more
carefully. A wide gate ran the whole length of the
boxed in section, designed to open out on one side to
allow full access to the trash cans within. That meant
there had to be a way to get the trash in there in the first
place, Kane realized, most likely a door on the inside
of the fenced-in area. He eyed the sharpened points of
the fencing again, weighing the options in his mind.

It was guesswork, of course, assumption and sup-
position.

His life as a Magistrate had trained Kane to think
through situations logically, to assess risks and to know
how to draw reasonable conclusions about a situation.
The only life they had found since they had arrived

in this ville had been the Magistrates, and it had been Mags who had chased after Grant. He and Baptiste had checked a half dozen of these buildings and all of them were deserted, the only life remaining was in the form of skeletons and old video recordings. But the Magistrate's Hall of Justice was abuzz with activity, Mags and vehicles bustling about.

"Heaven knows who they're looking to prosecute," Kane muttered, eyes still on the tall fence around the litter bins.

If Grant was anywhere, it would be here. Brought in for questioning, maybe, or medical attention. Or on a slab in the morgue, a dark voice whispered in the back of Kane's mind. Ignore it, Kane told himself. Live in the present.

Kane shrugged out of his tailored jacket. It was streaked with dirt now, from clambering down the side of the hospital and from crouching in the grass by the lake, speckled with dirt and frayed fibers from the other places he had been and the skirmish with the dead Mag. Kane turned the jacket around, putting his arms in the reverse ends of the sleeves so that the open front of the jacket was toward him, a little like a straitjacket.

Kane stepped back, walking foot over foot until he was as far back down the alleyway as he could get. There were windows above him, overlooking this service area, but there were no lights up there, no one looking down through the smeared and ruined windows that he could see.

Kane glanced down to the street end of the alley, confirming that no one was coming. Then he began to run, the jacket reversed over his hands in front of him, feet pounding against the chipped tarmac of the road, boots splashing in the puddles.

Kane ran at full speed, legs blurring as he sprinted toward the fenced-in area, the jacket swinging back and forth as his arms pumped like pistons. Three steps from the fence, Kane kicked off, leaping into the air and scrambling up the wall, driven upward by his momentum. He reached forward with his right arm, slapped his palm hard against the wooden spike that topped the post there. The jacket had bunched under his hand just as he had planned, creating a makeshift cushion as he pressed against the sharpened point.

With a grunt, Kane drew his body up, reaching over the fence with his left arm. Kane grunted again as the inside of his left elbow slammed against one of the pointed posts and was once again grateful for the protection granted by the rolled-up jacket. Kane's booted toes clattered against the wooden struts, and then he was over, swinging his whole body above the fence that barred his way, legs clearing the pointed posts by little more than an inch.

Kane sailed over the fence and crashed down an instant later on the large, wheeled bins that waited inside the trash corral. He winced, conscious that he was making a lot of noise as he rolled across the top of the bulging bin, bounced from its surface and tumbled into an identical trash can that stood beside it. Then he was no longer moving, and he pulled himself to a graceful halt atop one of the tall bins. His jacket was still caught on the railing, and when Kane pulled at it one of the sleeves tore. He had his shadow suit beneath his shirt, so he wasn't about to get cold.

Kane looked around him, the echoes of the hollow bins still loud in his ears. There were six large trash receptacles inside the area, each one almost as tall as a man, leaving just enough floor space for a single person to step into the fenced-in area to dump the trash. The area had not been emptied in months, Kane guessed, judging by the stink of the bins and the lopsided stack of bulging black bin sacks that lay strewed across the tops of the bins and the ground below.

The area was almost a perfect square, with fencing on three sides while the fourth wall was made up by the side of the justice building itself. There was a door set into the wall, with a grille over the window and a metal clip fitted below the handle. The metal clip could be affixed to the wall by a padlock, but the lock was missing.

Kane eased himself down from the trash can, dropping down among the bags of garbage. Several of them had split, and the stench of rotten food was heady in the air. Oddly, Kane noticed, there were no flies buzzing about. He had already noted the lack of insects in the ville, but seeing trash strewed about like this without the accompanying hum of insects' wings felt odd, almost surreal.

Kicking trash out of his way, Kane stepped over to the door and tried the lock.

"Please don't have an alarm," he whispered.

GRANT HAD BEEN SPEAKING with Roger Burton for over an hour by the time Baron Trevelyan came back for him. The baron had changed his clothes, and stood behind the barred door in a spotless white two-piece suit. Once again, Trevelyan was flanked by four Magistrates whose complexions left a lot to be desired. They reminded Grant of victims of some biological plague, but now he knew their secret. Dead Magistrates, walking under artificial power. It hardly bore thinking about.

Burton cowered at the back of his cell as Trevelyan stood in the open doorway, vertical bars blocking any entry or exit. "My baron," Burton said in a reverential whisper.

Grant winced as the gray-haired man fell to his knees, bowing his head to the floor. The hose that fed a solution of the guilt drug to his brain stretched taut, its metal covering clinking like a struck drainpipe as the man moved his head.

"Professor Burton," Trevelyan sneered. "Why aren't you working?"

Burton spoke into the floor, his forehead still bowed against it, the hose to the ceiling jiggling as he spoke. "You found a live subject, my baron," he said. "What was it you wanted me to do?"

"Live subjects are no interest to me," Baron Trevelyan told the professor. "I expected you to have worked him into something I could use by now."

Burton bowed lower, his head clunking as it struck against the cold, hard floor as one of the Magistrates unlocked the door. "Whatever you want me to do, my baron," he sobbed. "You need but ask."

"Useless," Trevelyan cursed as he stepped into the room.

Grant watched from his position on the cot, not bothering to hide his contempt. Without a word, two of the Magistrates crossed the room and placed themselves on either side of Grant.

"Stand," Baron Trevelyan commanded in his weasel voice. When Grant ignored the instruction, he elaborated. "You will stand."

Grant looked at the genuflecting figure of Roger Burton, realized that should he disobey it was likely that this man would suffer, not him. So, with his hands still bound behind his back, Grant got smoothly to his feet, showing remarkable agility in so doing. As he stood, the Magistrates to either side of him grabbed him by the elbows, ushering him toward the door.

Grant shrugged away from their grip, glared at them. "I can walk fine," he growled. "Don't need you dead creeps pawing at me."

Trevelyan made a clicking sound in the back of his throat and the two Magistrates brought their arms back, allowing Grant to exit the laboratory cell under his own power. Trevelyan followed, eyeing the broad-shouldered ex-Magistrate thoughtfully.

"Unhook the professor also," Trevelyan added, not even bothering to glance back into the cell. "I shall be needing his services. We launch tonight, within the hour."

One of the remaining dead Magistrates plucked an adjustable wrench from its housing in a molded unit just outside Burton's cell. Then, without a word, the Magistrate stepped back into the cell and took the wrench to the hose that connected with Burton's skull, working a catch there in a series of violent turns of the wrench. Still crouched on the floor, Burton whimpered, his head yanking back and forth as the hose arrangement was snapped loose of its ceiling housing.

Standing just beyond the cell door, Grant winced as he heard the hose hiss. The shrill sound was the whine of a tire's burning rubber.

KANE WAS SCUTTLING AMONG the trash cans outside the Magistrate Hall when the door in the wall began to rattle. He ducked down, hiding as best he could among the discarded garbage bags on the ground.

Kane held his breath as the door came open with a shunt sufficient to dislodge the nearest of the bulging black sacks. Standing there, framed in the doorway, was

a Magistrate in full dress uniform. His helmet was removed and his uniform stained with long-dried blood
the color of rust. The Magistrate's face looked like a
skull, graying bone visible through the few strands of
flesh still clinging to it, eyes dark pools in the recess
of black sockets.

Kane ducked back as the skeletal Magistrate brought
a black bag of trash from the doorway. He proceeded
to toss the bag in Kane's direction. The bag rolled over
several other sacks, and something hard inside clunked
against Kane's skull, causing him to let out an irritated
grunt. As he did so, the gruesome Magistrate spotted
Kane hiding in the litter. Kane seemed to be watching
in slow motion as the skeletal figure raised his hand in
a smooth, well-practiced movement. Kane knew that
movement well and watched helplessly as the automatic
pistol materialized in the Magistrate's bony hand and
his index finger crooked against the trigger.

Chapter 24

The Soul Eater spit bullets across the trash area with a wail like a sick child. Kane didn't even realize he was reacting but just ducked down as the first bullets strafed the area, bursting rubbish sacks and kicking rotting debris into the air in rancid explosions.

The skeletal Magistrate squeezed the trigger again, sending a second burst in Kane's direction even as Kane leaped out of the way. There was nowhere for Kane to go; all he could do was dive into the stinking trash bags and try to lose himself among them. Kane held his breath, trying to ignore the stench as he pushed his way beneath the garbage. It was dark down there, dark and warm as if he were inside something organic, a womb of trash.

The Magistrate was alone, Kane told himself, and that gave him a chance.

The area was so overloaded with trash bags that the Dark Magistrate found a half dozen of them tumbling toward him as Kane moved beneath them. He shoved them aside, took a step into the trash area, whipping the Soul Eater pistol before him. Then a hand reached up from the wealth of plastic black bags, grabbed the Magistrate's wrist and pulled, yanking him down into the stinking trash. The Magistrate lost his footing, and overflowing trash bags tumbled in his wake.

Beneath the heap of trash, Kane drew back his other

fist and drove it repeatedly into the Magistrate's face. The Magistrate struggled a moment, squeezing his pistol's trigger and sending another of those wailing bullets through two bags of garbage above him.

Then Kane shoved against the Mag, batting him down with his forearm and landing another blow with his other fist. The Magistrate sank down amid the refuse, plunging into the hot, stinking darkness.

Moments later, Kane reappeared, head and shoulders emerging from the mass of overstuffed garbage bags like a diver coming up for air. Beneath the shimmering plastic waves, the Magistrate had stopped fighting back. Kane still didn't know what the Mags were, but he was certain of one thing—they weren't human, not anymore.

Shrugging the last of the trash from his back, Kane waded through the piled litter to the open door of the Mag Hall of Justice. He stood there for a moment, catching his breath and surveying the interior through the narrow gap that the door allowed. Determining that the way was clear, Kane pulled the door wider and slipped inside.

WITH THE SWIFT PROFESSIONALISM born of need, Brigid Baptiste made her way through the ground floor of the hospital. She recalled the turns she had made here with Kane and Grant, and visualized the doors and elevator banks they had passed, searching her mind for possible routes up through the floors of the collapsing building.

There was no lighting inside the hospital, and the corridors were illuminated only by what ambient light reached them from the open doors into the examination rooms and the wards. And with the sun fading, that light was becoming fainter by the minute. Brigid moved on, holding her fear in check, ignoring the figure she saw silhouetted in the rooms and reflected on the glass windows of the wards. "He's not here, he's just a hallucination." She reminded herself of what Kane had explained back in the media suite.

Brigid soon found the main staircase. It flared out from behind the reception area a handful of corridors away from where she had entered the building itself. The wide staircase ran through the center of the building. The soft shade of green paint that illuminated its walls had been scarred with blood and smoke, rust-colored streaks marring its surface. Shotgun and radio in hand, Brigid jogged up the stairs, taking them swiftly as she made her way up into the hospital building. Burned signs on the walls gave weight to her theory that it had been a military facility, which went some way to explaining why the place contained a mat-trans unit on its third floor. The walls also featured dark patches where water had seeped in. Brigid kept clear of those damp patches, wary now of any sitting water. The water contained dark memories, she knew—memories that bit back.

Brigid passed the second floor, but as she rounded the right-angle turn in the staircase, she faced a hunk of machinery that blocked any further progress. The machinery was cylindrical and reminded Brigid of a torpedo. It had come crashing through a wall above the staircase, and part of it was still teetering above her, poking through from the wall overhead, creaking as the wind moved it to and fro. She stopped on the staircase, staring at the blockage for half a minute. It was balanced precariously, pivoting on the fulcrum of the ruined wall. Although there was a slim gap beneath the unit, Brigid didn't fancy her chances there. The balance was too exact, and if the machinery should slip it would crush or pin her in an instant.

"Time to find another road," Brigid muttered as she backed down the staircase.

Turning back the way she had come, Brigid jogged along the darkened corridors of the building's second story, keeping her breathing measured as she searched for another route. She didn't hear the soft footsteps behind her, didn't see the figure moving in the thick shadows by the damp walls.

PULLING THE DOOR CLOSED behind him, Kane found himself in an empty, unlit corridor in the Magistrate Hall of Justice. The walls were streaked with damp and the whole corridor had a dank smell. None of the bare lightbulbs overhead seemed to be operational. Whatever had hit the rest of the ville had hit this place, too; indeed, the carbon scoring that blackened the walls in a radial pattern suggested that this structure had been close to the epicenter, the thick black streaks running across the walls like isobars on a weather map.

Warily Kane edged into the corridor, listening carefully for any signs of activity. Shuffling noises came from nearby, but there were no voices, not from anywhere.

Making sure that the door at his back was locked—it wouldn't do to learn that his playmate in the trash area had revived to sneak up on him—Kane made his way deeper into the Hall of Justice, eyeing the charred walls with distaste.

He was at a T-junction now, but with nothing lit Kane had trouble deciding which direction to take. Spotting two uniformed Magistrates turn the corner to his right forced his hand, and Kane hurried down the left branch, rushing along with a silent tread. Kane recognized the door on his right, an equipment locker. He shoved against it, conscious of the Magistrates pacing the corridor just twenty feet behind him in the darkness, but the door wouldn't budge. It was locked.

THE HOSPITAL CORRIDORS WERE dark, the damp heavy in the air, clogging her breath. Brigid had been walking around for over ten minutes, trying to find a route up to the higher floors. The next staircase she tried was blocked off above the second flight where a ruined wall had left an impenetrable barricade of debris. After that, she had found a winding stairwell protected by a heavy fire door with a reinforced glass panel at its center. The door had refused to open, even when Brigid put her shotgun down and pushed her shoulder against it.

She moved on, looking for another way to ascend, passing the gloomy, burned remains of wards and X-ray facilities, lung function and recovery rooms. Sometimes, as she passed rooms where the overhead pipes had burst, she would see the figure standing there, his feet sinking in the pooling, stagnant water that carpeted the floor. She would turn away quickly, not acknowledging him, not wanting to see his face. She knew who he was—Daryl, waiting with his accusing gaze, ready to judge her for abandoning him. He wasn't real, she reminded herself; he wasn't here.

Magistrate East followed at a careful distance, tracking the red-tressed female as she did her manic dance through the corridors of the hospital. He knew this place from his old life and took alternative routes when he saw which direction Brigid was going. Sometimes East would cut through a ward, using the chief nurse's office as a shortcut into another corridor that ran parallel

to Brigid's path. He had backup on the way; he could
afford to be patient. Better to catch the living than to
scare and thus lose her.

Unaware of her tracker, Brigid moved on, working
her way logically through the stairwells until she located a bank of service elevators. There were two of
them at the west of the building, hidden down a corridor
that stood behind a decorative wall. The wall featured
a painting of a wheat field in summer, but the yellows
had been turned to gray and black from smoke damage, turning it into a nightmarish vision.

Brigid stopped before the twin elevators, their ac-
cordion doors wider than a normal elevator. To the far
right, an unobtrusive door crouched in the wall, painted
an off-white to match the paint job on the walls. Like
much of the hospital, the paint on the door had blistered where some incredible heat source had brushed
against it.

Tucking the radio receiver beneath her armpit, Brigid
pushed at the door, finding its hinges creaked a little as
she shoved it. The door swung open, revealing a pitch-
black staircase within. Brigid squinted, trying to make
sense of what little light trickled in from the corridor
beyond. Here was a staircase that had not been blocked,
leading up past the fourth and fifth floors of the building, apparently all the way up to the roof.

Brigid stepped inside, making her way carefully up
the stairs in the near-total darkness.

Magistrate East saw Brigid step through the doorway
from his hiding place at the side of the service elevators. Once she had disappeared from view, he began to
follow, stealthily pacing forward, ball and toe, ball and
toe, to ensure she would not hear his pursuit.

The door was still open where Brigid had entered,

and the Magistrate peeked in, the darkness made more complete by the tint of his visor. He needed no sight of his prey; he could smell her, the hot blood rushing through her arteries, the sweat smell of her skin. The dead saw differently, their senses refined in new ways.

In a moment, Magistrate East was inside the stairwell, stepping silently up the stairs as he pursued his prey.

Outside the hospital, two personnel carriers had arrived with an accompanying patrol car, disgorging their long-dead occupants in the regen apparatus suits of the Magistrates. Twenty-eight Dark Magistrates waited at ground level, eyeing the hospital from the road.

An angry sneer crossed Kane's lips as he stared at the locked door to the equipment store. There was a keypad to the side, caked with grime, its numbers almost worn through. Back home in Cobaltville this keypad would work the magnetic lock into the equipment store. Kane glared at it—there was simply no way of knowing the combination. Behind him, the twin Magistrates were striding closer. Unable to see him clearly in the darkness, they had likely taken him for one of their own, and had not raised the alarm yet, but Kane knew it was only a matter of time.

"Fuck it," he growled under his breath, punching in a code on the waiting keypad: 4-3-5-5

It was the same code he had used for the equivalent equipment locker in Cobaltville. And remarkably, it worked.

"Great minds…" Kane muttered as the lock clicked open and he slipped inside, out of the path of the approaching Magistrates. Strange, too, to find that the electromagnet that operated the lock was still functional. It meant that somewhere in this building there was a power supply. That was certainly interesting. Kane made a mental note to investigate that later.

Inside, the equipment room was stacked head-high with clothing and armaments. Stagnant water pooled in its darkest recesses. There were shelves of grenades, hand cannons and nightsticks, all stored behind protective grilles, each with its own lock. Kane ignored them, moving instead to the clothing area.

There were Magistrate uniforms there: helmets, leathers, boots and outdoor wear in various sizes. Kane grabbed one of the greatcoats, working his arms quickly through the sleeves until it sat on his shoulders. The coat was heavier than he remembered—clearly he had become used to the thin fabric of the shadow suit since his days as a Magistrate—and it stretched down past his knees to line up with the top of a Magistrate's boots.

Buttoning up the coat, Kane found a pair of boots in his size then added a Mag helmet to the ensemble. Sure, he didn't look half-past-dead, but he would pass for a Magistrate all the same, at least so long as no one peered beneath the coat.

After that, Kane scanned the lockers for things he could use. He broke two locks, nabbing a handful of grenades, which he shoved inside the pockets of the black coat, then snatched up a magnetic multikey.

A moment later, Kane was at the door, checking the corridor before moving out there. He was inside. And, if luck was with him, he could pass through the place unnoticed. Unconsciously, Kane brought his hand up to his face and brushed his nose with his index finger where it peeked out from beneath the Magistrate's visor; it was the old one-percent salute, and he wished Grant was here to see it.

Chapter 25

Brigid breathed a sigh of relief as she stepped out of the pitch-black staircase. She had been in there less than a minute, trudging up the staircase in the darkness, but she had started to get the feeling she was being watched.

"Stupid," she cursed herself. That nonsense with Daryl Morganstern had messed up her brain, put her on edge. This whole ville was empty, apart from a few spectral Magistrates wandering through the abandoned streets, and she had not seen one of them in hours.

She found herself in another boring corridor, its unimaginative paint scheme and lack of adornment a rather damning reflection of the practicality of the designers. If she had her bearings straight the mat-trans room was a little way ahead, located along a parallel corridor to her right.

Brigid trudged on, regretting her choice of the heavy shotgun as she made her way down another darkened corridor.

Behind her, Magistrate East peered from the darkness of the staircase, propping the door ajar with one emaciated hand. It was time.

Magistrate East took a step back into the stairwell, pushing the heavy fire door silently closed as he activated his helmet comm. The radio burst to life in a hiss of static, and East drew his lips back to reveal black-

ened teeth, unleashing a duo-tonal splutter of noise from
deep in his throat.

Downstairs, waiting in the streets outside the hospital, twenty-eight dead Magistrates acknowledged his
instruction as two more personnel carriers arrived.

KANE MARCHED DOWN A DIM corridor in the Hall of Justice, the Mag coat cinched tightly around his broad
chest. That there were so many other Magistrates
around surprised him—he had never seen so many
Mags on duty, even during the busiest periods at Cobaltville. Kane strode past a half-dozen Mags hurrying
toward the subbasement garage level located beneath
the sector house.

He walked proudly, slipping into the almost military Magistrate stride without effort. He couldn't be
timid if he was to carry off his ruse, he knew. A timid
Magistrate would stick out like a sore thumb, and the
legitimate ones would be on him like a shot. So he kept
going, striding in the opposing direction to the vast
wave of movement, keeping his head tucked low to his
raised collar.

As he passed a group of Magistrates on their way to
the garage, he saw their skin where the helmets ended
at the line of their nostrils. The flesh beneath their helmets was in varying states of distress, pocked and eaten
as if ravaged by locusts. They spoke in screeches, like
electronic static, cutting and starting without any discernible rhythm.

Up ahead, another group was marching in Kane's
direction, heading toward the subbasement garage as
if they were answering a call.

Good, Kane thought, means there are less here to fool.

He ducked into a handy stairwell to let the group

pass, his shoulder rubbing against the damp wall. Down, he told himself, descending the stairs. Find the cells. If Grant's anywhere, that's where he'll be.

Kane hurried down the stairs, feet padding silently in the darkened stairwell. A moment later he was at the foot of the stairs, pushing open the heavy fire door. As he did so, he heard footsteps and voices, and he drew back into the stairwell, holding the door ajar and peering out. Unlit, it was like looking around one's bedroom after being suddenly awoken. It took Kane's eyes a moment to adjust. He saw the walls, droplets of water glistening on their surface. Someone was coming. Not just someone—lots of someones, a whole troop of them working their way down the corridor at a slow pace.

Kane stilled his breath, trying to make out the words. A supercilious-sounding voice was making proclamations, high enough that Kane was not sure if it was male or female.

He waited, tucked into the alcove of the stairwell, eyes fixed on the moving shadows in the darkness, learning everything he could from the first new voice he had heard since arriving in Quocruft.

It had taken a while to hook Professor Burton up for mobility.

Even so, Grant was still woozy as he walked along the unlit corridor flanked by Magistrates, hands cuffed behind his back. Baron Trevelyan was leading the way, discussing matters with Professor Burton as they strode slowly from the cells toward the elevators.

Burton walked with a perpetual stoop, his head bowed in supplication to his baron. The metal hose that had been attached to the ceiling of his cell was now connected to a box on wheels that he dragged beside him like a suitcase. The box came up to Burton's hip and featured an illuminated display on its rear, along with a clear panel through which Grant could see cloudy liquid. The liquid was churning in the lights from the panels and was being fed through the hose via a small pump within the wheeled box, its repetitive hiss-gurgle a constant in the otherwise unlit corridor.

The corridors were grimy, streaks of dirt running across the walls and floor, the ceiling tiles stained brown where they had been marred with damp. There was water clinging to the walls, slowly running down them, beading there like sweat. It all smelled, stagnant and rancid, like a mixture of days-old food and disease.

"I expected him to be more…altered," Trevelyan told Burton in his high, clear voice.

"I cannot explain it, my baron," Burton replied fretfully. Burton looked over his shoulder at Grant for a moment, and Grant saw his expression was one of guilt. "How much did you say he was given?"

Trevelyan shrugged with a lack of interest. "He must have been under the water for three or four minutes at a time. I don't know—how long can you humans survive without air?"

Irritated, Grant spoke up then, butting in on the conversation as one of the Magistrates worked the pull-back door of the elevator. "Hey, Baron Troublemaker—if you want to talk to me I'm right here."

Standing before the elevator, Baron Trevelyan turned, shooting Grant a withering look.

"What?" Grant challenged. "You too frightened to talk to someone whose spirit you ain't broke? Huh?"

"Do you see?" Trevelyan said, turning back to Burton. "The subject remains unaffected by guilt. He was under the water for a long time—he should have reacted by now. I am at a loss to understand it."

"Maybe there are no reserves of guilt to tap in this man," Burton suggested meekly as he stepped into the elevator. Grant and the Mags followed, and Grant saw that the only lighting inside the wide elevator cage came from the circular buttons that identified the floors. "Perhaps he has nothing to be guilty for."

"That's right," Grant snarled. "I got no guilt. Whatever I did, I did in good conscience."

The others did not seem to notice him speaking.

"Sure," Grant growled, rolling his shoulders. "Just ignore me." The cuffs were starting to chafe, contributing to his already bad mood.

It appeared to be a freight elevator, leaving ample room for the seven-strong group inside. Grant was muscled over to one corner, as far from Baron Trevelyan as it was possible to be. Trevelyan paid him no attention— if the thought that Grant might attack him crossed his mind, he gave no sign that he was afraid.

KANE ALMOST GASPED AS HE recognized Grant's voice. He had not been able to see much from his hiding place behind the stairwell door, just a sliver of a gap through which he could peek. He had counted seven figures trudging toward him in the dark, but had not recognized Grant's bowed form where the cuffs restrained him.

But Grant was alive. At least, for now. Things did not look good for him out there. Suddenly Kane was even more aware of the urgency of his mission.

But what could Kane do? He could try taking on the group, perhaps even use the darkness to his advantage. But the corridor was too tight; it created too much risk.

Besides, the party was already entering the elevator, so that had power, too.

Kane waited, still eavesdropping on the conversation. "Just don't shoot him," he mouthed to the air in a silent prayer.

THE ELEVATOR DOOR CLOSED on its runners, and Grant waited in silence as the group ascended through the building. It was all starting to feel familiar to Grant. Very familiar. He was beginning to get a notion about this strange place where he had wound up.

"A human without guilt," Trevelyan said in a mocking tone that belied his disbelief. "Could such a creature really exist?"

Professor Burton stared at the floor, defeated. "It's only a hypothesis, my baron. With the right psychiatric tools and sufficient time, one might be able to prove or disprove it. Regrettably that's not my field."

"No," Trevelyan acknowledged. "What did happen to that psychiatrist—Baird, was it? I think he was reassigned as Magistrate Nees. It would be in the logs."

"No doubt," Burton agreed.

"Important to keep records of one's achievements," Trevelyan said to the elevator cage, as if making a proclamation about his superiority. "I'm looking forward to logging the next world when we take it. All those little boxes to fill in."

Grant listened to the conversation, his fury growing with every smug word. He would wipe that grin off the hybrid's face if it was the last thing he did here.

KANE PULLED THE DOOR TO THE stairwell a little wider and let out the breath he had been holding. They were gone, ascended in the elevator.

He stepped out into the corridor, eyeing the display panel above the elevator. The display was dim, just barely illuminated. Kane watched as it rose through the building, stopped at the top floor. Then he knew where they were taking Grant. But why the top floor? What would they want in the Magistrate archives?

Without pausing, Kane was back in the stairwell beside the elevator door, taking the dark steps two at a time as he hurried up to the topmost story.

"Hang in there, partner," he said to the darkness. "I won't be long."

"There you are," Brigid muttered, eyeing the door into the mat-trans area. "Who says women are no good with directions?"

She tried the door, knowing full well that it would be jammed, just as it had been when Grant had tried it earlier. She held out some sliver of hope that the door might have been locked from the outside, that there might be some catch that could be released from out here, but the door held, the handle turning and turning with no effect. She looked more closely at it for a moment, noticed a nasty dent in the door lock and the wall where something heavy had struck against it in the damp corridor—the tattered remains of a security touch pad. It looked as if the lock had been forced at some point, and now it wouldn't work at all.

Brigid turned back to the dim corridor, recalling the ruined wall beyond the mat-trans chamber itself. She felt confident that she could climb out of a window and work her way around without too much trouble; she just needed to find another room from which she could access some windows. As she turned she saw someone waiting in the corridor, standing amid the pooling water that ran down the walls. "Daryl," she muttered, shaking her head. "Quit bothering me."

The figure continued to watch her from the shadows. He was standing between Brigid and the next door, the obvious one to try, a line of rubble behind him. Brigid knew he was a hallucination, just the way Kane had described, knew she could overcome him. He had tried to kill her in the video room, had persuaded her to blow her brains out. Only Kane's intervention had prevented that. But Brigid could be strong. There's nothing to fear, she told her hammering heart.

Brigid began to walk toward the next room, trying to ignore the figure waiting there. But as she did so, the figure moved toward her, raising its right hand. It held something there; Brigid saw metal glint in the darkness. Gun.

Brigid's body reacted even before she had consciously realized it, ducking down as the man's blaster bucked in his hand. The bullet went overhead, wailing in that unforgettable scream in the manner of the Magistrate's guns. The bullet struck the wall where Brigid had been standing, kicking up plaster and fractured paint as it drilled its shrieking path there.

It was not a hallucination, Brigid realized as the breaking plaster dusted in her hair. Nor was it Daryl; it was one of the strange Magistrates, hidden from her by the darkness of the corridor. She was in trouble.

Chapter 26

The hospital wall exploded as another bullet struck inches from Brigid's head. She moved, hurrying back down the corridor as the Dark Magistrate chased her. His lumbering steps were heavy and robotic, balancing like a machine. The Mag's Soul Eater pistol boomed again, sending another of those hideous, shrieking bullets toward her in an ear-splitting scream.

Brigid leaped around a turn in the corridor, ducking her head down as the bullets crashed against the wall behind her. All the while she was cursing herself for her own stupidity. The earlier hallucinations had fooled her; she had become so convinced that this was just something in her mind that she had let her guard down. And almost paid the ultimate price for it.

Brigid slipped in the pooling water as she turned another corner, regaining her balance in an instant, picking up speed as she tried to create some distance between her and the Magistrate. Behind her, Magistrate East edged around the corner, the devil skeleton glinting atop his helmet, leveling his Soul Eater and reeling off a triple burst of screeching fire. Three bullets howled down the corridor, squealing like stuck pigs as they sought the living flesh of their prey.

Turning, Brigid slammed her back against the wall, swinging the Mossberg shotgun around in a one-handed grip. She squeezed the trigger as the Dark Magistrate appeared in the corridor, sending an angry burst of lead in his direction. The Magistrate staggered, the blast missing him by a foot. Brigid didn't wait to see what he would do next. Already she was working the handle of the nearest door, disappearing into the room beyond like a wraith.

Inside, Brigid crashed into something at waist height, sending metal bowls clanging to the floor and something heavier striking after them. It was a gurney, she realized as she jumped over it, recovering in an instant. She was in a recovery room, dark, but with a window at the far wall. The window was wide, looking out on the ville and the dark sky lit only by the sunken sun.

Window, Brigid thought

She didn't even bother to stop. Flipping the shotgun around, she blasted the smoke-streaked glass out of the window, taking most of the frame with it as she ran at the window

A moment later, Brigid was clambering through the broken remains of the window, bringing the shotgun around once more as the Magistrate appeared in the doorway to the room. Without a second's remorse, Brigid pulled the trigger, sending another ugly burst of fire at the Magistrate. The Mossberg replica held five shots, plus one in the barrel.

Brigid still had three bullets left before she would need to reload. Enough, if she was careful. There was no time to reload now, she had to get out of here, find her way back to the mat-trans a half turn around the building's facade. As Magistrate East ducked out of the recovery room, Brigid secured the radio in her belt and swung out of the window, her feet searching for a ledge on which she could balance.

Brigid's long legs stretched down beneath her past

the window's ledge, toes nudging the brickwork as she sought somewhere to tread—a ridge, anything. Out here, the swirling winds were howling like wolves through the artificial canyons of the streets. She dangled there for a few seconds, precariously balancing the shotgun as she gripped the window, feet scrabbling to find purchase. Then, almost as far as her body could stretch, her toes found an indentation in the wall's surface. Powder crumbled as the pointed toes of her boots kicked the loose stone, finally finding a ledge that ran a few inches above the windows of the story below.

Brigid's heart was racing, but at least she was safe from the Mag. It was at that moment that she heard more screaming bullets cut through the air, as the Magistrate's support unit spotted her climbing on the face of the building.

"Crap!"

WITH A SCREECH OF STRAINING cables, the elevator shuddered to a halt. Grant watched from the rear of the cage as one of the Magistrates who accompanied him opened the pull-back door. The Magistrate stepped aside to allow Baron Trevelyan to step through first, followed by Roger Burton.

Grant stumbled, shoved in the back as he followed them. He grunted, the world still swimming a little around him. His earlier dunking had left his senses reeling, and he could not quite shift the sense of seasickness he had. He knew now that Trevelyan had tried to poison him with guilt. Tried—and failed. Grant took a deep breath and held it, working through the sense of mental disorientation.

The party continued to walk, but with each step Grant was taking careful note of his surroundings.

Again, water darkened every surface, permanent dark patches blotching across the floor. Even unlit the layout was familiar. Grant knew this place, or one like it. It was a Magistrate Hall of Justice; he was sure of it now. He had not been able to say for certain while he had been in Burton's cell—one cell was much like another. But the corridors, the placement of the freight elevator—it all fit. It was a mirror image of the Mag Hall he knew in Cobaltville, but otherwise it was a perfect match.

Made sense, Grant told himself. All these Mags around, of course we're in a sector house.

Grant trudged on, mind racing as he puzzled through how this knowledge might help him. If he could orchestrate some diversion he might be able to break free, despite the darkness of the building's interior. But with his hands now bound behind his back in the plastic cuffs of the Magistrates, there was no way he could do that. He needed to find some way to trick them into releasing him, just for long enough that he could sow the seeds of confusion and bug out.

KANE HURRIED UP THE UNLIT staircase to the top floor. He met a couple of Magistrates who were using the staircase to get down to the basement level and stepped aside to let them pass, his head down. It was very dark in the staircase but the Magistrates did not seem to be affected by that.

A few steps after they passed Kane they halted, scenting the air. Kane had begun his ascent as they started twittering, strange discordant tones emanating from their throats. Disguised as one of them, Kane hurried on, boots clattering on the cold steps. They had noticed something was wrong. He would need to stay alert.

Reaching the top floor, Kane pressed open the door

and warily walked through. The staircase opened on the hooked recess of a corridor behind the service elevator, granting Kane some shelter before he stepped into view.

Confirming that the corridor was empty, Kane made his way down it toward the double doors at the end. As he recalled, the top floor of the Magistrate Hall had been dedicated to the archives. Paper reports were filed and refiled here and it also held the main servers for the Magistrate computer system.

Kane pushed himself up to the double doors, pressing his face against one of the cool glass panels there. The glass was streaked with dirty water. What he saw there made Kane regret not acting when he first saw Grant down in the basement level. Kane had expected to see the regimented shelving units of the archive, but instead the shelves had been removed, leaving one vast room the size of an aircraft hangar.

Although underlit, the room was bright thanks to the glowing apparatus at its far end. There were Magistrates patiently lined up along the walls and more working at a variety of unfathomable tasks in the vast room. All of them showed signs of decomposition, their flesh colorless and rotting. His eyes hidden behind the Magistrate's visor, Kane blinked quickly; for a moment he had seen not Magistrates in the greenish light but women, girls— the dirty-blond tresses of Helena Vaughn on two-dozen helmeted heads. He closed his eyes, willing away the vision, then opened them again. "Leave me alone," he murmured.

Grant stood with his back to Kane, close to the doors, along with several dark-clad Mags and two other figures. The first of these was a brown-skinned human with what appeared to be some kind of dialysis machine on a wheeled frame beside him. The apparatus was connected to the man through a thick tube in the base of his skull, reminding Kane of a hookah pipe. Beside this man was a shorter figure with a narrow-shouldered frame, his long spindly arms waving elaborately in the air. The figure was dressed in a white tunic, its lines carefully pressed and somehow at odds with this dirty ville. Kane recognized what the figure was instantly— it was a hybrid, one of the old barons who had ruled the villes. But they were all dead, weren't they?

Kane peered through the glass, trying to make sense of the illuminated thing at its far side. It looked like a showman's ring, the kind one might see at the circus that a lion would jump through. Just like the showman's ring, this one glowed with a fire, albeit a fire made of electrical sparks with the blue glow of a burning acetylene torch.

Standing upright, the ring was taller than a man. Kane guessed it was twelve feet in height, almost scraping the ceiling. The ring sat on a thick base of elaborate machinery, with power hoses running to and from it in great cords like sinew. Magistrates worked diligently at these machines, running diagnostic checks through eight computer terminals positioned in a semicircle around the left side.

Kane saw dark windows behind the ring, placed high in the building. The windows were open, showing the deep indigo darkness of the night sky.

For a moment, Kane was paralyzed, the sight overwhelming. There had to be seventy Magistrates in that room, perhaps more. He patted at the pocket of the greatcoat, feeling for the handful of grenades he had stashed there. No, the odds weren't good.

Warily, Kane slipped into the room, his helmeted head down as he walked toward the gathering Magistrates. The hybrid was talking, his voice a grating whine echoing in the vast chamber.

"Humans," the baron said, speaking the word like a curse. "So simple to manipulate, all that guilt locked away inside their monkey shells."

Grant glared at him defiantly, straining at his bonds. There was a Magistrate standing to either side of him, two more close by and ranks of them all about.

Kane walked past the group, positioning himself a little way back from the baron where he could watch proceedings without drawing any obvious attention to himself. Grant looked tired, standing before this wretched, pale-skinned hybrid.

"I was born to rule them," Baron Trevelyan continued, pacing a small circle before Grant. "More than that, I was specifically evolved to rule them. But there are so many of them that a leader must make decisions. If you or your kind had any notion of what real leadership is you might understand." He glared in disdain at Roger Burton for a long moment, where the man stood humbled with his feeder unit.

"Humans have such capacity for resolve," the baron continued, "that it makes things tricky sometimes. But the one thing man cannot conquer is his own guilt.

"I set things in motion—weaponized guilt," Trevelyan continued. "In the water, an additive that plucked at human emotions, working like a depressant. It infiltrated the reservoirs and, from there, the water cycle took over. Before we knew it, it was in the crops, the seas, the rain. While it worked in the ville, the efficient natural system took it outside, into the world beyond. My world."

Listening to this, Kane realized what had happened out in Quocruft to both himself and Brigid. They had been plagued with visions from their own pasts, nagging worries that kept coming to them, tugging at their consciences. For him it had been Helena Vaughn.

The hybrid baron was shaking his head as if contemplating an impossible task. "So many humans to rule, and me their master."

"What about the other barons?" Grant asked.

"Other barons?" Trevelyan repeated, bemused. "What other barons?" He looked disturbed at the thought, a chess master finding himself tricked by a move he had not anticipated. "There are no other barons."

OUTSIDE THE WALLS OF THE hospital, the winds were moaning like the restless dead. Night had fallen now, and it was dark outside the brutal building, the sky painted a deep shade of indigo touched with purple where the sun nudged beneath the horizon. High above the ground, the masonry felt cold against Brigid's face as she pressed along the tiny ledge, feet scraping warily to retain her balance on the narrow lip that ran above the window frames of the second floor.

Bullets streaked the air all around her, their hideous screams moaning like a prisoner being stretched on the rack. Brigid took a deep breath, shuffling along the precarious ledge. They could not see her, she realized—not well, at least—and their weapons were a poor choice at this distance. That was something; she was hidden from the Mags below, and if they hit her it would be by chance rather than superior aim. Not very reassuring, though, not when at least a dozen bullets were cutting the air around her as she hurried along the narrow ledge.

Brigid scuttled on, clutching the Mossberg as she worked her way along the outside of the building, three stories above the road. She could see the corner of the building up ahead, a dark and solid absence against the night sky. She needed to get around that corner, out of the immediate line of fire, and also around to the side where the building had collapsed to expose the room with the mat-trans.

A bullet clipped the masonry close to her ear, and Brigid reared back automatically, without thinking. Suddenly she was slipping backward, reaching for the wall ahead before she tumbled from the building's face. Her right arm thrust out, the shotgun still clutched in her hand, jabbing into the slick reflective surface of a window. The window clinked and held, the toughened glass repelling Brigid's stabbing Mossberg.

Brigid's other arm windmilled for a moment, her feet skidding along the ledge as another hail of bullets shrieked past close to her face. The world seemed to spin around her as she reached out desperately with her left hand, grabbing for the wall or the ledge. For a moment she was falling, everything spinning. Then her bare fingers found the rough surface of the wall and she clenched her hand, grabbing the lintel of the window she had tried to break.

For a moment she hung there, her breath coming in thundering gasps. Then another bullet struck the wall close to her breast, and she came out of her trance, forcing her shaking body to move.

She peered back as she walked ahead, saw the Magistrate clambering out of the same window she had used not two minutes earlier. He must have been waiting there, confirming that she was not poised to shoot him the moment he appeared. He poked his head out, demon baby glinting on his helmet, his weapon aimed and ready, face emotionless in the darkness. Brigid saw the Soul Eater flash as another of those awful, screaming bullets popped from its muzzle and streaked toward her. She clung tightly to the edge of the building, holding her breath as the bullet zipped past, clipping through her lion's mane of hair as it went.

"Too close," Brigid whispered to herself. "Way too close."

Her head felt hot where the bullet had passed, a friction burn searing against her skin. She ignored it, driving her body onward as her heart beat a tattoo against her ribs. Behind her, Magistrate East had drawn himself out onto the same ledge, arms splayed as he scratched for a grip with his skeletal claws.

Brigid hugged the building in a solid hold, switching the shotgun from her right hand to her left. It was not an easy maneuver, not up here three stories above the hard tarmac of the street with the winds howling in her ears and the screaming bullets cutting holes all around her. But Brigid zoned out everything, determined to get the gun into position.

Magistrate East pulled himself up and began working his way along the building in the shuffling crab walk that the narrow ledge demanded. Brigid's eyes narrowed, framing the Mag in her sights. Then her shotgun boomed, the sound muffled by the furious winds all around her. The shot missed the Magistrate, but that didn't matter. It was close enough, and Brigid watched regretfully as the man suddenly lost his grip amid the strike of buckshot, slipped and tumbled backward away from the building's face.

Brigid turned as he fell, urging her body to keep moving. She heard the loud crunch of metal as the Mag struck one of the personnel carriers parked outside the hospital, denting the metal beyond repair. It was done. Swiftly Brigid scrambled to the corner of the building, doing her best to ignore the bullets that screamed all around her, pulling herself around the side of the block.

Brigid breathed a sigh of relief as she swung around the corner, clinging tightly to the building's face. Then she turned her head, searching for the holed section of the hospital. And there, framed against the darkness of the night sky, Brigid saw fifty Magistrates climbing up the side of the building on fixed lines, like a troop of monkeys climbing a tree. They were coming for her. And she had just two blasts left in the replica Mossberg shotgun.

Chapter 27

In the aircraft-hangar-size room atop the Magistrate Hall of Justice, Baron Trevelyan was shaking his head, a cunning, lizardlike smile on his thin lips.

"The most wonderful thing about leaders is...I'm the only one." He laughed.

Cuffed before the hybrid baron, Grant began to see it all now, piecing the clues together from everything this Baron Trevelyan had said. The barons of Grant's world had been hybrid shells designed for one purpose—to house a genetic template that would one day be activated, securing new life for the long-dead Annunaki royal family. That process had involved a download catalyst from a starship called *Tiamat*, the mythical dragon mother.

But here, in this world—so like and yet so unlike Grant's own—things had gone a different way. In the wake of the Deathlands era, the hybrid program had stuttered, creating not nine barons but just one— Trevelyan. Alone, Baron Trevelyan had created the lone ville that dominated the Earth: a megaville called Quocruft, where Grant and his companions had accidentally emerged when they'd engaged the quantum phase inducer of the mat-trans. In this world, the baron's call to arms had never come from the dragon mother. Or, when it had, it had failed somehow, leaving Trevelyan a half-born thing with a purpose but without the knowl-

edge of his Annunaki past. Without the competition of
the other barons, Trevelyan had been able to turn all of
his attention to the decimated remains of humanity—
a human population that had been pared down by the
nukecaust and the Deathlands period that had followed.
Trevelyan's own inhuman streak had clearly encouraged
him to experiment in methods of control.

In Grant's reality, the nine barons had been a thorn
in the side of the Cerberus organization during its early
days, and Grant had often wondered how much better
the world would have been without those inhuman hybrid rulers. Seeing this world with just one baron made
him realize it was a case of "better the devil you know."

"The Magistrates are dead," Trevelyan gloated. "You
realize that, don't you?"

Grant looked at the black-clad figures who flanked
their baron, their rotted faces masked behind the helms
they wore, each exhibiting a different stage of decay.
"Yeah," Grant said, recalling what Professor Burton
had told him. "But why?"

"Technology," Trevelyan said. "You know, it has
been a long time since I've had someone new to speak
to. I'm rather enjoying the feeling of liberation it brings.
Bask in my glory, apekin."

"So what now?" Grant asked with a sneer.

"For you? Or for me?" Trevelyan quipped.

Grant remained silent, letting the hybrid enjoy his
moment of triumph while he could. He had spotted
something familiar when he scanned the Dead Magistrates faces a moment ago—a figure who looked an
awful lot like Kane. Furthermore, the man looked de-
cidedly alive, much to Grant's relief. And if Kane was
here, that meant that surely Brigid wasn't far behind.
Grant's eyes flicked in that direction again as Treve-

lyan spoke, trying not to make it too obvious where he was looking.

"There are other worlds out there, ape-thing," the baron stated, gesturing wildly with his bird-thin arms. "Other Earths held in pockets, one beside the next, each one populated by millions of humans just like you. In galactic terms, only the lightest fabric separates us."

Again, Grant put this together with what Burton had told him, realizing that Trevelyan had been seeing with his Annunaki knowledge, peering into dimensions without quite realising why or how. Properly born, the Annunaki were multidimensional, their battles fought across many planes. This one saw those planes, those other levels of the great game board, and didn't know why.

"I have spent—" Trevelyan paused thoughtfully, his oily eyes wistful "—*time* breaking that fabric, tearing it aside so that I could travel there. To rule. The personnel, the power needed—it all takes so much time."

"You're deranged," Grant growled.

Standing amid the Dark Magistrates, Grant's partner Kane could not help but smile at his friend's statement. Brief and insightful as ever, he thought.

Trevelyan inclined his head in mocking acceptance of Grant's insult. "Our first attempt almost destroyed this settlement," he stated, emotionlessly. "The power required to pierce dimensions is more than you could possibly comprehend. We channeled the sun's rays across a dozen separate capacitors and still it blew out the ville like a bomb. The shockwaves rocked through every mat-shifter on Earth, wiping out great chunks of the globe.

"I'm surprised to see you still alive after so long. It's hideous out there."

"And then?" Grant encouraged.

"The trouble was there was no port," Trevelyan explained. "Nothing to dock onto. We were flinging our dimensional anchor out there, but there was nothing to hook, you understand?"

In response, Grant glared at the baron. He had a nasty feeling he knew where all of this was leading—his very appearance on this world at this time was the only evidence he needed.

"Eventually, we found a receiver platform out there, on one of the worlds," Trevelyan said. "Which meant we could send our explorers to that one specific point. Much more chance of survival, you understand?"

A chill went through Grant's spine, already knowing what the baron was referring to when he spoke of "a receiver platform"—he meant the mat-trans. Trevelyan's dimensional transmission was utilizing the same basic tech that Cerberus employed, which was how Grant had arrived here with Kane and Brigid, plucked from the quantum ether during an energy spike from this plane. Grant might not be a science guy, but he had spent long enough around the Cerberus brainiacs that he could imagine the basic process—it was the same as a crossed-line telephone call or a stronger radio signal interfering with a weaker one. *Shit*.

"You want to go conquer another Earth," Grant said. "Is that it?"

"Not conquer," Trevelyan said sneeringly. "Man is a plague, a cancer. I wish to eradicate him. Surely even you can see the simple truth in that.

"Which brings us to what is to happen to you, I suppose. As you have witnessed, my Magistrates are robust. But they waste away in time, as the rot sets in. One can only hold back time for so long. We remained on this Earth rather longer than I had envisaged, and between natural wastage and the loss of test subjects while we refined the procedure, my army is beginning to dwindle. So, I would like to offer you a position—as a Magistrate, working for your baron."

Grant eyed the rotting figures who were moving about the room, each one further decomposed than the last. "And what if I refuse?"

"That won't matter to you for very long," Trevelyan assured him with a hideous reptilian smile. "The brain functions are halted during the conversion, and your physical system is rewired so that it can gorge on itself, a self-perpetuating loop that grants you a reasonable period of servitude. Two years, I believe we said, didn't we, Professor?"

Professor Burton nodded without enthusiasm. "Yes, my baron."

"But they're dying," Grant said angrily.

"No, they're not dying," Trevelyan told him. "They're dead. But they serve me, anyway. You'll learn, in time, that the demarcation between life and death is a lot less solid than you had been led to believe."

Hiding among the mingling Magistrates, Kane eyed the nearest of them warily, spying the rotten skin on their chins where their helmets left them exposed. Dead Magistrates. It was so monstrous that it hardly bore contemplating.

BRIGID CLAMBERED IN THE indigo darkness, hurrying along the ledge outside the deserted hospital. The Dark Magistrates had secured fixed lines up the side of the building using launching devices with grappling hooks on the street below. The nearest of the Magistrates was less than ten feet below her and just a little way along from where she scrambled.

Brigid halted for a moment as she passed the safety of the building's corner, drawing her shotgun around and pulling the trigger. The Mossberg replica boomed above the howling winds in the concrete canyons, a vibrant burst of propellant lighting the night for just a flickering second.

Two Magistrates were caught by the blast. The one nearest Brigid took the brunt of it, a gob of flesh bursting from his flank and spattering across the wall like spilled paint, joined a moment later by a hissing burst of gas. Behind him, a second Mag was clipped by the wide-spread burst of fire, and he let go of his fixed line, sailing back to the ground from two stories up. On his way down, the falling Magistrate knocked two further Mags from their lines, while a third went spinning in place as his grip was jarred.

Brigid smiled grimly as she saw the first Mag dangling from his line, his head now just a bloody ruin. The immediate path was clear, but she only had one shot left in the shotgun's breech—better make it count. At least everyone out here was her target, which made it marginally easier.

Brigid's feet skipped along the narrow ledge running atop the windows, the soles of her boots barely making contact as she urged herself to greater speed like some crazy high-wire artist. Her left side was against the wall, hand tapping along it, pressing against it as she drove herself on, shoulder brushing its solid surface. She had to get to the mat-trans unit; that was the only priority. Once inside that room she could put her back to a wall giving her some chance, however slim, of defending herself. Out here she was so vulnerable that she may just as well have had a target painted across her back.

Brigid kept moving, foot over foot, driving herself on toward the jagged cavity in the wall. The facade of the building had taken a major blow at some point in the past, taking out a huge section between the fourth and first floors. Looking at it from the outside like this, Brigid realized that it could very well have emanated from the mat-trans itself, some rogue surge of power firing through the hospital building. Just what the hell had they been doing in there?

Around her, the unlit ville was a ghostly presence, a shadow crouching in her field of vision like a big cat stalking its prey. It looked large, larger than any ville she had ever seen. The night sky was a deep gray now, and no stars showed through the cloud cover. It was almost as if she were running under the bedcovers.

Another bullet clipped the wall close to Brigid with an agonized scream as it drilled through the stone. As it struck, Brigid's body trembled, and for a moment she thought she might lose her balance on the precarious ledge. She stopped, steadying herself, calming her rapid breath. Her heart was slamming against her rib cage, pulse pounding in her ears so loudly she could barely hear the bullets streaking through the air all around her. The darkness was hiding her for now, but she could not stay lucky forever. No one could.

"Keep moving," she told herself. "Don't stop."

With those words of encouragement, Brigid started moving again, stretching out her feet in her boots, balancing on the soles of her toes, making as little contact with the ledge as possible.

The wall pressed against her left hand, cold to the touch. The gap in the wall came upon Brigid abruptly, so much so that it almost caused her to fall. Its ragged edges had been hidden by the night's darkness, and she found it purely by the fact that her left arm no longer had anything to support it.

Brigid swayed in place, the shotgun swinging out like a trapeze artist's swing as she struggled to keep from falling. Her left foot skittered on the ledge, and she levered her body through the gap in the wall. Even in the faint light, she knew she was in the wrong room. It was small, a narrow aisle running between high shelves.

She stood there just a moment, catching her breath. Outside, the fixed lines of the Magistrates cut through her view of the ville like bars on a window, another launching as she watched. She saw something flash in the distance as one of the buildings in the center of the ville came to life, as if lightning had struck within its walls.

"What on earth—?" Brigid muttered, watching the distant windows sparkle.

But there was no time to worry about that now. She needed to get to the mat-trans, tap its power supply, send a message through the quantum ether to Cerberus.

A hand reached up as Brigid stepped toward the destroyed wall. She'd been planning to step out again, run across the building's facade and get to the mat-trans chamber that way. It could only be a room or two over, she knew—her eidetic memory granted an impeccable spatial awareness.

The gloved hand reached up, followed by its partner, scrabbling across the cratered floor inches from Brigid's feet. The Magistrate's head appeared a split-second later, and Brigid seemed to be watching in slow motion as the Mag called his Soul Eater pistol to his palm. The weapon revealed itself from its hidden sheath above his right wrist, barrel extending as it popped into his hand. His black lips pulled back over yellow-gray teeth that hung in receded gums.

Brigid kicked out even as the Magistrate fired, a screeching bullet cutting the air above her head before planting itself in the ceiling. Brigid's kick struck the Magistrate full in his rotted face, the side of her boot ramming into his nose in a burst of fluids and dusty skin. The Mag's helmet was shunted askew with the blow. Brigid followed up with a second kick, this time using the solid heel of her boot to drive a powerful blow into the Mag's exposed chin.

Crack!

The Magistrate slipped and fell, losing his grip on the ragged ruin of exterior wall. But as he fell, a second and third pair of hands materialized along the edge, then a fourth, a fifth and a sixth. The Dark Magistrates had caught up with her, and there was no time left to escape.

PERHAPS THE DARK MAGS could sense the living, too, Kane pondered, as something alien to them. That would explain the confusion in the stairwell when he had brushed past the two Magistrates on their way to the basement, and it might also be the reason that they had found him and his companions so easy to track in the abandoned ville.

Wary now, Kane took a step away from the other Mags, watching them from the corner of his eye as he listened to the baron's continued bragging.

"Of course, by then your opinion will be very much irrelevant," Trevelyan was telling Grant as he leaned toward his bound form. "Much as it is now," he added with a braying laugh.

Grant stared straight ahead, eyeing the glowing ring

that dominated the far end of the room. The ring had begun to crackle with witch fire, bursts of electricity firing from one side to the other, over and over. It was charging up for something, the power thrumming through the floor in a rapid drumbeat.

"After that," Trevelyan continued, "you'll be sent on your way, just one more loyal warrior in my conquering army as we mount our invasion." He pointed to the upstanding hoop. Four figures stood before the hoop now. They were dressed in matte black, all-in-one coveralls that hooded over their skulls, hiding their faces. Grant guessed that they were Magistrates, seconded to do exploratory work. In unison, the quartet checked the weapons attached to their wrist holsters.

As Trevelyan spoke, Grant saw something flickering within the hoop, an image blurring into place inside the inner rim of the circle. He watched as it took hold, showed a room seen through a brown sheen as if viewed through sunglasses. The room was busy, figures silhouetted through the bottle-brown glass as they hurried about their tasks.

"My scout found a 'port' earlier today," Trevelyan explained. "A beachhead for my army's initial landing."

Grant saw the image come into sharper focus then, lightning still playing across it where the dimensional breach rocked with incredible energies. He recognized the view, knew the room that waited beyond that tinted armaglass wall. It was Cerberus.

TRAPPED INSIDE THE TIGHT hospital storeroom, Brigid was dancing backward, getting out of reach of those scrabbling hands as five dead Magistrates pulled themselves up over the lip of ruined wall. She had the shotgun, of course, one bullet chambered.

No, Brigid realized. That won't be enough.

She spun around, sweeping an armful of items from the nearest shelf and sending them at the Magistrates' helmets. A bottle slapped against one Mag's helmet with a clunk, another took a box of disposable wipes on his chin, knocking him backward with surprise more than force. But Brigid needed something better, and she needed it quickly.

She reached around in the darkness, found a stool waiting between the shelves close to the storeroom's door. Two feet high, the stool was designed to help people reach the higher shelves. The metal stool had wheels to make it easy to maneuver, but was spring-weighted so that it would not slip while it was in use. Brigid grabbed it, swinging it around her with one hand. Metal and rubber, the heavy stool clunked against the chest of the first Mag who had revealed himself through the wall, knocking him back and out before he got his legs over the lip.

Brigid followed through, using the momentum of her swing to bat another of the Dark Magistrates from the wall even as his blaster materialized in his hand. The Magistrate never had a chance to fire it, as he was already toppling from the building's face, falling to the street with a burst of stuttered screeches from deep in his throat, his regen suit hissing with expelled gas where Brigid's strike had punctured it.

Still swinging in Brigid's hand, the heavy stool struck one of the shelving units, knocking it from its housing so that it came crashing down against its supports. Once upon a time, the metal frame of the shelving unit had most likely been secured to the exterior wall on one side. Without that wall to support it, the whole unit went caroming out the gap, taking two more

Magistrates with it, and clipping a third, on its journey down to the street.

Brigid was back at the gap in the wall now, where one last Magistrate was climbing in. Peering over the side, she could see more of the dark-clad figures clambering up the walls on their fixed lines, death shrouds hurrying to stop her. The nearest Mag reached out for Brigid's ankle, but she sidestepped, driving the heel of her boot into his grasping fingers. The Mag let out a squeal of pain, the noise a popping hiss.

Brigid stamped again, kicking out at the Mag's withered fingers until he lost his grip. She watched grimly as he went plummeting to the street. This wasn't how she had wanted to play it, but there was something about these Magistrates that was inhuman. Their presence made her flesh crawl.

More of the Dark Magistrates were hurrying up the wall. Holding the stool close to her chest, Brigid took careful aim and dropped it, letting it plummet down the side of the building and onto the unsuspecting head of one of the Magistrates a floor and a half below her. He tumbled from the wall, arms flailing as he lost his grip, stool following.

Brigid was out of the hole in an instant, scampering along the narrow ledge as she rushed to the room containing the mat-trans. As she ran along the outside of the building, Brigid felt something cold and wet hit her left cheek. It was rain.

IN THE UPPERMOST ROOM OF the Magistrate Hall, a gateway to another world had opened. Kane and Grant watched from their separate positions as the dimensional rent tore wider, the image of the Cerberus ops room becoming more pronounced inside the illuminated hoop at the farthest end of the room.

Baron Trevelyan looked overjoyed as lightninglike energy flitted across the surface of his gateway. "The first strike must be quick," he told Grant as more of his dead warriors prepared themselves before the crackling gate, securing the hoods on their protective environment suits, hiding their rotted faces. There were men and women among them, some too short or too weedy to have ever made Magistrates in life. Grant knew then the full horror of Burton's creations: the professor had given the baron an excuse to exterminate everyone on the planet so that they might serve him in death with unswerving loyalty. Every human being on this Earth was dead except for Burton, and every corpse had been reanimated to serve in the baron's invading army.

"Do you really think the people there will just lie down and let you do this?" Grant demanded.

"Whether they will or they won't will not matter," Trevelyan gloated. "In two days everyone on the planet will be consumed and indoctrinated into the glorious army of your baron. Praise me."

Grant and Kane watched helplessly as the first squadron of reanimated dead men stepped into the dimensional breach to invade their home.

Chapter 28

"Something's coming," Domi said, the words more certain this time.

Lakesh and the Cerberus ops team were already moving into action, ready this time for Domi's alert. The last time, they had been caught unawares, with the mysterious woman appearing via the mat-trans before anyone could really comprehend or process what was happening. The woman had died within a minute, dissolving as if her body had no stability. Since then, Lakesh had ordered his team to trust Domi's instincts, putting his faith in her incredible ability to detect things at the very limits of human sensitivity.

"Where, my love?" Lakesh asked as the ops room went into high alert all around him. The main lights switched to an orange hue, warning everyone that they were now in alert mode.

"Same place," Domi said, her scarlet eyes narrowing as she stared at the armaglass-walled chamber. "Mat-trans."

"Mr. Farrell—report!" Lakesh demanded.

At his monitor beside the mat-trans doors, Farrell was nervously running a full scan, searching the receiving patterns. Sweat beaded on his brow, droplets glistening on his shaved head. "Nothing showing as yet, Dr. Singh," he stated. But as he spoke, his voice seemed to falter and he watched the digits on his screen with marked intensity as they altered before his eyes.

"Mr. Farrell?" Lakesh prompted, striding across the room from his desk with Domi trotting along at his side. Domi had drawn her Combat Master handgun from the waistband of her shorts, flipping its catch to check for the reassuring shine of brass in the chamber.

"Is there something?" Lakesh asked.

"Temperature's dropping," Farrell said, still reading from his screen. "Rapid. Real rapid."

As he continued, Lakesh was indicating for the security team to join them from the rear wall of the ops room. Two men hurried over with Edwards joining them from where he was operating the coffee percolator. "Shape up, team—this is it," Edwards barked.

Domi looked vexed for a moment as her loyalties were split. She loved Lakesh and her instinct was to protect him by remaining at his side. At the same time, she wanted to be where the action was, wanted to be more than her lover's personal bodyguard. As if sensing this, Lakesh glanced up from where he stood analyzing Farrell's terminal and gave Domi a nod. "Go," he mouthed with a reassuring smile.

Domi strode over to meet with Edwards and his team, making her way toward the smoky armaglass walls of the mat-trans itself. At the rear of the room, more sec men were hurrying through the doors into the operations center while the nonessential personnel were ushered out.

Standing before the mat-trans, Domi could feel coldness emanating from the smoky-brown glass, radiating toward her with a physical presence. It felt like a haunting. She reached forward, bringing her splayed fingers close to the glass.

"Temp's falling ten degrees a second," Farrell warned. "More'n that."

Lakesh looked up, advising Domi to take care. "What is the reading now?" he asked Farrell.

"Minus ten, minus fifteen, eighteen, twenty." Farrell couldn't read the figures fast enough, they were changing so rapidly. "Now at…minus thirty and still dropping."

"If it keeps plummeting at that rate," Reba DeFore said, watching the mat-trans, "it'll soon be below the temperature that a human could withstand." More Cerberus personnel had joined Lakesh and Farrell before the mat-trans computer link, including Brewster Philboyd and Donald Bry and his team. Lakesh was grateful for their show of camaraderie, but he worried for their safety. If it came to it, he would clear out the whole room.

Lakesh looked at the stocky blonde Cerberus physician as she ran her eyes over the plummeting temperature gauge. "How low would it need to drop before human survival became impossible?" he inquired.

"Off the top of my head? I couldn't tell you," DeFore admitted. "But temperatures in the Arctic Circle can go below minus-one-hundred degrees Fahrenheit. Cold that intense can affect a person's mind before they realize it. You'd die mad as a hatter of the ultimate brain freeze."

With that revelation, Lakesh made a decision, ordering all remaining nonessential personnel from the room. "Donald, I need this area evacuated. Security personnel only, along with myself, the good doctor here and…Mr. Farrell?"

Farrell nodded, but his expression was one of gratitude. Lakesh may be a hard taskmaster at times, but he did so with the support of his staff. Had Farrell wanted to leave he knew that his chief would not stop him or respect him any less.

Lakesh continued to discuss the survival probabilities with DeFore, while his second-in-command, Donald Bry, led the staff out of the room, hurrying everyone to the doors and ushering them through.

Within thirty seconds the ops room had been evacuated, with only Lakesh, DeFore, Farrell, Domi and eight security personnel remaining. Brewster Philboyd, who had been monitoring the communications and satellite feeds, had nabbed a radio headset before leaving. With it, he could operate away from his desk, running the feeds quickly through a portable laptop-style computer for the duration. He took up residence on the floor just outside the ops room door, transferring the essential functionality to his portable deck as he sat there with his back propped against the wall. If anything happened, he did not want to be too far from the action.

"Temperature's just hit minus eighty," Farrell reported. "Minus ninety. Shit, this can't be right. Gotta be a glitch in the sensors..."

Farrell's words died in his throat as the mat-trans came to life, its mechanics whirring as the unit booted up.

"I'm not doing it," Farrell announced, his eyebrows raised. Beside him, Lakesh and DeFore were watching the counters blur on his screen.

A crackle of lightning appeared inside the armaglass chamber, visible through the smoked glass of the walls, cutting from ceiling to floor like a lash of spilled white paint in the air. Edwards was barking orders at the sec team, while Domi had her Detonics Combat Master .45 in a two-handed grip, thrust steadily before her, targeted on the sealed door of the mat-trans. With a dull silver finish and a stubby nose, the weapon was a small, compact pistol but it still looked large in Domi's petite hand as she trained it on the mat-trans door.

"Now at minus one-twenty," Farrell stated emotionlessly, holding himself in check. "Minus one-forty and dropping."

There came an almighty grinding sound then as the armaglass of the mat-trans chamber began to crack, frosty air seeping from the rent.

"Everybody back," Edwards ordered, motioning to his people. "You, too, Domi."

With reluctance, Domi took three steps back, still eyeing the fissure that was opening on the surface of the mat-trans wall. It was not deep enough to crack right through; in fact, it appeared to be only on the inside of the glass.

The ops room was silent, all eyes but Farrell's on the mat-trans chamber now. The lightning continued to fire through the mat-trans chamber, thunderclaps emanating from the contained room.

A WORLD AWAY, KANE WAS powerless as the dimensional portal throbbed and bulged before his eyes at the end of the long room. Its circular proportions were shifting as the space around the gateway hoop began to lose integrity, metanormal energies spitting and fizzing around its edges. The first four dimensionauts stepped into the fiery window and their bodies were racked with coruscating energy as they began to shift from one world to step into another.

Standing a few feet before the cuffed figure of Grant, Baron Trevelyan gestured grandly at the dimensional rift, a hideous grin on his lips. "It begins," he squealed. "The keys to the multiverse—mine to turn."

Grant moved, angling his body forward and head-butting Trevelyan right in the nose.

"Do you never shut the fuck up?" Grant growled.

Baron Trevelyan staggered backward with a shriek as blood began streaming from his pale nose.

Three Magistrates hurried to restrain Grant, grabbing him from behind as the ex-Mag lunged a second time at the hybrid baron. Grant ducked, barging with his shoulder into the baron's chest, shoving the shorter man off his feet.

Hidden among the Magistrates, Kane saw his cue. As three Mags struggled to restrain Grant, Kane commanded his Sin Eater to his hand with an instinctive flinch of his wrist tendons.

Despite having his hands still cuffed together at his back, Grant was making a good show of tangling with the Magistrates. He rose from the floor, driving head and shoulders into the first Magistrate, flipping him over his body. The second was upon him by then, bringing a nightstick around for a brutal swing at Grant's face. But Grant was faster, drawing his leg around in a sweep, yanking the Mag off his feet before the blow could connect.

The third Magistrate took no chances. His Soul Eater was already in his hand as he crept behind Grant, finger squeezing the trigger. But as he did so, the weapon exploded in his hand where Kane shot it, the blaster and two of the Magistrate's desiccated fingers spiraling to the floor in an instant. The Mag turned at this new attacker, a strained squawk emanating from deep in his throat as putrid-smelling gas began to stream from the stumps of his missing fingers. Kane snapped the trigger again, running across the room to create a moving target as the other Magistrates began to react to the infiltrator in their midst.

The Mag went down in an instant, a single, perfectly placed bullet lodged in his forehead, splitting through the protective armor of his helmet.

"Grant?" Kane yelled as he dodged an attacking Magistrate's outthrust fist. "You okay, partner?"

"Forget me," Grant snarled as he heaved himself up off the floor, driving his head into the gut of another Dark Magistrate. "They're attacking Cerberus. Close the gateway."

Kane knew good advice when he heard it. He spun on his heel, drawing his Sin Eater around toward the glowing hoop at the far end of the room. Grant was on his own.

INSIDE THE CERBERUS operations center the lights were flickering as the whole facility suffered an enormous power drain.

"These readings are impossible, Dr. Singh," Farrell uttered as the maelstrom continued to build in the mat-trans chamber.

"Go ahead, Mr. Farrell," Lakesh ordered with remarkable calm. His eyes were still fixed on the light show that played through the mat-trans in the corner of the ops room, turning it into a lightning cage.

"The sensors are indicating the chamber is now at minus four-hundred-and-sixty degrees Fahrenheit," Farrell reported, staring at his monitor screen in disbelief.

"Absolute zero," Lakesh said, his breath catching in his throat. The cold could be felt here, several feet away from the chamber's door. It was bleeding out across the room, a coldness almost beyond comprehension.

"Has that ever been proven?" Reba DeFore asked.

As a physician she had an understanding of such principles, though nothing compared to Lakesh's knowledge.

"According to the laws of thermodynamics," Lakesh recalled, "said temperature is impossible. We are below absolute zero, where the thermal energy of matter ceases."

"Meaning?" Domi asked, her Combat Master still trained on the door to the mat-trans chamber as a wave of cold energy swooped over them all.

"Entropy halts," Lakesh said. "The laws of our universe cease to operate at below minus 459.67 degrees. In essence, nothing is possible, no movement, nothing."

Domi continued eyeing the fissure in the mat-trans chamber, with the eight-man security team behind her. Even if the concepts themselves were beyond the albino girl, she knew what Lakesh was saying. "We're in trouble," she deciphered.

"The readings can't be right," Farrell said with false conviction. He sounded for all the world like a man trying to convince himself.

"Right or wrong," Lakesh said, "there can be no doubting that something is happening here that is beyond our current level of understanding."

The orange-lit ops room fell to silence, the only noise coming from the commotion within the mat-trans chamber, muffled to a dull tapping by the protective armaglass. The Cerberus personnel watched as the crackling lightning coalesced into a figure standing dead center of the mat-trans floor's grid.

"Impossible," Farrell muttered.

As he spoke, another figure appeared, then a third, a fourth, dark silhouettes behind the tinted glass.

"Lock the mat-trans," Lakesh commanded. "Now."

Farrell's fingers danced across his keyboard, shutting down the mat-trans. For all the good it would do them. Already the network had been infiltrated, and their mysterious user had shown complete contempt for any of the security protocols put in place by Cerberus.

"Unit's powering down," Farrell stated. "Door's locked."

As he spoke, a clacking sound came from the chamber's door where its magnetic locks slid back and forth in their housings, as if rattling to escape.

"Mr. Farrell?" Lakesh prompted.

"I locked it," Farrell said. "I swear I..."

The chamber door rattled in its housing as the lock snapped apart in a shower of sparks.

A DISEASED HAND REACHED FOR Brigid Baptiste as she tottered along the rain-slick ledge, and she felt herself skip a step, recover and keep going. There was no turning back now, not when she had come this far. The Magistrate who had grabbed for her pulled himself up onto the same ledge that Brigid was using.

Brigid didn't hesitate. She swiveled her torso as she continued to run on the precarious ledge, raising the shotgun in her right hand and sending a booming shot through the spitting rain.

Final bullet.

The 12-gauge round streaked from the Mossberg's thirty-three-inch barrel, burning through the air in an explosive boom of propellant. Poised behind Brigid on the ledge, Magistrate Sweet took the shotgun burst full in the face, his protective helmet disintegrating with the impact as the bullet drilled through his skull and out the far side in a shower of withered brains.

IN LIFE, MAGISTRATE SWEET had not been a Magistrate at all. He had been a protestor at a rally against the experiments that Baron Trevelyan's science division had conducted, worried about the damage that could be seen in the weather patterns, the undeniable fact that they had not seen the sun through the clouds in almost two months. Trevelyan's people had corrupted the weather by then and, though the protestors didn't realize it, Trevelyan was using the rain as a weapon, adding chemicals to it that could turn a man's mind.

The man now known as Magistrate Sweet had been captured at that rally, cuffed and driven to the Mag Hall of Justice in the back of a secure truck, its windows crisscrossed with a strengthened grille. He had not been known as Sweet then, that name had come later, after the baron had finished with him. The name was taken from a compass point—Southwest. The baron named all of his regen Mags after the nodes of the compass; he had once explained it was purely out of boredom, because human names meant so little. The names were reused as Magistrates died, just as in the old days of the villes. The only difference was that the supply of fresh Magistrates was endless now, made up of whatever citizens the baron and his bully boys chose to enlist.

Magistrates had taken Sweet to the Sector House, kicking and cursing as he was slung in a cell. He had been left there for three days and two nights, with nothing more than water to sustain him. He had not had a single visitor; no one from the protest had come. Nor had he seen another prisoner or a Magistrate. What happened here—a new jug of water, cleaning of the evidence of his bodily functions—happened while Sweet was asleep.

Finally, when he had begun to wonder if he was going to die in that cell, Sweet received a visit from Baron Trevelyan. The baron was angelic in his appearance; his pale skin almost seemed to glow as he stood before the cell's bars with his entourage of scientists and Magistrates for protection. He had stared at Sweet a long time, as the protestor cowered before him, hunched over against himself where his empty stomach clawed at his will. He had been studied for almost ten minutes, the baron simply watching him in silence. Finally, Baron Trevelyan had spoken, his voice high with a nasal quality. "He will suffice."

Then the cell had been opened and Sweet had been walked out, taken down a corridor to a medical bay where he was checked over and fed. Sweet was not fed in the normal manner, however—they placed a tube directly in his stomach and pumped specific nutrients there to sustain and strengthen his body. The doctor explained this was being done prior to his enlistment in the Magistrates, where he would serve as one of the new breed.

Sweet had spat out a curse at that, naming the doctor's mother for a whore. He would never serve the baron, never be a Magistrate. Once the Mags had protected the people, ensuring that the world never reverted back to the horror of the Deathlands. But in the past decade, Baron Trevelyan had been turning them into something more attuned to his vision. They were "the enemy"; Sweet knew this for a fact.

Dr. Langdon had simply shaken his head, tsking between his pursed lips. "The Magistrates are the future," he said. "Our beloved baron will take us to new heights, new glories. And you are to be his first salvo, to make the first gains in the future world."

Sweet had had no idea what that meant, and in his delirium he had not the wherewithal to fight back, either verbally or physically. "Kill…thing," he had muttered, drifting into unconsciousness.

Langdon had offered an ironic smile at the words. They were so very appropriate, after all.

Sweet had only woken once more. He had been in agony; something was being wrenched from his insides. He looked down and saw that his guts were open, the flesh pinned back by great metal nails. The nails shone red where they had been daubed with his own blood.

Baron Trevelyan peered at him, a superior smile on his smug face. "No, you're right—kill him," he had instructed. "It will be easier to complete."

Sweet had been about to respond when something cold slapped against the left side of his skull, followed by another a moment later to the right. He heard a buzz, felt the jolt as electricity was passed through his head. Then nothing.

Dead, Sweet had been reawoken in a regen suit, the adapted uniform of the new Magistrates. He functioned without breath, operated without question. He existed to serve his baron, without need for sleep or sustenance. Even as his body decayed he continued to serve the barony, hunting and killing those he had once protested beside. The executions meant nothing to him; he had no emotional attachment to the world around him anymore. The regen suit kept his body moving, and Baron Trevelyan filled his mind with instructions, a life lived by rules and counterrules.

Sweet died a second time serving his baron, the way he had "lived" for the past two years. Brigid's shotgun blasted in his face, shattering the visor of his helmet, driving shards of safety plastic through his eyes and into his wasted brain stem as particles of brain and bone were sown into the rain. He had died right this time, serving his baron. Magistrate Sweet felt no pride in this, however, no joy. He simply served, and when he stopped serving he merely stopped. A death guided by rules and counterrules.

BRIGID SWUNG HER LITHE body through the gap in the wall, scarcely breaking step as she moved from the narrow ledge to the mat-trans control room. Even in darkness, it looked just as she had left it a few hours before—dust lining the control panels, the battered row of metal lockers running up one wall, the insect-eye armaglass concealing the mat-trans itself.

Brigid took a moment to reload her shotgun, breaking the weapon open and pulling the spare cache of bullets from her pants pocket. Outside, through the missing chunk of wall, Brigid could hear the rain getting heavier, caroming from the skies in thick sheets. It hit the walls and the hard surfaces of the streets with a death rattle, drilling against them relentlessly.

It felt like the end of the world.

Chapter 29

In the Cerberus redoubt, the door to the mat-trans opened and four dark-clad figures stepped from the swirling teleportation mists. Undoubtedly masculine, the four figures wore padded suits of jet-black with a metallic thread running through it that caught the orange warning lights of the ops room. The metal weave made a netting pattern where it ran through the protective garments, its lines flowing with each step the strangers took in deadly unison. The one-piece garments were accompanied by heavy boots into which the legs of the pants were tucked and sealed. Masks covered their faces entirely, enwrapping them in a black shroud, like rubber pressing tightly against their features.

"Stay where you are," Edwards ordered, raising his Sin Eater pistol in an unwavering two-handed grip. "Not another step."

Beside him, the sec team did likewise, training their own weapons on the intruders.

The black-clad figures continued their advance, each step placed in clockwork formation with a thud.

Behind the deathlike figures, the armaglass of the mat-trans was crackling with cold, a layer of ice running across its surface, outside and in. Domi could feel it from where she stood over to Edwards's left, ten feet back from the nearest plate of glass. The cold seemed to emanate from the mysterious intruders, too, a cold so intense it felt more like an emotion than a temperature. The intruders stank, too, a musklike burning mixed with damp. Domi knew exactly what it was: the smell of stagnation.

At his desk, Farrell was transfixed by the incursion, watching openmouthed as these new figures stepped from the mat-trans into his world. Lakesh grabbed his shoulder, shaking the man.

"Snap out of it," Lakesh commanded. "Let's go— go."

Behind Lakesh, Reba DeFore had already anticipated his instruction, scooting back from the mat-trans terminal and scurrying to the far wall where the Mercator map glowed with lights. A moment later, Lakesh and Farrell weaved through the desks to join her.

"What are they?" Farrell asked breathlessly.

"They're trouble, Mr. Farrell," Lakesh told him. "Nothing but trouble."

The wraithlike intruders continued their entry into the operations room, raising their right arms with practiced precision as Edwards ordered them once more to halt. Each of them moved at the same moment, like some dance troupe from hell.

In front of the cracking walls of the mat-trans, Edwards began barking orders to his security team, instructing them to select their targets as the intruders ignored his final warnings. As he spoke, weapons appeared in the strangers' raised hands, materializing from the holsters strapped to their inner arms. They looked like Sin Eaters to Edwards, but the tooling was more elaborate, ammo feeds expanding on the weapons' sides like a stag's horns.

After that, the whole room descended into anarchy as the intruders began their extermination of life on Earth.

BRIGID BAPTISTE STOOD IN the unlit hospital room, trying to calm her breathing. There were still at least thirty Magistrates out there, she guessed, working their way up the side of the hospital on their fixed lines. This respite could only last half a minute at most, barely enough time to clack the barrel of the Mossberg closed on the reloads. She turned to the hole in the outside wall, propped herself over the edge and began picking out targets. They were hard to see in the darkness and the rain, their black uniforms the ideal camouflage for the night. But Brigid watched for their movements, saw the way their beetlelike silhouettes skittered against the solid planes of the hospital walls.

Her shotgun boomed, swatting the first of the Magistrates from the wall. The man was just starting to fall when Brigid fired again, loosing another blast at his nearest ally, sending both Mags spinning to the street.

Screaming shots pierced the air as the Magistrates returned fire, realizing that they were under attack. Brigid did not stop. She swung her weapon toward the next Mag as he reached for the broken wall, blasting the vile bastard in the face, his head exploding in a melange of protective helmet, skull and brains.

Her teeth gritted, Brigid turned the shotgun around, blasting the next, the next and the next.

Reload. Fire again and again. Keep them back; keep them away. Reload again. Fire. Reload again.

Brigid kept to the grim pattern, the rain-slick lip of the holed wall the only protection she had against the screaming discharge from the Magistrates' guns.

KANE CHARGED TOWARD THE throbbing dimensional gateway, weaving past the reanimated Magistrates as they grasped for him, their nightmarish, screaming bullets zipping all around the vast room above the Hall of Justice. Somewhere behind him, he knew, Grant was struggling to hold his own against at least a dozen Mags, his hands still cuffed together behind his back. He would have to take care of himself for just a minute more.

For an instant, Kane saw that other face before him, the face of Helena Vaughn, her dead eyes rolled up into their sockets. He hadn't killed her, he reminded himself. Kane willed the image away, using it to feed his anger and his determination. This was no time to let misplaced guilt get the better of him.

Realizing where Kane was running, the black-clad Magistrates formed a cordon before the glowing hoop of metal, their ranks closing like the midnight wings of a crow. Kane's pace didn't slow. He drove himself at the nearest Magistrate, just one more obstacle to saving the world. The dead man had a ring of blisters marring his lips, a webbed crack across his visor. Kane kicked out, delivering a snap-kick to the man's chest, shunting him back.

But the next Magistrate was already taking his colleague's place, bringing up his Soul Eater pistol to blast Kane in the face. Kane ducked as the Mag's bullet chambered, then he punched with a left-right combo as the man fired. The Mag's bullet exited the muzzle of his pistol with a tortured howl, scooting over Kane's head and embedding itself in the chest of one of his own colleagues. The Magistrate, meanwhile, fell to Kane's one-two attack, collapsing to the floor with an awful clicking in his throat.

Thirty feet away, Grant was tussling with Magistrates, too, using a series of kicks and head butts to keep them at bay as a mass of the dark-robed figures tried to overpower him. Baron Trevelyan was lying at

Grant's feet, clutching his bloody nose, and his face looked paler than ever.

Two of the reanimated Magistrates came rushing at Grant from different directions. Grant eyed them both, instinctively timing their approaches in his head.

The first came at him with an outthrust fist. Grant moved his body into the blow, effectively blocking it with his chest before it could gain enough momentum to hurt him, turning it into a weak jab. He shrugged the blow off, powering forward to strike the startled Mag with the crown of his lowered head.

The second Magistrate had two nightstick batons in his rotted hands, and he wielded them like a flag waver. Grant knew that if either of them hit they could result in a fracture. As the Mag approached, Grant leaped high, kicking out with his left leg and clipping the Magistrate under his chin with a clack of breaking teeth. The dead Mag was knocked off his feet, tumbling backward into one of his colleagues.

But as Grant recovered his footing, he almost barrelled into the cowering form of Roger Burton, who lay crouching amid the action. Tears were streaming down the man's face; he was sobbing uncontrollably. The metal ribs of the skull hose shuddered with each sob, glaring as they caught the reflection of the sparking dimensional gateway.

Grant did not stop to think about it; he simply reacted, lashing out with his foot, driving his boot into Burton's hose attachment. The hose rang with a clang of metal as Grant's boot connected, and Burton was sent tumbling to the floor. The hose snapped at its base, where the metal ring met with the portable dialysis-type machine that Burton had been forced to carry around with him like a sick badge of honor. The display lights flared, liquid churning behind the clear panel of the feed unit. Grant kicked out again, making sure this time that the hose broke off. His kick sent the glowing box skittering across the room into an approaching Magistrate, wrong-footing him as he tried too late to avoid it.

Roger Burton looked up at Grant with querulous eyes, the tears dancing on his cheeks. The feeder hose swung at the back of his skull dripping fluid, no longer connected to anything.

"No more guilt," Grant told him. "Get up and start living your life."

Somewhere behind him, Grant could hear the angry voice of Baron Trevelyan barking orders.

"Execute him," Trevelyan screamed. "Serve your baron, Magistrates."

Grant backed away as a horde of Mags turned toward him and Burton. He was rapidly running out of places to run.

At the hoop-shaped gateway, four more figures stepped through the breach into a parallel world.

FINALLY, THE HOSPITAL walls were clear. Once they had seen the futility of their position, the Magistrates had retreated. Brigid turned back to the darkened room, wiping sweat from her eyes. Her hair was soaking wet, rain and sweat mingling, pouring in streaks down the sides of her porcelain face. Her bright emerald eyes flickered around the room, reorienting herself after the bloodbath she had caused outside the hospital. She had not enjoyed killing Magistrates, even dead ones like these. Worse yet, she had seen many of them pick themselves up after being blasted, recovering from falls and wounds that would kill a living man.

Brigid checked the breech of the shotgun as she

strode to the mat-trans, confirming it was empty. Her pockets were empty, too—whatever ammo she had grabbed from Pellerito's factory was spent.

She put the shotgun down as she reached the mat-trans console, leaning it against the waist-high pillar that stood before the chamber's doors. The pillar was black in the darkness, as if standing to attention, while the doors to the mat-trans chamber were still open.

Brigid ran her hand over the flat glass screen, bringing it to life with her touch.

"Hell-o, operator," she mocked in a quiet voice as the podium's display lit up, a series of grid references appearing on its glass surface.

She tapped at the keys, running her fingers over the fingernail-like implements through which the machine could be liaised. She felt the hackles at the back of her neck rising with the touch, as if with a static charge.

The podium screen ran red on black, information marching across the screen like an army trudging to war. Brigid typed in a simple command: "Display power source location."

The screen flashed for a moment before bringing up a schematic of the mat-trans with an area at its base highlighted. Brigid eyed the mat-trans in the darkness, searching for the access panel that was displayed on the blueprint. She wished she had more light, but all there was came from this control podium a few feet in front of the transportation chamber itself. Exposed copper piping glinted in the dull illumination where the floor had been holed like Swiss cheese, capturing the light of the display.

There.

Brigid scurried forward, sinking to her knees before the armaglass wall of the mat-trans. There was a tiny seam at the base of the unit, where the vents worked to pump gas from the transitions. It was barely discernible in the darkness. Brigid ran her fingers along it until she found the catch, plucking it toward her until the access hatch dropped open. The whole thing was just sixteen inches square, with the door opening onto a set-back unit with a glowing light off center.

Brigid smiled. "Bingo."

She had power. Now she just had to run it through the radio and start broadcasting across the quantum reach.

EDWARDS, DOMI AND THE other security officers blasted back as the black-clad intruders raked the Cerberus ops room with bullets. The bullets howled, screeching through the air like living things, the screams dying on impact.

A blond sec officer called Tatlow went crashing to the floor as one of those howling bullets struck him dead center of his chest, piercing the light armored vest he wore. Edwards leaped over the falling figure of his colleague, bringing his Sin Eater around and blasting a stream of 9 mm bullets at the intruders. Bullets flew all around, slapping against the walls and the furniture in the room, shattering computer terminal screens as they struck.

Nearby, Domi ducked for cover as a cluster of strange, shrieking bullets cut the air toward her. She dove behind a computer desk as the bullets hit. The computer screen shattered and wooden chunks kicked up where bullets raked the desk.

Wary, her breath coming fast, Domi scampered down the aisle of computer terminals before peering over the top of another desk. The strange interlopers were shooting wildly, targeting anything that moved in the orange

illumination. Lakesh, Farrell and Reba were at the back
of the room now, close to the exit doors. Domi willed
them to go out there, to get themselves out of the line
of fire. But there was no time to give orders. Better to
take action.

Bringing her Detonics pistol above the lip of the
desk, her head so low that only her ruby eyes and white
hair were visible, Domi took careful aim at one of the
intruders and pulled the trigger. A steel-nosed 230-grain
bullet launched from the gun's snout in a burst of propellant.

In the corner of the operations center, the mat-trans
chamber was powering up again, lethal bursts of cosmic
energy rushing through the glass-walled room.

It was chaos.

BRIGID SLID HER THUMBNAIL under the open section at the
front of the mat-trans, shoved her thumb in the groove
and snapped the panel back as far as it would go. This
was no time for delicacy; she needed to get in there
and tap the power unit. A moment later, she had recovered the radio from where it was securely held under
her jacket. It had survived intact, at least; maybe that
was a good omen. With similar efficiency, she pulled
the front panel of the radio off, working the holding
screws with her nail.

Leaning down until her head almost touched the
floor, Brigid stared at the guts of the mat-trans where
a little power light glowed green. There was wiring
there and a whole load of mechanics. A hoselike attachment corded out from the left-hand side, clipped into the
door panel on molded housings. She recognized it as a
test pipe, a way to reroute the energy during the necessary maintenance periods that the mat-trans would be

expected to go through. She plucked the hose free, ran her exposed hand over the metal prongs that were positioned at its tip. The attachment was designed to slot into a portable analysis unit. It was not live, but with a flick of a switch and a command to the podium, she could make it so.

Brigid glanced behind her, watching the hole in the wall for a long count to ten. The rain continued to lash at the wound in the wall, pooling water at the far edge of the room. Nothing was coming yet, just a lot of noise out there where the Magistrates were regrouping.

"Come on, come on," Brigid urged herself, turning back to the test feed line beneath the front panel.

With deft movements of her fingers, Brigid had the radio unit wired into the power hose, allowing her to pump power into it. She turned back to the podium, pushing herself up from the floor and tapping in a coded sequence to run the power test. It would send power to the radio, linking it to the mat-trans's quantum field generator. In theory, she could use that link to jump a radio broadcast across dimensions. As she triggered the power, two Magistrates appeared in her field of vision, clambering over the rubble at the edge of the room. Behind them, more hands were appearing as their colleagues ascended their fixed lines and swarmed on their prey. The lead Magistrates brought their Soul Eaters up, squeezing the triggers. Brigid was all out of time.

IN THE CERBERUS REDOUBT where the sounds of gunfire filled the air of the ops room, Domi's attention was drawn for a moment to the mat-trans chamber looming in the corner of the room. Her eyes widened as she saw the cosmic energies swirling there. It looked like a whirlpool of electricity and dark matter, spinning around and around within the armaglass box.

Edwards, meanwhile, found himself drawn into hand-to-hand combat with one of the intruders as he tried to dodge flying bullets. His own weapon had clicked on empty, but before he could reload one of the black-clad strangers was bringing his own weapon up to execute him. Edwards lurched back, kicking as he moved out of the faceless figure's line of fire. The intruder's Soul Eater bucked, firing another blurting bullet in a ghostly burst of propellant mist. Edwards saw a face flash in the expelled gas, imprinting on his mind's eye. The face was in agony.

The bullet sailed over Edwards's arched body, and then the shaven-headed Cerberus man jabbed out with his right leg, smacking the intruder a sharp blow behind the knee. The stranger wobbled but stood firm, Edwards's kick bouncing from him with a dull thud.

The dead man turned on Edwards, bringing his Soul Eater up to blast the Cerberus warrior in the face. Edwards moved fractionally faster, slapping the gun aside as the barrel spit its screaming discharge at him. Then with a yell of sheer effort, Edwards brought his other hand around in a fist—his empty Sin Eater back in its holster—jabbing the black-clad figure in the chest.

The infiltrator toppled backward, crashing into a computer terminal and knocking it from its perch.

But Edwards was struggling, too. His leg felt cold where he had touched the intruder and he was losing the feeling in his right hand. He staggered back, stumbling blindly against a chair as bullets zipped all about him.

Close by, Domi sensed the change in the air. The whirlpool of quantum energies was slowing down inside the mat-trans chamber, coalescing into something solid. Something else was coming, she realized. More of the invaders.

Chapter 30

Standing at the control podium, Brigid jabbed at the final key and leaped. At the same instant, six Magistrates shot at her, launching a half-dozen screaming bullets across the room.

But Brigid was a blur of motion, leaping across the room to where the power cable was hooked into the radio unit. As the bullets struck all around her, Brigid kicked, breaking the power cord's connection with the radio even before it had begun to charge. The hoselike cord flopped free for a moment as power began to surge through it. Brigid was still running, muscles pumping as she leaped into the open door of the mat trans itself. The mat-trans had been designed to contain the quantum energies involved in moving objects through folded space; it should protect her from what she hoped was about to happen.

Bullets clattered against the pebbled armaglass panels as Brigid ducked inside the chamber. Outside, the flailing power hose danced in the air for a moment, as if it were a snake hypnotized by a snake charmer, before sinking to the floor. As it struck the floor, the sparking jack brushed against one of the exposed copper pipes that ran the length of the room beneath the broken floor tiles. Suddenly the whole room was lit as if by lightning as the floor came to life. The pooling water began to dance and pop as electricity streaked through the room.

From the safety of the mat-trans chamber, Brigid felt those first jolts tremor through the floor, felt the crackle in the air as static played across her skin.

From outside, it appeared that the hospital was trying to contain lightning as electricity sparked across the floor of the room, running through the copper pipes and sending jolts up high in the air, crackling up and down the thick metal struts that had been used to support the ceiling.

Six Magistrates had been hurrying through the main room as Brigid kicked the hose, peppering the tinted armaglass of the mat-trans with screaming bullets as the first shocks struck. The electric current zapped through the floor tiles and surged through their dead bodies, striking them down like a glowing electric scythe. Five more Mags had just entered the room via the ruined exterior wall. As their booted feet touched the pooling water, they were caught up by the electric current and tossed high in the air, their bodies smoking as they slammed against the ceiling or went flying back out of the room and down into the street through the open wall.

Two more Magistrates were caught up as their colleagues tumbled into them, while another was sideswiped by an electric lance that zigzagged through the air.

Closeted within the mat-trans chamber, Brigid huddled down, watching the electricity spark and flame through the multifaceted armaglass. Magistrates were still pouring through the open rent in the wall, hurrying inside after their prey, irrespective of the danger. Several managed a few steps into the room before the sparking electricity struck them down or sent them up into the ceiling or across the room until they hit a

wall. Their Soul Eaters coughed as they were hit, sending great streams of bullets across the room in hideous
screams until they finally fell to silence.

Brigid continued to hide in the secure mat-trans
chamber where she was safe. Her hair was raised with
the static buzzing through the air and her skin tingled,
but the electricity didn't reach into the chamber itself.
The exposed copper piping didn't run inside here, and
the pooling water was all out in the main room, close
to the opening that dominated one wall. Brigid watched
as Magistrates went down like tenpins. Suddenly, her
shotgun sailed past the door as a streak of electricity
caught it, whipping it across the room before slamming
it against the line of metal lockers with a resounding
clang. The lockers, too, were alive with electricity, shaking in place as white lightning played across them.

The room seemed to shake as Brigid watched, the
reanimated Magistrates being swept from their feet before they could get more than a few steps inside. The
water at the edges of the room was leaping and boiling
under the pressure, misting in the air as Magistrates
were thrown back. For a moment, there in the mist,
Brigid saw Daryl standing, watching her with accusing eyes as the reanimated Magistrates were destroyed
in the electrical cataclysm.

"Don't judge me," Brigid told him. "You'd have done
the same if you were still alive."

KANE ELBOWED ANOTHER sickly-looking Magistrate out
of his way as he forged a path to the gateway. Cosmic
energies crackled all around the gate, causing Kane's
hair to stand on end as he headed toward it.

Up close, Kane could see that the device was more
elaborate than he had initially registered. It was con-

structed of layered metal, jointed like an ancient suit of armor with thin tubes of glass running across its surface connecting all the joints. The glass pumped cooling fluids through the system from a barrellike block at the base.

As Kane stared at it, the hoop seemed to expand and contract, shimmering in place as figures moved in its impossible depths. He could see the Cerberus ops room from the perspective of their mat-trans chamber, saw the sheer chaos this infiltration by dead Magistrates was wreaking. He had to stop it. If only he could figure out where to shoot the darn thing.

Kane had been standing still just two seconds, his gaze racing across the many sections of the gateway, searching for a weak spot. From his right, another of the dead Magistrates launched himself at Kane, drawing his Soul Eater and preparing to fire.

Kane whipped his own pistol up, blasting the dead Mag full in the chest.

The way now clear, Kane turned his blaster on the gateway itself, targeting the control stand with a narrowing of his eyes. "Show's over, people," he muttered as reality seemed to quake and bulge before him.

As Kane squeezed the trigger he heard Baron Trevelyan scream a defiant curse somewhere behind him, the words echoing through the vast chamber. Kane's Sin Eater bucked in his hand as he held the trigger down in continuous fire, playing the barrel left and right, peppering the whole of the control unit and the barrellike cooling system with 9 mm rounds. Bullets laced the casing, kicking up sparks as they struck against the metal, several of them deflecting away at tangents through the room. Kane's lips were pulled back in a sneer, his eyes narrowed to slits as the circular gateway crackled and throbbed, sending shock waves of fearsome energy through the room.

Without warning, the view of Cerberus winked out and was replaced by a different view, one that showed a sun-scorched desert, its dry earth cracked and broken. Kane watched as the second wave of Magistrate travelers was pulled from his world into this new one, their bodies stretched into new and impossible shapes. The gateway glowed with the intensity of a miniature sun then, and Kane was forced to turn away as the image flickered and changed again, the desert becoming a concrete-walled bunker, a restaurant, a star field.

On the far side of the room, Baron Trevelyan watched with horror. "No, he can't…"

Grant kicked the baron in the ribs as he ducked past another Magistrate who tried to grab him. "Keep it down, Baron Bozo," he snarled. Then he was running through the room toward Kane. It was possibly the most foolish thing Grant had ever done, placing him closer to the source of danger as the dimensional gateway began to erupt in a wreath of crackling witch fire. But he knew that whatever happened now, he should be beside his partner, fighting the good fight.

Behind Grant, Roger Burton was eyeing the hybrid baron with something other than fear for the first time in years. He felt a new emotion rising in his chest, an emotion he had been denied as he was fed his own self-loathing. The emotion was hate, hate for the inhuman thing who had perverted his inventions, who had wasted his genius on new methods of cruelty. As Baron Trevelyan recovered from the kick to his ribs, he saw Roger Burton reach down for him, as if to help him up from the floor.

"Yes, yes," Trevelyan encouraged. "Help me up. We can still rectif—"

But Burton didn't allow the baron to finish the sentence. The baron flinched as he saw something thick and metallic snap at his head, smashing him in the face; it was the hose that had fed guilt into Roger Burton's brain, still connected to his skull like a tentacle. Burton leaned down, his hands around the midsection of the hose, striking with it again and again at the baron's bloody face.

All across the room, the Dark Magistrates seemed disoriented by the sudden outpouring of cosmic energies, the sum total of everything the sun shield had trapped to power this incredible hole through the universe. The floor seemed to buckle as a burst of radial energy spit from the dimensional hoop, running through the room and knocking a dozen Mags off their feet, shattering the windows behind the gateway. Grant leaped as the wave of force came at him, felt it buffet his body as the floorboards were torn from their housings.

Standing before the blaze, Kane continued washing the machinery with bullets, doing his best to ignore the wild forces that were playing out before him. The view through the hoop had become a jumble, a thousand flashing images streaming across its tesseract depths, a window into a thousand different realities.

"Dunno what you did," Grant said breathlessly, appearing at Kane's side, "but I think it's time we made our exit."

Kane watched as the impossible window flickered and changed views once more, out-of-control energy playing across its surface. "Couldn't agree more," he said. "You got a friend?"

Grant glanced back into the room. Professor Burton

had the metal hose stretched across Trevelyan's throat, cinching it around the hybrid's neck, crushing his windpipe. The professor was wide-eyed, blood on his clothes. He looked deranged. "I think he has some things he still wants to work out here," Grant admitted.

As the dimensional gateway hit critical, Kane and Grant made their way to the rear of the room, clambering up onto the desks there before launching themselves out of the broken window. Sure, there were better ways to exit the building, but they both knew that they didn't have the time to spare. The gateway was about to blow.

A WORLD AWAY, WITHIN the Cerberus ops room, Domi waited behind the cover of a bullet-riddled desk. Her eyes were fixed on the mat-trans chamber door as four new figures began materialising inside. "Come on," she muttered. "Bring it."

The very second that door opened, Domi would shoot them, she vowed; there was no way that she would allow herself or her people to be put in any more jeopardy.

Behind Domi, the ops room was alive with fighting. The Cerberus security team was doing its utmost to hold back the first invaders, four black-clothed figures with masks over their heads.

One infiltrator had fallen thanks to Edwards's relentless attack, but the others were proving durable even under heavy fire.

"Their suits are deflecting bullets," Lakesh realized from where he watched with Reba and Farrell, crouching beneath the Mercator map by the room's doors. "I'd guess they're wearing…Kevlar."

Even as he said it, he and DeFore exchanged a meaningful look. According to DeFore's analysis of the mysterious woman who had emerged from the mat-trans a few hours earlier, she had been wrapped in a mixture of Kevlar, Mylar, Nomex and nylon. It confirmed that these people came from the same source, even if it did nothing to inform Lakesh what that source was.

DeFore looked helpless as another howling bullet zipped by the trio before embedding itself in the wall six feet from Farrell's dangling gold hoop earring. "I don't know what to do, Dr. Singh," she admitted with a shake of her head. "I just don't know."

Ignoring the madness around her, Domi emerged from her hiding place close to the mat-trans as the door eased back on its greased tread. She had her Detonics Combat Master held out before her, and as the door slid back she began to fire, driving 9 mm slugs into the figures revealed within the swirling transport mists.

But as the door drew back, the sound of cracking ice filling the air, the figures seemed to sag, caving in on themselves even as Domi's first bullets struck them.

"What th—?" Domi muttered, easing the pressure on the trigger for a moment.

Inside the mat-trans chamber, four dark-clad figures seemed to wither, their bodies caving in on themselves as they collapsed to the floor. Domi watched incredulously as they lost integrity, once-hard muscles turning to gelatine.

Across the room, Lakesh peered up into the barrel of a pistol as one of the remaining intruders prepared to blow his brains out.

OUTSIDE THE HALL OF JUSTICE, Kane and Grant were clambering down the side of the building. Kane had used the multikey he had acquired to free Grant from his handcuffs. The multikey was designed to work any set of Magistrate cuffs, though Kane had never known quite how useful that would prove when he had stolen it from the storeroom.

The two men moved swiftly down the building's facade, their hands and feet skimming over the rain-slick masonry as, above them, the glowing dimensional gateway reached a crescendo. A moment later the Cerberus warriors were on the ground, running hell-for-leather away from the Magistrate Hall as a mighty shock wave rippled through it from the top floor.

They had landed behind the building, in a fenced-off area where Magistrate vehicles were parked. The area included Land Rovers, two hover tanks and a half-dozen personnel carriers, as well as several bulky Sandcats. Kane ran the magnetic multikey over the door of the nearest Sandcat to unlock it, while overhead great chunks of the building started to crack as incredible cosmic energies sought release. The driver's gull-wing door swung open.

Grant slipped into the passenger seat as Kane ran the multikey over the ignition, starting up the engine with a satisfying purr.

Part tank, part wag, the Sandcat had a low-slung, blocky chassis supported by a pair of retractable tracks that could negotiate the most challenging terrain. The durable design also featured an armored bubble at the center rear of the vehicle, from which jutted the twin barrels of two USMG-73 heavy machine guns capable of inflicting incredible punishment on anyone who challenged the Mags. The hull was composed of a tough ceramic-armaglass bond.

All around, lightning fired into the sky from the topmost level of the Magistrate building, its electrical fingers clawing at the sky.

"Time to leave," Grant urged as a chunk of stonework came toppling from the building's roof, crashing through the hood of a parked personnel carrier two vehicles over from them. The personnel carrier sunk on its tires as the weight broke its suspension.

"Definitely," Kane agreed, gunning the engine and shoving the Sandcat into gear.

A moment later, the Sandcat barrelled through the thick wooden gates of the restricted area, tracks wailing as it hit the road.

"No word of thanks?" Kane challenged Grant as he wrestled with the wheel, bringing the Sandcat around a corner over the traumatized tarmac there, its headlights carving a path ahead of them.

Grant glared at him, rubbing at his wrists where the cuffs had bound him. "I almost died," he snapped. "So, what kept you?"

Kane smiled. "You know me, partner—fashionably late's how I play these things."

Grant nodded. It was good to be back among friends. He watched the road for a few seconds as Kane urged more power to the engine, eyeing the streets for landmarks. "You have any idea where we're headed?" Grant asked.

"Hospital," Kane told him. "Brigid had an errand to run there. I promised I'd pick her up when I was done here."

LAKESH LOOKED AT THE black-clad infiltrator who was bringing his pistol around to shoot. Lakesh tried to scramble away, pushing DeFore and Farrell out of the line of fire as the intruder pulled the trigger.

A shot rang through the air, sounding close as Lakesh tried to get out of its way. But the shot did not scream the way that these nightmare guns seemed to. It came instead with the clean whizz of a 9 mm slug, cutting through the air and embedding itself in the black figure's skull. It struck with a shattering crash as the intruder's head broke apart, chunks hurtling in all directions.

Lakesh turned as the infiltrator collapsed to his knees, just a headless corpse now. Gas was pouring from the stump where the masked head had been, chugging into the air in a gray-green cloud. The cloud smelled awful.

It took a moment for Lakesh to process what had happened. His eyes were fixed on his would-be killer, watching as the foul-smelling gas hissed from his suit. Then his eyes flickered, scanning the room where his security force was battling with the last of the intruders. He stopped, spotting the figure on the far side of the room standing with the outthrust Combat Master in her chalk-white hand. It was Domi—and Lakesh realized that she had shot his would-be executioner, once again playing the role of his guardian angel. Lakesh inclined his head in a nod, mouthing words of thanks.

Domi nodded back, returning to the mop-up as the last two invaders were penned in by the Cerberus forces.

In the hospital room, the air smelled of ozone. The power hose was still skittering across the floor, writhing back and forth where the under-floor piping was exposed, its sparking end firing as it snagged the last remaining water droplets on the floor tiles. Brigid's improvised plan had worked better than she could have hoped. None of the Magistrates were moving and nothing appeared to be coming through the gaping rent in the wall other than that relentless rain.

Brigid watched for a half minute longer, waiting to be sure that the Magistrates' attack was over. Her long red hair stood out like a halo around her head where the electricity in the air caught it, shimmering in place. No one was coming. The attack was over; she had repelled it.

Outside the mat-trans chamber, the room still buzzed where the current played across the floor and metal lockers, the pooled water all turned to steam. Brigid watched the lightning trails, eyeing the hose that fed them from the front of the mat-trans chamber itself. Steeling herself, Brigid stepped out onto the lip of the mat-trans door and kicked out as far as she could to hook the flailing hose up off the floor. As soon as it ceased to make a connection with the copper piping the artificial storm stopped, the smell and the smoke still churning in the air.

Standing on one leg, Brigid drew the hose toward her with her other toe, pulling it close enough so that she could grab it. The hose felt hot and Brigid winced as she touched it with her bare hand. It was like touching the side of a hot oven. She grimaced, holding the hose aloft. The two metal prongs on the front had turned black, and smoke poured from their ends. No matter, the thing was still pumping power, it could still be made to suit her purposes.

With the circuit broken, the room had ceased its sparking storm. Brigid stepped out onto the burned floor, leaned down and tucked the hose carefully back into its housing beneath the armaglass panels where it could do no further harm. Then she strode across to the control podium, flattening her hair with one hand as she stepped over the singed body of a fallen Magistrate. The dead figure lay still, the chunky Soul Eater

weapon still clutched in his hand, its firing pin clicking on empty. Brigid ignored him as she tapped out a
command sequence on the podium, instructing the unit
to power down.

A moment later she was back at her radio, examining it for damage. Miraculously, despite some singed
exterior panels, it had survived the unleashed electricity. She only hoped it still worked.

Chapter 31

The Sandcat bobbed and weaved along the street as Kane floored the accelerator, hurtling away from the Magistrate Hall as a shock wave raked through the upper floors from the damaged dimensional gate. Kane glanced in the rearview mirror. The upper stories of the building were glowing green and white, the pressure growing as the power leaked out.

Beside Kane, Grant was securing his seat belt as the Sandcat hurtled along rain-slick streets. "At least traffic won't be a problem," he said as Kane took a corner at sixty miles per hour, following the twin cones of his headlamps, urging more power from the engine.

"One advantage of driving in an abandoned ville," Kane agreed as he fishtailed out of the turn, driving the Sandcat onward toward the hospital by the lake.

Two blocks behind the Sandcat, a great explosion shook the Magistrate building, vaporizing the upper levels in an instant. Green-gold energy churned forth, blazing into the heavens and firing outward into the ville. The building collapsed amid the deafening outburst, destroying the last remaining Magistrates before they could exit through the gateway. An avalanche of masonry struck the street with a roar like thunder as the building collapsed in on itself, a further great hunk of mass disappearing through the dimensional vent.

Inside the Sandcat, Kane and Grant felt the shock

wave as the building was leveled, the impact shaking the street as they hurried away from ground zero. The only lights in the ville came from Kane's headlamps and the dimensional rift behind him; the rest of rain-drenched Quocruft was left in absolute darkness. The treads squealed as Kane pulled at the wheel, jouncing over the cracked ruins of the roadway.

As Kane sped over a crossway, swerving the steering wheel left then right to avoid a large hole in the road, something slammed against the driver's side of the Sandcat.

"The hell?" Kane spit, yanking at the wheel.

Kane's head turned, glancing down the cross street where it stretched at right angles to the one they were traveling on. With the loud roar of a straining engine, a Magistrate wag appeared just three feet away from his wing, swerving to ram them a second time, its only lights coming from the driver's displays.

CERBERUS WAS CLEAR AT LAST. The last of the invaders had been dealt with. Edwards's security team had trapped the last two, penning them in so they could do no further damage. But before they had been able to detain them, both black-clad figures had crumbled like crushed ice, flopping to the floor as quaking wrecks. Across the ops room, their fallen colleagues were exhibiting a similar reaction. It was as if they were watching a spilled slushie in the midday sun, black shards twinkling as all of their bodies turned to liquid.

Lakesh and Domi were joined by Reba DeFore as they stared at the sharp fragments of blackness that were all that remained of the intruders from the mat-trans.

"Any idea what happened to them?" Reba asked.

"They arrived at absolute zero and shattered like ice sculptures," Lakesh mused. "I'd say that whoever sent them didn't do his calculations right, wouldn't you?"

"Tapping into the mat-trans can be a tricky business," Domi added.

DeFore nodded in agreement. "Question is, where did they come from?"

Lakesh turned his head, fixing the physician with his penetrating blue stare. "That, my friends, is a question we may never have an answer to," he said with an air of defeat, "and you both know how much I dislike a mystery."

Evacuated personnel had just started filtering back inside to take up their posts when Brewster Philboyd came hurrying through the ops room doors balancing a laptop computer in his outstretched arms.

"Dr. Singh," Philboyd blurted excitedly, "I have CAT Alpha. Brigid's on the Commtact right now."

Lakesh did a double take. It had been a strange few minutes, so much so that he had almost forgotten that Kane and his team were still somewhere off the map. "Brigid, my dear," he said, bringing his mouth close to the upraised laptop's microphone pickup. "How are you?"

Brigid's voice came back through the portable computer's built-in speakers, faint and a little distorted, peppered with the hiss of radio static. "Feeling kind of lost," she admitted. "Brewster tells me you've been having some trouble there."

Lakesh's eyebrows knitted in consternation. "Nothing to worry you with," he told her. "Where are you exactly? We've rather lost track."

"That's just it," Brigid told him. "I'm going to need a remote pickup."

Lakesh was the bona fide expert of the mat-trans, and Brigid's request did not faze him at all. "Give me the location," he said. "I take it you're near a mat-trans."

"I'M BROADCASTING THROUGH one," Brigid told Lakesh as she sat on the floor before the mat-trans.

The door to the mat-trans was sealed shut, and the unit was chugging over in a sending loop, running power to its quantum phase circuitry. Brigid had been relieved to find that the mat-trans still had power, despite the rest of the ville being seemingly left without any. It seemed that the mat-trans ran on a different circuit, one that tapped into a separate grid running through the ville. Someone somewhere must have been pumping a lot of power through the linked network.

With the power running, Brigid had hooked the portable radio unit to the testing jack and, with a little inspired rewiring, got the two systems cross-talking well enough that she could broadcast to another world.

"When we accessed the mat-trans in the Panamint range, we were batted sidewise through space-time," Brigid explained, "emerging not on our world but on another, a parallel casement. We came out at something that equates to our mat-trans, but the unit can't send us back."

"Didn't you say you were running this broadcast through it?" Lakesh asked. His voice came with a burbled, distorted edge from the radio speaker, as if heard through the end of a vast metal pipe.

"Yes," Brigid confirmed, "but I don't see any way to send humans. It's not powered to do that, only to receive."

Through the radio's static buzz, Brigid heard Lakesh *humph* to himself. "So we need a power supply strong enough to hook you and your team out of another reality," he mused. "This will take some doing." He didn't need to add "if it's possible."

"I have faith in you, Lakesh," Brigid said, staring at the radio speaker in the pitch-dark room in the abandoned hospital in the dead ville.

KANE WINCED AS THE personnel carrier struck them again, fighting with the steering wheel to keep the Sandcat on the road.

"If it ain't one thing, it's another," Kane growled, spotting the grim visage of the dead Magistrate at the wheel of the other vehicle. The Mag's helmet had a wide split running from crown to eye, and his expression was a fixed lunatic's grin.

"Guess I spoke too soon about the traffic situation," Grant quipped, snapping open his safety harness and ducking back into the rear of the Sandcat. A moment later the big man clambered up into the armored port at the top of the Sandcat, seating himself in the gunner's bay. Rain lanced against the clear bubble as he took his position behind the machine guns.

As an ex-Magistrate himself, Grant knew how to handle the Sandcat's weapons. He powered up the twin USMG-73 heavy machine gun array as the Sandcat was buffeted again by the heavier personnel carrier, scanning the street for more hostiles. It seemed their nemesis was alone—probably a straggler from some op across town.

Grant brought the guns around, swinging them in the direction of the personnel carrier as it raced beside them, kicking up a wall of water as its tires tore through the puddles at high speed. "I'm gonna need some space to get in my shots," he shouted down to Kane. "See what you can do."

Kane scanned the street ahead through the narrow beams of the headlamps, looking for some maneuvering room. The personnel carrier was heavier and faster than his vehicle, and while the Sandcat was built like a tank it was not immune to being knocked into a wall or, worse still, rolled onto the uneven road surface.

The Dark Mag pulled back for a moment, swinging his vehicle away before coming back at Kane's wag from the side.

Grant tapped the twinned triggers of the heavy machine guns, sending a stream of bullets from the armored turret. The heavy rounds punched into the road with eerie screams, kicking up great hunks of tarmac but missing the fast-moving Mag's vehicle by six feet or more.

"Bastard weapons got the same screaming report as their Soul Eaters," Grant muttered to himself as he targeted the fast-moving personnel carrier. "Like that's helping anything."

The Mag floored his accelerator at that moment, ramming into the Sandcat's back wing, the nose of the personnel carrier striking the port-side treads. Kane gripped the steering wheel, battling with it as the Sandcat threatened to go into a skid on the wet road.

"More space," Grant shouted from above him.

"I'm trying," Kane growled back, willing the Sandcat to more speed.

No matter what he did, there was no escaping the fact that the personnel carrier had greater acceleration and was far more maneuverable in this urban environment. As Kane scanned the street ahead, searching for some way to outdrive his assailant, Grant's raised voice came to him again.

"Kane, you want to check the mirror right about now," he said.

"What?" Kane asked as he zipped over another empty intersection, passing the burned-out wrecks of automobiles on either side. "Why?"

By then, Kane was looking in the rearview, and he saw what Grant had seen a few seconds before. The shock wave from the Magistrate Hall of Justice was expanding, ripping through the streets in a tidal wave of energy, obliterating everything it touched.

BRIGID WAS DRAWN TO THE hole in the wall by the light. She scurried over to take a closer look. She could see an explosion had obliterated the central area of the ville some blocks away. The explosive force glowed a sickly gray-green and it seemed to be spreading in a towering whirlpoollike swirl, like a twister on the horizon. Brigid did not know what it was, but she figured she had a pretty good idea who had caused it. "Kane and Grant," she muttered with a shake of her head. "Every time you boys get together, something like this always happens."

She watched the cloud of swirling force, trying to judge if it was getting closer. She only hoped that her absent partners were somehow okay out there.

Brewster Philboyd's voice crackled over the radio as Brigid continued to watch the force wave, drawing her back to its speaker. "Brigid, we have a lock on your transmission using a four-dimensional mapping program," he explained. "We can find you, but we're having trouble generating enough power to bring you home."

"Acknowledged, Cerberus," Brigid said into the microphone. "Anything I can do?"

"Hang tight, Lakesh is working on the equations now," Philboyd assured her.

Crouched on the scuffed floor, Brigid stared at the power indicator light on the radio as the transmission went silent. All she could do now was wait—wait and hope.

But as she sat there, Brigid heard a scraping noise behind her. She reacted automatically, honed instincts kicking in from long hours in the training gym. A figure was standing in the gaping hole of the exterior wall, his tortured pose backlit by the explosive wave that was barreling through the ville. It was a Magistrate, one of the dead. His helmet was missing and he was clutching something that Brigid recognized—a twisted length of cable. It was the same length of cable that Kane had used to tie the dead man up when they were in the office building downville.

"You were dead," Brigid stated, staring into the rotted face of Magistrate South.

Even as she said it, Brigid realized that death posed no obstacle for these revived Magistrates. Magistrate South moved with lightning speed, sprinting across the room with the cable stretched taut between his claw-like hands.

Brigid ducked, rolling out of the way as the Magistrate lunged for her throat. She didn't have any ammo left for the shotgun and was too far away to try to electrify the floor again. As she ticked off the options in her head, Brigid found herself avoiding the Magistrate's relentless attack, her boot heels skidding on the water-stained floor.

Once he had broken free from his restraints, Magistrate South had tracked Brigid's signature across the ghostly ville of Quocruft, scenting her obscene livingness the way a dog scents a fox. He had been dead when Brigid and Kane had checked for his breathing back in the office cloakroom, but then he had also been dead before that—for the past eighteen months of his awful period of servitude to the baron. All he knew was to hunt for the baron, to kill for him and so replenish the ranks of the dead Magistrates. He had followed Brigid's trail to this building, missing the main firefight by minutes. When he had arrived, the bodies of his fellow Mags were piled up all over the street but there was something else that caught his eye—fixed lines, dozens of them, rushing up the front of the building and leading right to the signature of the living woman. Magistrate South had climbed.

KANE WATCHED IN HIS rearview as the churning wave of energy surged down the street from the ruins of the Magistrate Hall. The shimmering wave of unrestrained energy was tall enough to peek over the lowest rooftops as it roared down the streets, six blocks behind Kane and his partner in the speeding Sandcat, consuming everything it touched. Beside them, the Dark Magistrate's vehicle slammed against the Sandcat's wing again in a bid to knock Kane from the road. Even if he managed to somehow outdrive the dead Mag, there was no way Kane could outrun that wave of energy for long.

Kane eyed the street, his mind racing, searching for some inspiration that might save their lives. He was in the business district again, the place where he and Brigid had found the abandoned media station full of video tapes. The buildings in this sector featured decorative quadrangles, open spaces with statues and fountains designed to calm their occupants. Up ahead Kane could see one of these open spaces tucked behind a series of decorative Grecian-style columns, a metal sculpture acting as a centerpiece in its concrete haven. The sculpture flashed bronze as Kane's headlights touched it.

"Hang on," Kane called, pumping the accelerator and pulling the steering wheel in a tight turn to send the Sandcat threading between the closest set of pillars.

Grant bucked about in his seat, clinging to the handgrips on the USMG-73s as the Sandcat left the road and leaped over the paving stones. The personnel carrier followed, the dead Mag's eyes fixed on the Sandcat's rear with deadly intensity.

The Sandcat zipped past the stone columns, clipping them with its right side as Kane goosed more power from the straining engine. Suddenly, his right-hand wing mirror disappeared in a crash of splintering plastic and glass, and Grant shouted a warning down from his vantage point.

"Go left!"

"Just get that monkey off our back," Kane shouted back, his eyes fixed on the courtyard they now found themselves in where it materialized in the headlamps. The courtyard was littered with decorative features: wooden benches, water troughs and a giant chess board sitting in the shadow of the metallic sculpture at its center.

Kane wrenched the wheel, clipping a wooden bench with his front wing, knocking the seat from its restraining posts. The personnel carrier followed, keeping barely a car length behind him, rising and dipping over the cracked paving slabs. The distance was not much, but it was enough for Grant to line up his target and flick the triggers of the heavy machine guns once more, sending a stream of heavy-duty bullets into the hood of the personnel carrier, just beneath the nightmarish corpse face of its reanimated driver.

Grant's bullets strafed the chasing vehicle as Kane weaved between benches, whipping the back of the Sandcat around as he roared past the metal sculpture in the center of the courtyard. Each bullet let out a hideous shriek as it tore from the muzzles of the USMGs as if in terrible pain. Grant ignored the noise, eyes fixed on the target.

The Sandcat kicked into the air, leaping over a raised section of the courtyard, slamming down again with a heavy bounce, bullets streaking from its top-mount turret. Kane yanked the wheel hard, forcing the vehicle toward the line of columns at the edge of the quad once more.

Grant tracked the personnel carrier that followed, keeping it dead in his sights as they raced through the paved area that fronted the office block.

The dead driver was struggling to keep up with Kane's driving prowess, his heavier vehicle proving no advantage now in the tight space. Bullets were streaming before his armored windshield, kicking up debris and obscuring his vision.

Grant dipped the guns lower, targeting the grille of the chasing wag, his fingers never easing on the triggers. An unbroken stream of bullets slammed into the personnel carrier, rattling across the grille, staking it again and again with their pointed tips.

Suddenly, smoke began pouring from the personnel carrier's hood, but Grant did not let up for even a moment—he kept strafing the engine cover with bullets, hitting as often as he could with the bouncing path that Kane was taking.

Kane pulled at the wheel again, hurtling around toward the bronze sculpture, shifting gears as he fought to keep traction. He heard something explode behind him, and Grant let out a cheer at the same moment. Behind them, the personnel carrier was on fire, its strengthened grille shattered by the relentless assault of the USMGs.

Kane hooked the Sandcat around, weaving back through the columns and onto the street. Behind him, the personnel carrier became a fireball before slamming against one of the pillars. Flames licked up the pillar, black smoke souring the night air.

"Nice work," Kane congratulated as he watched the fireball in the rearview mirror.

But there was no escaping the ominous show of energy that powered through the ville from the direction they had come. It was getting closer all the time.

They were back on the road, but there was no time to let up.

DEAD MAG SOUTH LUNGED for Brigid again with the cable, his dead eyes staring into hers. Brigid side-stepped, gasping as the length of cable snapped against her like a whip. She danced out of the way, feeling the pain in her side where the cord had struck.

The Magistrate came for her in the darkness, lashing the whip-cord up and back so that it snapped in the air.

At least he no longer has his gun, Brigid thought. That's something.

She ducked around a ceiling support strut as the cable slashed through the air at her face, almost stumbling over the fallen body of another Magistrate blackened from electrical burns. Mag South slapped his palm

against the metal strut, unreeling the cord at Brigid's
face. She felt it lash against her cheek, stumbled back
at the sting.

Her face was throbbing around the cut, and when she
touched her cheek she found that the cord had drawn
blood. She looked up as the shadow of the Magistrate
fluttered past her vision, skipped back as he grabbed
for her…and slipped.

Suddenly Brigid was falling, the broken wall at her
back, just two inches of floor under the toes of her
boots. She reeled in place, bringing herself back from
the brink and right into the arms of the dead Magistrate. The Mag cinched the cord around her throat in an
instant, shoving her down to her knees with a violent
thrust. He stood over her, the electrical cable wrapped
around Brigid's neck, one hand on each end as he pulled
it tighter.

Brigid made a gagging noise, felt the pressure on her
windpipe. She grasped for the electrical cable, tried to
hook her hands under it to alleviate the pressure. Standing over her, the Magistrate just pulled harder, using
his leverage to force her back to the edge of the floor
where the outside wall was missing.

Brigid's back arched, her head tilted backward out
of the wall, rain falling against her face. The Magistrate would kill her now; she had nothing left to give,
no way to fight back.

Her hands skittered on the floor seeking purchase,
her head reeled. There had to be something she could
do, some way to stop this monster that she and Kane
had left in the offices.

In the offices.

Of course, that was it. As black spots swam before
her vision, Brigid's right hand reached behind her, feel-

ing desperately along her waistband until she found the
snub-nosed .38 she had jammed there, discovered in the
skeleton hand of Bryan Baubier.

Brigid pulled the weapon free, brought it around
without really seeing anymore, flipping the safety off
as she guessed where the Magistrate was—and pulled
the trigger, all in the space of a second. The .38 boomed
loud in the darkened room, expelling its bullet in a flash
of explosive.

The Magistrate took the bullet to the side of his skull,
no longer protected by the lost helmet he had worn.

Brigid felt the pressure on her neck ease as the Magistrate's grip slackened. She wrenched the cord from her
throat as the reanimated Mag stomped backward clutching the gaping wound in his desiccated face.

Her mind still whirling, Brigid tried to make sense of
the scene before her as the Mag stumbled back, the glow
of the approaching energy wave behind him. Brigid lev-
elled the .38 and took another shot, blasting the Magistrate from her crouching position, driving a bullet
through his forehead, right between the eyes. The Mag
stumbled back with the hit, and then suddenly he was
gone, his feet on empty air, tumbling over the side of
the building through the missing wall.

Brigid stood up and ran across the room to the space
where the Magistrate had disappeared, watching with
satisfaction as he struck the street below in a jangle of
limbs. The tidal wave of energy was edging ever closer.
And down there, among the abandoned buildings, she
saw twin headlights traveling at high speed toward her,
bumping and weaving past the wrecked vehicles that
lined the deserted streets.

Brigid smiled, shaking her head. "Got to be Kane—no one else drives like that," she said, her throat raw from the attempted strangulation.

Chapter 32

"So, who was the old guy I saw you with?" Kane asked as they pulled up outside the hospital. The street was littered with the broken bodies of Magistrates. Their limbs sprawled at painful angles and many exhibited awful blaster wounds on their rotted torsos and ruined faces. Not one of them moved.

"Scientist," Grant told Kane as he climbed out of the Sandcat's cab. "Professor type. He was a plaything of a baron. Just like all of us were, once."

Kane surveyed the dead bodies of the Magistrates where they lay in the rain, their vehicles abandoned. Two-dozen fixed lines were attached to the ruined front of the hospital building, swinging in the wind. "Looks like Brigid has been busy," he deadpanned, reaching for one of the dangling fixed lines. He gave it a hard tug to test it. "Cords seem secure. Gonna be our easiest way up."

The two friends looked back down the street for a few seconds. In the distance, the roads were rippling with energy as if an earthquake were shaking them apart, great gouts of lancing electricity crackling into the air in plumes as it carved a path outward from the Magistrate headquarters. In the far distance they could see a glowing column of fire, the Magistrate Hall burning itself into oblivion, folding in on itself as the overloaded gateway seared through the dimensional rift it had carved.

"Easy's good," Grant acknowledged, reaching for a rope. "Quick's better."

The two men hurried up the fixed lines, pulling themselves up with their hands and ankles, grips tight despite the wetness of the cords from the rain.

THEY FOUND BRIGID TALKING into a deconstructed radio unit beside the mat-trans chamber. Lakesh's voice was coming from the tiny speaker, sounding small and distorted by an overlay of static.

"We need to get more power to pluck you from your current location," Lakesh was explaining.

"There's nothing here," Brigid told him in her hoarse voice. "I'm sorry. If I could figure out how we'd been misrouted here then maybe I could find us a way back." She looked up as Grant and Kane came trudging in out of the rain, the fierce energy churning in the streets behind them.

"Hate to admit this," Kane said by way of greeting, "but I think I may have blown up our only way home." He gestured to the green-gold column of fire that could be seen billowing through the missing walls.

Brigid shook her head thoughtfully. "No," she insisted. "If I can send a signal to Lakesh then I can send a person. There has to be a way. What did you blow up?"

"Dimensional gateway," Kane said, brushing a hand through his rain-soaked hair.

Brigid eyed the gold-green column that was blasting into the atmosphere. "Which means those energies…" she began.

"Already ahead of you," Lakesh's voice said from

the tinny speaker of the radio unit. "How long do you think you have there?"

Brigid, Kane and Grant watched as the fiery column cut through the ville like the sword of some great, mythical god. "Not long," they agreed in unison.

"Sooner's better," Kane added.

"Always," Lakesh agreed, his voice beamed to them from another Earth.

IN THE CERBERUS OPS ROOM, things were getting back to normal. Cleanup teams were already packing up the ruined computers and bringing in replacements, while Donald Bry ran a subroutine check on the mat-trans. A team would replace the armaglass before the day was over.

"We're tracking a major power spike in Brigid's immediate vicinity," Brewster Philboyd related as he studied the readings on his laptop. His fixed computer had been trashed by a Magistrate's bullet somewhere during the firefight.

Lakesh looked up from his own screen, studying Brewster's for a few seconds. "Whatever that energy source is, it appears to be expanding," he observed.

"It is," Brewster confirmed. "Exponentially. I don't know what it is but it's cutting a hole right through dimensions. My guess is it has something to do with how Kane's team ended up on that other Earth."

"Agreed," Lakesh said, but he was already figuring out a way to tap it. "Reroute power through the CJ-GS circuit cluster," he commanded, leaping up from his desk.

Donald Bry shook his head. "Those circuits can't take much," he stated dourly as he ran the systems check.

"Precisely," Lakesh replied. "I want to overload them. We're going to route everything through them and during the power spike we should be able to hook CAT Alpha up, bypassing the normal safety protocols."

Bry began rechecking Lakesh's calculations, tapping figures into his calculator pad. "I really think—" he began.

"No time for that," Lakesh warned as he pushed Bry gently from his seat at the mat-trans terminal and took over. "Reroute the circuits, Donald. And as soon as he's done, Brewster, transfer the power. No stalling, we do this now."

Bry ran a power switchover from his adjoining computer, the one he had been using to double-check his adjustments to the compromised mat-trans. With so many bullets flying, half the equipment had been compromised. It took just ninety seconds, and Bry told Lakesh the second his change was live. An instant later, Lakesh had toggled a run of virtual levers on the control computer, activating the corresponding circuits deep inside the mat-trans itself. Suddenly, the mat-trans was running through its power-up cycle, the chamber's internal lighting brightening.

Domi was standing over Lakesh now, watching the lights power up through the tinted armaglass. "This will work, won't it?" she asked.

Lakesh smiled grimly as he reprogrammed the mat-trans on the fly, drawing on his incredible knowledge of the system to reposition its command protocols. "We live in hope," he told her breathlessly.

Bry checked his terminal screen, waiting for the switchover to complete and take effect. "We're ready," he announced.

"And we're live," Brewster said a moment later.

"Power diverting now." He watched his laptop screen for five seconds before looking up to where Lakesh sat poised before the mat-trans console. "Readings are… off the chart, Dr. Singh. We have thirty seconds, at best, before the system burns out."

"That's more than enough," Lakesh said, striking a switch on his console. "Brigid?" he called over the Commtact. "We're scooping you out of there now. Get into the mat-trans and lock the door. And inform the others that it may hurt."

"ROGER THAT," BRIGID SAID before ripping the power lead from the radio.

The room seemed suddenly silent without the radio's buzz, even though the mat-trans was beginning to cycle through its prep sequence.

"We'd better get inside," Kane said.

Brigid nodded, tapping the door code into the keypad of the matter-shifter's chamber. She took one last look out the holed wall of the hospital as the door slid open. Out there, the column of cosmic energies was widening, ripping through whole buildings as it expanded across the ville. It burned brightly, lighting the ville like the noonday sun.

"How long do we have?" Grant asked, seeing the look of consternation on Brigid's face.

"Less than a minute," Brigid estimated as the shock wave ripped through a building just a block away.

Together the three Cerberus warriors stepped into the mat-trans and locked the doors.

"THEY'RE IN," BRY CONFIRMED as he watched the changing digits on the control screen.

"Power's being channelled," Brewster explained. "Scoop is ready."

At the mat-trans control console, Mohandas Lakesh Singh jabbed the button that would scoop Kane and his team out of the other world. And held his breath.

THROUGH THE ARMAGLASS wall of the mat-trans, Kane, Grant and Brigid could see the energy wave plowing through the ville toward them, a hundred broken lines of green-gold lightning blistering across the pebbled safety glass, brighter and brighter.

"This better work," Kane said as the mat-trans began to shudder beneath them, the power sequence engaging via remote.

The tidal wave of energy swooped closer, crashing into the hospital with the power of a thousand suns. In the street, the Magistrates and their vehicles were consumed in the cosmic whirlpool, and the missing facade of the building was torn through in an instant. Inside the mat-trans chamber, the Cerberus warriors gritted their teeth as the wave struck.

The mat-trans glowed brilliantly for a single second as it shunted its three occupants to another destination. And then the wave hit and the mat-trans, the room and the whole hospital disappeared in a burst of cosmic static.

The wave continued its rapid expansion, carving a searing path through the abandoned ville of Quocruft before blasting outward, consuming everything in its way. From a distance, Earth looked like a beacon, a shaft of energy sticking through it like an olive on a cocktail stick.

MILLIONS OF MILES AWAY, as she crossed through the orbit of Jupiter, *Tiamat* witnessed the great conflagration that impaled Earth, consuming the planet too soon for the dragon mother ship to complete her final download and bring the Annunaki back from extinction. Her last child was dead, she knew, stillborn before he could ever know life.

THEY WERE SURFERS on the cosmic wave, multiple worlds racing before their eyes. Kane, Grant and Brigid could only strain as a billion different images vied for space in their brains, their bodies hurtling across the time-less stream.

And then they were home.

They stood in the hexagonal chamber, the familiar brown-tinted armaglass walls arrayed before them, new cracks visible in the old panes.

"Everyone okay?" Kane asked through rasping breaths. He was leaning over, pressing his palms to his upper legs as he tried to shake the vertiginous feeling of movement that buzzed through his body

Brigid nodded very slowly while Grant muttered a few words of agreement before vomiting in the corner of the Cerberus mat trans. They were home.

LAKESH'S TEAM WERE READY with thermal blankets and rehydrating drinks when the mat-trans doors were fi-nally opened once the power flux had dissipated. The system was powered down entirely, and Lakesh in-formed everyone that it would be out of commission for a week while they recalibrated everything and re-placed the burned-out components.

"A normal facility would require *three weeks* to re-cover from something like this," he reminded his team, "which is why I'm telling you all we'll be back online inside of seven days. Don't make a liar out of me." He smiled then, knowing that his trusted personnel would step up to the challenge. They always did.

Domi took pains to tell Kane, Grant and Brigid about everything that had happened while they had been away. They had missed an other-dimensional invasion and it had been that invasion that had tapped into their mat-trans journey and thrown them to the abandoned ville of Quocruft.

They had visited a dead world and lived to tell the tale. That was all that really mattered. Donald Bry promised to recalibrate their Commtacts as soon as everyone had caught their breath.

As the others got themselves sorted out, filed their reports and caught up on a much-needed meal, Brigid Baptiste excused herself. She headed through the corridors of the Cerberus facility alone, wrapped in her own thoughts. Brigid made her way to the residential area where a whole run of self-contained suites and rooms was arrayed along a corridor like an apartment block. Like the rest of the Cerberus facility, the corridor had been carved directly into the mountain and it had a cold, rocky feel, reminding Brigid of cave exploring.

The beautiful redhead strode past the doors, acknowledging the occasional familiar face as she passed other personnel. Two-thirds of the way down the corridor she stopped, gazing at the door before her. There was nothing remarkable about it; it looked much like the others that lined the corridor. If anything, it had less character than the others, where some occupants had painted decorations or hung charms on the doors.

Brigid reached forward and tried the handle. It was unlocked—of course it was unlocked, why wouldn't it be?

She pushed the door wide, stepping into the darkened room that sat silently behind it.

"Lights," Brigid said to the empty room, and the automated lights came to life with a momentary dimming.

Inside, the suite was very simple, just a couch, a desk and a bed. There was a door to one side that led to a private shower cubicle and toilet, a small nook where coats could be hung and a simple fitted wardrobe. Brigid walked over to the desk, eyeing the notebook that lay open on it. The page was filled to the halfway point with complex equations written in a neat, precise script. Brigid smiled as she saw that a line had been crossed through and corrected beneath by the same hand. Typical of Daryl Morganstern, to correct his own work before he showed it to anyone else.

Brigid took a moment just to take in the atmosphere, to feel the man's presence one last time. "I'm sorry, Daryl," she said to the dead man's living quarters. "I didn't mean for you to die. You were so kind, so brave, even in the end. You died a hero's death to protect me. And to protect Cerberus.

"I know I should have said all this earlier," she finished, "and I'm sorry that I didn't."

Brigid remained in the room the rest of the night, tidying and boxing the man's possessions so that the living quarters could finally be given to someone else when the time was right.

* * * * *